CHASING LIES

BRANDT LEGG

By Brandt Legg

Chase Malone Thriller

Chasing Rain
Chasing Fire
Chasing Wind
Chasing Dirt
Chasing Life
Chasing Kill
Chasing Risk
Chasing Mind
Chasing Time
Chasing Lies
Chasing Fear
Chasing Lost

*As always, this book is dedicated to
Teakki and Ro*

*This book is also dedicated to
the memory of
Saul Martin "Marty" Goldman: 1935-2022*

*And
to the memory of
Mollie Gregory: 1937-2022*

Vinci Books

vinci-books.com

Published by Vinci Books Ltd in 2025

1

Copyright © Brandt Legg 2022

The author has asserted their moral right to be identified as the author of this work in accordance with the Copyright, Designs and Patents Act 1988. This work is a work of fiction. Names, characters, places and incidents are the product of the author's imagination or are used fictitiously. Any resemblance to actual persons, living or dead, places and incidents is entirely coincidental.
All rights reserved. No part of this publication may be copied, reproduced, distributed, stored in any retrieval system, or transmitted in any form or by any means, including photocopying, recording, or other electronic or mechanical methods, nor used as a source for any form of machine learning including AI datasets, without the prior written permission of the publisher.
The publisher and the author have made every effort to obtain permissions for any third party material used in this book and to comply with copyright law. Any queries in this respect should be brought to the attention of the publisher and any omissions will be corrected in future editions.
A CIP catalogue record for this book is available from the British Library.
Paperback ISBN: 9781036705299

Chapter One

On a cold November day, at a busy truck stop along Interstate 35, outside of Ames, Iowa, a dead man dropped down from the cab of a Peterbilt tractor-trailer and walked around inspecting the first of the eighteen wheels. He recalled learning that the word "dead" from the Middle English 'ded,' originally simply meant "having ceased to live."

Light snow flurries blew haphazardly as the dead man walked the perimeter of the truck. In his jeans and flannel shirt, a John Deere cap, and cowboy boots, no one gave him a second glance. They would never imagine he was the brilliant tech billionaire, Chase Malone, because he had died more than six months earlier.

Or had he simply ceased to live? Chase didn't particularly *feel* as if he'd stopped living, but as far as his enemies were concerned—the Chinese MSS, various multinational corporations, and a secretive group known as *the shadow people*, Chase Malone was no longer alive.

Yet for Chase, being dead actually left him feeling more alive than ever.

As a semi pulling a load of live hogs rolled by, Chase made a quick check of the remaining tires, although he knew they were fine. He'd actually gone out there to have a look around the area. Scanning past a pair of Kenworths, one a tanker loaded with milk, the other hauling Amazon—the pale blue arrow seeming to be smiling at him—the coast appeared clear. There was no sign of the two killers they were expecting.

There were cameras mounted on all sides of the big rig, so his "tire-check" was not only risky, but completely unnecessary. But he liked to be sure, liked to see it with his own eyes.

He climbed back inside the cab. Wen, processing security issues through the sophisticated computers onboard, had watched Chase's excursion, making sure he encountered no problems. He went through the well-camouflaged door connecting the cab's sleeping area to the fifty-three-foot trailer. The trailer, more like a command center, was outfitted with every bit of technologically advanced surveillance equipment available. It was from there they monitored not just their immediate surroundings, but the world.

The first six weeks after they'd died, they'd stayed on a remote island in the South Pacific, healing as much as hiding. However, they both knew there was work to do. "We can't pretend the world doesn't exist forever," Wen had said. Chase hadn't argued. Part of him would've been content to live on that island for at least another ten years, to be sure the shadow people had forgotten about them, to avoid the bullets, bombs, and chaos that had been their lives for so long. But he would've missed Tu, the little boy they had rescued from China, who had become like a son to them.

Wen said they might have brought him to the island, but Chase didn't believe that would be safe. So in the end, he'd agreed, and they'd built the truck.

Then they got ready to go to war.

Several monitors showed their expected "guests" approaching. Chase checked the date time stamp on the feed and whispered, "November seventeenth, the day the shadow war officially begins."

Cranson looked like a schoolteacher, not a killer, but that only made him better at his job. He was a hunter; a *bounty* hunter, but he never brought anyone back alive. It wasn't his objective, ever.

He waited for Belfort on the veranda of the fully restored antebellum mansion a few hours outside of Atlanta, and wondered again what Belfort's first name was. He didn't *need* to know it, but Cranson was a curious guy. He didn't like mysteries, and Belfort was a big one.

I'm not even sure if Belfort is his last name... might be his first, probably isn't real anyway. What the eff is his real name? Cranson cared because Belfort could easily screw something up and get him killed, or if Cranson screwed something up, Belfort might *have* him killed. *I'd sleep easier if I knew this slug's name...*

Cranson didn't much care for Georgia—*too effin' humid*—but in the middle of November, it was almost bearable. He didn't much care for Belfort either, but the money . . . oh the money was *so- way- too- good* that he would put up with about anything.

"Cranson, you look a bit watered down," Belfort said as

he came through the two huge oak doors and crossed the brick floor. "Want a lemonade?"

Cranson looked at the African American butler trailing Belfort. The man was dressed all in white, appearing as a slave might have two hundred years earlier. Cranson thought Belfort might like it that way. The butler extended a silver tray with two glasses of freshly made lemonade balanced upon it. Cranson took one and thanked the man.

"What's going on with the team hunting Chase and Wen?" Belfort asked. It was always his first question. Cranson didn't get the obsession. Those two were dead. Bigtime dead and buried deep—*really* deep—under a zillion tons of rubble.

Besides, there are bigger fish to fry.

"Nothing new," Cranson said. "Chase and Wen are dead."

"Are they?" Belfort asked. "I see no bodies."

"No one could have survived that blast. They were there, *inside*, we know they were. They *are* dead. *Very* dead."

"I don't think they can be killed."

Cranson laughed.

Belfort's face went from serious to annoyed. "Did I say something funny?"

"You've seen the footage, the reports . . . Inside that facility, it was equivalent to a nuclear blast."

Belfort's expression remained skeptical.

"More than six months, and not a trace of them," Cranson tried again. "Someone would have seen them by now. They're dead. It's *over*."

"*I* decide when it's over."

Cranson suppressed a sigh. "I'll keep at it."

"Yes, you will."

Chapter Two

Even though Chase and Wen both recognized their visitors, they waited until the AI system made a positive ID before they opened the door to the trailer command center.

Grimes always seemed to appear as if he'd just walked off a beach, and that was often the case. His sandy, perpetually messy hair, stubble, and tan gave him that beer commercial look.

"Brought a box of chocolates," Grimes said, handing a multipack of Reese's Peanut Butter Cups to Chase. "And a long-stemmed rose." He handed the single flower to Wen.

"Thank you," she said, thinking the gifts a little odd. They hadn't seen Grimes and Shelby for months, but they'd stayed in regular contact.

"Peace offering," Shelby said.

"Peanut butter cups are always welcome," Chase said, unwrapping one and slipping it in his mouth. "Mmm. Nothing like it."

"So why are we risking this face-to-face?" Grimes asked.

"It's time to start the war," Chase replied.

"Excellent." Grimes reached for a peanut butter cup. "But if we start this, we're on a one-way track . . . there'll be no turning back."

"This war has been in the planning stages ever since the day we died," Chase said.

"Last chance to walk away," Wen added, looking at Chase. Their deaths had given them a kind of freedom they hadn't known since they'd begun fighting those who used technology to harm and control. Shadow people had, for unknown reasons, been pursuing them for years.

"We sure aren't going to just ride off into the sunset," Chase said. They'd had this conversation many times, they didn't need to have it again. They both knew the answer. Even if they weren't determined to right the wrongs, there was no denying that the world would eventually catch up to them. "The only way to make them stop is to face our demons," Chase said bitterly. "To find the shadow people and destroy them."

"Same," Shelby said. "Ending Belfort and his people is also our only hope at a normal life."

Chase studied her. Shelby, still attractive, looked older. Grimes, as always, unless he was on a beach somewhere, looked tense, ready for a fight. "You two look terrible," he said, smiling, but also concerned. "Been tough?"

"Yeah, well..." Grimes began. "The difference is they *think* you're dead, but they *want* us dead."

Chase nodded.

"They know we're alive," Shelby added. "And it's driving Belfort crazy!"

Belfort was the mysterious man behind the shadow people. He had hired Shelby, Grimes, and a whole lot of others to kill Chase and Wen, but instead, through an odd series of events along the way, they had saved each other's lives. Now the four of them shared a common enemy . . . the Circuit.

Belfort snapped his fingers twice, summoning the butler. "Is that sandwich ready yet?"

"Sir?"

"I'm hungry. Where's my sandwich?"

"I didn't know you wanted—"

"No excuses, boy! Bring me my damned sandwich."

"Yes, sir." The butler placed the silver tray on a wicker end table and quickly retreated into the massive home.

"Grimes and Shelby are still eluding us," Cranson said, preemptively bringing up another unpleasant topic. *At least they're alive and can be found and killed.*

"Yes. Impressive they've avoided us, but they're probably hiding under a rock in the Middle East somewhere. Eventually, they'll come out." He downed his lemonade. "But I didn't ask you here to talk about those two traitors."

Cranson was relieved. "A new assignment?"

Belfort nodded. "There are six key people in US intelligence that we don't own, that won't play ball . . . "

The butler appeared with the sandwich. Cranson guessed it might have been egg salad. Belfort snatched it from the silver tray with one hand, then waved the butler off with his other.

"This one is first," Belfort said, his mouth full. "Tess Federgreen."

"She knew Chase and Wen," Cranson said, recalling Tess's name from Chase and Wen's files.

"Quite well."

"Is that why she's on the list?"

Belfort scoffed. "I must admit, it gives me extra pleasure to kill a friend of Chase Malone. However, she's on the kill list for a more important reason."

ANC - Always News Channel - Top Story

"Stu Lemon reporting. Our top story at this hour: Researchers at the University of Maryland have discovered a new and dangerous computer virus dubbed NoLiv, that they say could not just harm your computer, but is capable of causing catastrophic damage to the economy. We have Bill Doorset, who made his fortune in the computer industry before turning to philanthropy, here to explain."
"Thanks, Stu. This really is the perfect storm. For anyone who remembers Mydoom, which was the world's fastest spreading computer worm, or viruses like Sobig, or the ILOVEYOU worm, this is something far more lethal."
"'Lethal' seems an unusual term to use for a computer virus."
"This is a very unusual virus. It can literally kill your computer, and NoLiv has all the necessary components to be able to self-replicate at speeds we've never had to deal with."
"Sounds terrifying."
"It is."
"Can we stop it?"
"We don't know yet. Finding solutions for something this sophisticated takes time. Fortunately, the government, universities, and numerous tech companies have been preparing for something like this, running simulations, looking for ways—"
"When do you think a patch will be available?"
"This is way beyond a patch. I'm optimistic that eventually we'll find something to stop NoLiv, but your viewers need to be prepared. This is going to get a lot worse before it gets better."

Chapter Three

The *Destino* creaked in the wind. The name they'd given the truck—Spanish for destiny—had been inspired by the inevitable showdown with Belfort and his shadow people. "Our life comes to this," Wen had said. "It begins or ends with the final breath of the last shadow person."

Yet they both understood that it also went beyond the shadow people. Their true enemies were the people who *paid* the killers.

The small sounds and movements outside, brought on by the weather as a front moved across the flatlands, made Wen nervous. She checked the cameras while Chase, Grimes, and Shelby continued talking.

"For better or worse, the four of us are uniquely qualified to go after the shadow people," Shelby said.

"We're doing more than going after them," Chase replied. "We're going to find out who the Circuit is."

Shelby and Grimes exchanged a glance. "Nice little truck you got here," Shelby said, changing the subject. "Does NASA know you stole it?"

Chase laughed. "NASA doesn't have anything *this* sophisticated." Then he explained the name, the reason behind it, and vowed again that they would never stop.

Grimes studied a section of controls closely.

"Hey, don't touch that," Chase admonished him.

Grimes pretended to push a button. "Why? If I do, will a satellite fall out of the sky?"

"Maybe," Chase said impatiently. "Let's get to it."

"We've got some interesting information to share," Shelby said. For the past six months, she and Grimes had been methodically pulling leads together. "But it hasn't been easy navigating all this. Getting help from past associates when there's a price on our heads has been exceedingly difficult."

"Welcome to our world," Chase muttered.

Grimes squinted, as if this didn't amuse him. "We've been working hard to convert a few more to our side."

"Shadow people?" Wen asked.

"Well, we don't really call ourselves that, but yeah, contractors. The ones we know who don't like Belfort, who might have the guts to cross a line. Know what I mean?"

"I think so," Chase said. "How's it been going?"

"We've lined up a few," Shelby said, rubbing at her forehead. "It's slow work."

"There are others who we're close to turning," Grimes added. "But we have to be extremely cautious or Belfort will get wind."

Chase started adjusting settings on a large control board.

"So what's all this stuff *do*?" Grimes asked, pretending as if he might start pushing buttons again.

Chase looked up from the keyboard. "Give me some-

Chasing Lies

thing to go on," he said. "That's why we're here, right? You finally have something? A breakthrough?"

"Yeah, we do, but first, how are we doing with following the money?"

Chase and Wen had been tracking the funds around the shadow people and the mysterious group funding them known as *the Circuit*. "We're into financial transactions amounting to hundreds of billions of dollars. There's nearly a million separate transactions—we call them *MEs*, for monetary events. Our programs can uncover the faintest trails, but the walls are high, and every time we think we've reached an endpoint which might result in an identifying feature, the walls close in on us."

"Try this," Shelby said, giving him a name. "We've been running down Belfort's complex web of hitmen, fixers, and others who have operated within the influence of the Circuit."

Chase fed the name into SEER, or the Search Entire Existence Result program. Chase had developed SEER in strict secrecy, and was not about to share its details with Shelby and Grimes beyond that he was using a machine learning program to assist in finding the Circuit and their assets.

However, SEER was way beyond simple machine learning. It employed advanced photonic quantum information processors and utilized deep learning, AI, quantum algorithms, and virtually every data point in digital existence to predict the future with stunning accuracy. It was their best weapon against the Circuit. As Chase told Wen, "It's how we're going to bury the Circuit."

"Who's that?" Chase asked as SEER began processing the name.

"We were hoping you could tell us," Shelby responded.

"Is there a physical location?" Chase asked hopefully. "Something I can pair with the photo?"

"There's a web address." Shelby spouted a string of numbers from memory.

"That should help." Chase typed it in. "Here you go," he said a couple of seconds later. A photo of a man filled one of the screens.

"That's him," Shelby confirmed. "He's as close to Belfort as we've been able to get."

Chase spoke several voice commands to the computer.

Wen continued monitoring the Destino's cameras. She felt exposed, vulnerable, with the truck just sitting out in the open. *Not many places to hide in Iowa . . .*

Twenty seconds later, when results began filtering through, Chase said, "It's not his real name."

"We know *that*," Shelby said. "That's where we got stopped, but you're the computer genius."

Chase flashed her a smile and began instructing the computer again. The AI took over.

"What's happening?" Grimes asked. "Are you developing some sort of profile on him?"

Chase shook his head. "It's building a net."

"Meaning?" Shelby asked.

"'Net' is a simple term for what the AI is really doing," Chase explained. "It's more like a giant filter. It's creating potential links for this name, this photo . . . it's verifying, checking, connecting more and more . . . "

Wen scanned nearby traffic cams—not for the man, but making sure they were still safe, scrutinizing each vehicle.

"Which databases is it searching?" Grimes asked. "I mean, how does it decide?"

"All of them," Chase said. "It's searching everything that has ever appeared anywhere."

"*Everything?*" Shelby echoed. "Wow. Is that even possible? What about all the records that haven't been digitized?"

"There are ways to get into them, too. Just because it's not on the Internet, or even the dark web, doesn't mean we can't find it and see what's going on."

Additional images of the man began appearing on the biggest screen. They seemed to be mostly from various surveillance cameras around the world.

"Incredible," Grimes said. "Those are all photos of him."

"Just wait," Chase said. More photos streamed through, now showing the man with other people. "Are any of them Belfort?" Chase asked.

"Trouble!" Wen announced.

"What?" Chase asked, immediately hitting the keys that would upload all the data to a safe spot in the cloud.

"Men with guns!"

Chapter Four

On a brisk, overcast day, two operatives codenamed Leia and Luke blended into their surroundings so well, a hunter in the area might have accidentally stepped on them. Then, of course, the hunter would die. However, there were no hunters, or anyone else, around since the Secret Service had cleared the area in preparation of the presidential motorcade about to pass through the wooded section of rural Maryland.

Although the Secret Service had missed the two operatives, the man and the woman were part of a covert group known as the Regulators, and had no idea if the Secret Service had missed them "on purpose," or because they were outmatched. It didn't really matter. They were there, and the president's motorcade was on the way.

The president rolled his eyes at the aid sitting next to him in the limousine, speaking into the cell at his ear. "That's not going to happen," he said to the Secretary of State on the other end of the call. "Turkey is misinterpreting."

"Sir, Tess is holding," another aid said quietly.

"Mike, tell them to move. No mercy, got it?" he said, ending the call with the Secretary. "Tess, what the hell is this?" he asked, the same thing he'd asked the Chairman of the Fed and his Treasury Secretary, but from Tess, he expected a different answer, a *real* one, one that he could understand, act upon. "Where is the economic push coming from?"

"It's not good," she said.

"How bad?"

"End Game."

The president's face went white.

The man and the woman buried in the underbrush, waiting for the president, had worked together numerous times. Both had considerable experience with this type of operation. They had shot enough people that a certain numbness had set in. However, she was much better at long-range targets. With all their combined kills, neither had ever faced a situation where the stakes were this high. The president of the United States was either going to live or die today, and everything afterward depended on which of those two options happened.

"I don't have a target," Leia's voice whispered into Luke's ear. He could hear the tension in it; almost panic, but not quite. She would never allow panic. He couldn't see her even if she wasn't buried in leaves and dirt. She was thirty yards away, with an entirely different viewpoint.

"Eagle is still more than two minutes out," he

responded, knowing she knew down to the second when "Eagle," the operation's name for the president, would pass them.

"I *don't* have a target," she repeated as if he'd said nothing.

"Two minutes," he repeated while still searching. They were in the right spot, the time was good, but a hundred things could throw it off. A thousand things could have changed. In an operation like this, everything was fluid. The chain of decisions, as he called it, meant any variable affected by a choice anyone made could create a new reality.

Ninety seconds.

The president looked at his most trusted aide. He, too, had heard Tess utter the words *End Game*. The aide closed his eyes and exhaled, allowing a final moment of normalcy.

"Are you sure?" the president asked, trying to buy his own moment to decide what to do. Now, gazing out the window, he watched the woods blur by. It had been a mild autumn, and many of the trees clung stubbornly to their brown leaves.

"Of course I'm sure. It isn't just Turkey, it's NoLiv and something else . . . "

"What?"

"The Circuit."

"Oh, good god," he said to his aide after muting the call to Tess. "The Circuit . . . why has she done this?"

The aide shook his head. "Her funeral."

"Let's hope so," the president said before unmuting the

call. "Okay, Tess. Give me everything you've got by the end of the day."

"In person?"

The president looked at his aide. The aide nodded.

"Ty will get back to you with the arrangements." He ended the call. "I can't have that meeting."

"Of course not," the aide said. "She'll never make it."

ANC - Always News Channel - Breaking News

"KiKi Carlyle reporting. Breaking news, Turkey's president Dogan announced minutes ago that his nation is pulling out of NATO. However, he said Turkey would be keeping more than thirty US nuclear missiles stored in his country. According to high-ranking, unnamed sources at the Pentagon, those thirty are not part of the previously known fifty B61 nuclear bombs held at Incirlik Air Base. This is a breaking story. Please stay tuned for further updates."

Chapter Five

Wen switched the big screen over to one of the traffic cams. "Two vehicles. Six armed men in each."

"Who are they?" Grimes asked, leaning in to get a better look.

"Were you followed?" Chase barked at him.

"No way," Grimes replied.

"Then how did they find us?"

"We don't even know if they're coming for us."

"They're heading straight here," Chase said, pointing at the screen.

"So are hundreds of other cars. We're on a frickin' interstate!"

"I've got a read on the license plate. I'll send it to the Astronaut," Wen said, referring to Nash Graham—a silver-haired math savant dubbed *the Astronaut*. His computer-like mind made him a target of the world's intelligence agencies, and meant he lived as a fugitive from those who sought to control his unique and powerful gift. For the past couple of years, he had worked almost exclusively with Chase and Wen.

Chase also fed all the vehicle plates, locations, and photos into SEER.

"None of those are Belfort," Grimes said, pointing to the images of the man with other people as more continued to come across the screen. He seemed unfazed by the approaching danger.

"We have more immediate concerns," Chase said, nodding to the screen showing the SUVs.

"Maybe, maybe not. But it's too late to run." Grimes looked around the trailer. "I'm betting this spaceship of yours has some impressive defenses."

"Nothing I'm interested in using right *now*," Chase gritted out.

"Now's as good a time as any." Grimes glanced at Wen, and then back to the images of suspects. "Still no Belfort."

"These folks may not be Belfort, but they're someone," Chase said.

"Yeah," Grimes agreed. "I recognize a few of them . . . Hey, there's me in one of the photos with the guy."

"Kinda scary," Chase said, then noticed the next photo coming up. "What do you know... there's a man I recognize. The target's standing next to the former Attorney General of the United States. Interesting." Chase looked at the monitor showing the SUV, then back to the photos. "Let's see when that photo was taken. If the Attorney General was still in office, it's a lot more damning than if he wasn't. In either case, it's interesting nonetheless."

"Chase, we definitely have a problem," Wen said. "The two SUVs approaching from the West are FBI."

Chase looked at Grimes accusingly.

"They *didn't* follow us," he repeated.

"You wouldn't know."

"Yes, we *would*."

Chase held Grimes' gaze.

"Chase doesn't think they followed us," Shelby said. "He thinks we led them here on purpose."

Grimes scowled at Chase. "You don't really believe that, do you?"

Chase lifted one shoulder, glaring right back. "I don't know, should I?"

Grimes squinted, but never took his eyes from Chase. "Hell, if I was going to sell you out, it wouldn't be to the feds. It would be to Belfort to save my own ass—and that's not happening either. Geez, and this after I brought you peanut butter cups!"

"If we're going to take down the Circuit," Shelby began, "we better start trusting each other."

"You all can argue later," Wen said. "Right now we have to prepare to survive whatever's about to come down on us."

Chapter Six

Leia narrowed her focus. "I see something," she said.

Luke looked through his scope, which had been treated to avoid catching sunlight, not that there was much sun today. His vantage point afforded him the long view, and he spotted the first vehicle in the motorcade. "Eagle doesn't know he's about to roll into an ambush," he said. "But someone in those cars does."

"Cut the chatting," she hissed.

Traitors fascinated him, but back to business. "Visual, vehicle one . . . two . . . three . . . star," he said, "star" indicating "the Beast," the nickname for the president's "indestructible" limousine. The thing was a tank that could handle almost any attack. The Secret Service had thought of every contingency, prepared for every kind of onslaught, but not what they were going to get today. A new, shoulder-mounted weapon that, when it obliterated the most well-defended passenger vehicle on the planet, wouldn't just kill the leader of the free world, but might well change the balance of power.

That prospect was why the Regulators had shown up. Luke and Leia were there because geopolitical balance was critical to maintain, especially when one was about to wage a revolution.

It's important to know which way the chips are going to fall when they fall.

"I don't have a target," she said again.

"Easy." He could hear her trying to suppress the panic. It was harder now. If she didn't obtain the target in the next forty-one seconds, their job would be blown, they would miss their one chance, and everything would be different after that moment.

Luke thought about what history would say of this day. *Will it know what happened in these woods?* If all went well, no one would ever learn they had been there.

As he watched the president's motorcade approaching, Luke gave up thoughts of destiny and history even as the symbol of power—at least symbolic power—was moving toward them at 65 mph, unknowingly facing grave danger.

At least no one inside the president's limousine knows, but someone in the rear vehicle sure knows, because he sold out.

Luke looked up, not with his head, just with his eyes. It was a reflex. He knew it was impossible to see the satellite, but it was sure as hell up there, and he and Leia were counting on it. Counting with precious seconds.

"Come on, *come on*," he whispered.

Normally Leia would never have tolerated anything other than mission facts breaking their radio silence, but she was also waiting. She also knew it was not possible their communications could ever be intercepted; their equipment was far too advanced for that.

"Seventeen seconds."

Chasing Lies

Luke could practically hear her heartbeat. She had the big weapon. There was, of course, still time. It was a precise operation, and he knew her nerves would hold; her muscle memory and nerve control were truly remarkable.

"*Two-seven-nine* . . ." a computerized voice entered their ears. It was almost soothing. The artificial female that relayed the coordinates continued giving numbers.

Leia took the information and began aiming the weapon. "Ready," she announced, now having the precise coordinates lined up and set. There was no way to miss. Still, timing the president's limo presented a challenge. The Beast had to be in just the right place when she fired...

Luke didn't dare say anything now, Leia's concentration too vital to risk. His concentration was only a little less important, as he was the backup. He adjusted the computerized sites. Killing someone he could not see was something he'd never get used to. However, in this case, it would likely not fall to him since Leia never missed.

I rarely miss either, he thought. *At least not in many, many years.* However, Leia was in the lead not for her accuracy, but rather for her nerves, her legendary control.

The digital readout counted down:

Seventeen

Sixteen

Fifteen

Fourteen

Thir—

The explosion was nowhere near as loud as he expected.

Chase clicked a button, and all screens went to exterior views of the Destino. "What do you want to do?"

"What's the ETA?" Wen asked.

"Four minutes."

Wen, who accumulated weapons like other people collected stamps, opened a large locker at the back of the trailer.

"Damn," Shelby said, looking at all the weapons inside, a veritable small armory—machine guns including numerous H&K MP7s, MP5s, Thales EF88s, Tavor TAR21s, FN P90s, FN Scars, VHS-2 Hellions, Kalashnikov AK 12s, a few AT4 rocket launchers, grenades, a Vulcan mini-gun, a sizable assortment of pistols, including Faxon FX19 Hellfire, Glock 19 and 21s, Beretta 92s, Sig Saur M17s, several sniper rifles such as the M110 SASS, Ruger Rimfire 22LR, Tikka T3X TAC AL 6.5 Creedmoor 24, a box of high-end tasers, various combat knives and throwing stars. "You planning a rebellion?"

"We're dead, remember?" Wen said. "The dead can never be too careful."

Shelby and Grimes each already had handguns, but Wen gave them MP5s.

"You okay with this?" Grimes asked Chase.

"If Wen thinks handing you a weapon is a good idea, who am I to argue?"

"Inside or outside?" Shelby asked. "Feels kind of like being trapped in a tin can in here."

"The walls are PCV armor plated," Chase said. "We have gun slots."

"Inside, then," Shelby said. "It's actually quite lovely in here."

"Three minutes," Wen announced.

"That's an eternity," Grimes said. "Might as well go back to reviewing mug shots."

Chase shrugged and clicked a button. One of the screens brought up more images of the man with friends and associates. "Recognize any of these?"

"That dude's a senator," Shelby said.

"And those two . . . " Grimes pointed at different photos, obviously stills from a video feed. "Those two are decent snipers. Not as good as Shelby is, but better than me."

"So we've got a former US attorney meeting with our mystery man just after he left office," Chase said. "We have a US Senator... let me check the date seen with him... oh, our Senator is still in office. Seems our boy is very well connected, and you're sure he's *under* Belfort?"

Grimes nodded.

"I'm hoping to get a name before the FBI comes in here and tries to arrest us," Chase said, hitting keys.

"Ninety seconds," Wen said, still watching the screens.

"Anything from the Astronaut?"

"Just dots," she said, meaning he was live, but not ready to respond yet. She glanced at the computer, and then at the door.

"Where should we be?" Shelby asked.

"There and there." Wen pointed to the gun slots on the south wall.

"There's a name," Chase said. "This one might be real."

"Sixty seconds."

"What is it?" Grimes asked.

"Hampton Brown. Ring any bells?"

"No," Grimes and Shelby said in unison.

"Let's see what else we can get . . . " Chase gave SEER a list of commands about Hampton Brown.

"Thirty seconds," Wen announced. "Be ready, be ready."

Chase looked from the photos to the SUVs.

"Ten seconds to heat."

"Slots opening."

ANC - Always News Channel - Top Story

"Stu Lemon reporting. For our top story at this hour, Retired General Abe Sanatkous is joining us. General, thank you for being here today. Can you give us a little background as to how we find ourselves in this tense standoff with a former NATO ally?"

"Dating back to 2017, we saw an increasingly unstable relationship between the US and Turkey. The pentagon began looking at options for removing fifty tactical nuclear weapons stored at Incirlik Air Base."

"Why do we have nukes in Turkey in the first place?"

"This was a program that began in the late 1950s as a deterrent to Soviet aggression."

"Shouldn't they have been removed after the Cold War ended?"

"The Cold War didn't end as much as it rested. The Russians are interested in regaining their former Soviet territories."

"For security concerns, a buffer zone against NATO expansion?"

"They claim this is for security concerns, and there is an element of truth to that, but make no mistake, this is specifically for oil, gas, minerals, and other resources."

"But Turkey is the issue."

"Turkey's president Dogan is dismantling democratic institutions and shifting to an authoritarian rule. Turkey has multiple disputes with the EU and the US. Dogan is moving closer to Russian President Boris Stupler, as their two countries have more in common together, and we believe they have already formed a federation of sorts."

"What does this mean?"

"With Turkey no longer the guardian of NATO's southern European

flank, the US is left with a large void. This move would clear any constraints, allows Turkey to build a vast army, and, with the help of Stupler, dominate in the Middle East."
"Dangerous times."
"Indeed."

Chapter Seven

The president of the United States wrenched his neck looking for the source of the noise he'd just heard. "Was that an explosion?" he asked the aide as the limo lurched forward

"Secret Service confirms," the aide responded, touching the receiver in his ear. "We are under attack."

A fleeting thought entered the president's overstressed mind that somehow Tess had heard them talking about her, that she had orchestrated an immediate response and ordered him killed. He knew it was a ridiculous idea, but Tess was a force to be reckoned with, and the timing seemed incredibly coincidental. As the motorcade roared up the empty highway, reaching more than ninety miles per hour, he pushed the notion from his thoughts.

"Are we out of danger?" the president asked.

"For the moment," the aide responded, but they both knew the president was never out of danger, especially now that they were in the End Game.

Chasing Lies

Leia allowed herself a smile as the president's motorcade raced by her position. She had not missed. She never missed. Air support would be there in mere minutes, but Luke and Leia would already be gone, having successfully killed the man who was going to assassinate the leader of the free world.

And no one would ever know they were there.

The incident that could have changed everything would not even be a footnote in the Secret Service manual, would never make any history books, the evening news would make no mention of the incident. Officials would bury it. Should some local farmer or Boy Scout mention hearing an explosion, there would be an explanation that made perfect sense and had nothing to do with the truth. Steps were already being taken. It had never happened.

But somewhere, a man was cursing the Regulators for foiling the assassination.

"Twenty seconds," Wen announced as she, Chase, Shelby, and Grimes all had guns at the slots. "Stop!" she suddenly yelled. "Astronaut says FBI not for us!"

"Are you sure?" Grimes snapped.

"Stand down," Wen insisted.

"Nothing like waiting until the last second," Shelby said, handing her weapon back to Chase.

The Destino's exterior cams showed the FBI vehicles cruising by, never exiting I-35.

"Apparently they're here for some major drug bust. Chinese/Mexican connected operation."

"In the middle of *Iowa*?" Chase said, surprised.

"In the middle of everywhere," Grimes replied emphatically.

"Maybe we found our new mission," Wen said.

"We don't need a *new* mission, we already have one." Chase pointed at the image of the man on the screen.

"ID him," Grimes said, "and we'll be able to ID Belfort. ID Belfort, and we'll ID Belfort's boss, and so on up the food chain until we get to the kingpin."

Haris Tane's blue eyes flashed with fury as he momentarily fantasied about flinging his laptop across the room, in this case a fourteen-thousand square-foot seaside villa.

Better, he thought, *I should throw the man responsible for this monumental failure, this full fiasco of an operation, off the roof of one of my buildings.*

By "buildings," he meant skyscrapers. He owned dozens of gleaming towers around the world.

He liked those scenes in movies, when the loser got tossed off the roof like a sack of garbage. But this wasn't a movie. It was real life, and he was a little too dignified to pull off such stunts. Instead, he repeated what the man had just told him.

"The president is still alive."

"Yes."

"I thought I'd be watching the news coverage of his death right now, but instead I'm looking at you."

"Sorry."

"Sorry?" Tane narrowed his movie star eyes. "*Sorry?* I should toss your sorry ass off the roof!"

"What?" the man asked nervously, having never heard his boss talk like a mafia don before.

Tane shook his head. "What happened? Timetable slip up? Weapons malfunction? How did this perfectly planned operation go bad?"

"Our shooter was eliminated."

Tane moved his head back in surprise. "Secret Service found him? How?"

"It wasn't Secret Service."

"Then *who*?" Tane asked, his mind already moving past the answer to form a list of who might have arranged such a bold move against his agenda, a move against *him* personally. He quickly came to one name, and the real question became how that person had obtained such valuable information about his plan to assassinate the president . . . *precise* details down to the exact location and the specific means of attack. Tane had worked out all those answers and formed an entirely new list of questions even before the man replied to his first one.

"It could only have been the Regulators."

Chapter Eight

Shelby and Grimes parted ways with Chase and Wen in Iowa. The two former shadow people would continue working to turn others against the Circuit. "It will be a lot easier once we identify the guy in the photo," Chase had said.

"He's a nobody," Grimes had replied. "But with an organization as big as the Circuit, a nobody to them is a somebody to the rest of us."

A remote stretch of Texas coastline owned by a marine biology research non-profit, seemed an odd place for Chase and Wen to go. The twenty-nine acres of pristine marshlands bordered a state park, and except for a few single-story buildings that had been designed to fit into the environment with minor impact or notice, the area seemed devoid of human presence. Hardly visible from the air, anyone who *did* catch a glimpse of the structures would not give them a second thought, even if curious. The three buildings would appear to be unimportant. This was the spot Chase and Wen had chosen to hide that which was most precious to them: Wen's grandmother and Tu, the little boy they had rescued from China.

Chase pulled the rig into a large "garage" that had been specially made from a pair of modified metal RV enclosures topped with enough foliage to render them invisible. They could not see Sepio, an elite, private security force who exclusively served billionaires and whose exorbitant fees matched their skill level, but they knew the operatives were embedded across the acres, ready to defend against any attack.

"Chase Bank!" Tu said, using his favorite nickname for Chase and sharing hugs with him and Wen. "I've been working on the problem with the program for shadow people."

The product of a Chinese experiment, he was not a normal boy. While still an embryo, he'd been part of a highly classified medical experiment conducted and controlled by Communist Chinese government scientists. His genes had been manipulated for increased intelligence. The results were both stunning and disturbing. Chase and Wen had rescued and "adopted" him when he was seven.

Now ten years old, Tu easily worked incredibly complex math equations in his head, and could quickly reason through intricate problems with machine-like precision, aided by a photographic memory.

"Did you come up with anything?" Chase asked.

"Of course," he said, as Wen's grandmother, Zǔ mǔ, greeted them.

"He works too hard," Zǔ mǔ said in broken English.

"Oh, Zu-ey, it's not work when it's fun. Besides, we have to beat the bad guys."

Tu had *loved* working for an anti-China Think Tank, helping with children's issues, but after Chase and Wen "died," Tu and Zŭ mŭ had needed to go into hiding again. Tu, who had also grown close to the Astronaut, collaborated often with the savant to solve big problems facing Chase and Wen. The Astronaut and Tu shared a bond of super intelligence. However, both were aware that where technicians had altered DNA to make Tu's advanced brain, nature had made the Astronaut's super mind.

"The way we are tracking them is linear," Tu said. "That means whenever they cut something out, we lose them. It is easy for them to stop. We need to be following them in circles."

"What does that mean?" Wen asked.

"Imagine looking at the Circuit's operations from above, like in a plane. I love to fly in planes. From that vantage point we could see everything, all the connections, and whenever they cut one, we will have already seen the other side, so we can keep following."

"Okay, but . . . " Wen began.

"I know what you mean," Chase cut in, excited. "If we write the program to immediately take a full perspective look at any data point—"

"Yes," Tu said. "Connect the dots the moment a dot appears."

"Send your idea to Bull and Dez," Chase said. The Astronaut and Tu were just two of the odd collection of people Chase had accumulated since his flight from "the real world" began. Dez, his original business partner, and Bull, a wild and gifted hacker, were already leading the development of AI-run computer systems that would track and counter the Circuit.

"Already did," Tu said, smiling, then racing off to circle the rig. Tu loved the truck, and thought *Rolling Thunder* was a better name than *Destino*, but Chase didn't agree. "You will change your mind, once you drive it long enough," Tu told him.

The ten-day visit was much shorter than any of them would have liked, but it was all they dared.

As usual, Tu wanted to leave with them, even though he knew he couldn't. But they promised to keep him up to date on what they were doing.

"The news is scaring me," Tu admitted.

"Don't worry," Chase said. "There won't be a nuclear war."

"I don't think about that," Tu said. "It's the computer virus. It could destroy our projects. Stop us from finding the shadow people."

"Better create a way to protect us then." Chase winked at him.

The boy nodded, giving him a slight smile, but his eyes still showed his worry.

Chapter Nine

Wen looked up from a paper map in her lap as Chase drove the Destino. "We are truly in the middle of nowhere," she said.

"That's the idea."

They passed through Wheeless, a tiny, forgotten town in the western most part of Oklahoma, where the dust bowl met the Santa Fe trail and the plains climbed into New Mexico's high desert, the last place one would ever look for a high-tech command post that was the headquarters for the most lethal private army ever amassed in America.

"There's nothing here," Wen said as they passed another abandoned farmhouse, its flaky, chalky white paint looking like the only thing keeping it from collapsing completely. "Are you *sure* this is right?"

"We're not there yet," Chase said. "Look for Camp Nichols."

She searched the internet. "'Camp Nichols,'" she began, reading the entry out loud. "'Under orders from Colonel

Christopher "Kit" Carson, Union soldiers constructed the outpost in 1865 to provide protection to travelers on the Cimarron route of the Santa Fe Trail.'"

"I like history."

"'Forty thousand square feet enclosed by native stone walls,'" Wen continued. "'Roughly three hundred troops were quartered in dugouts and tents. The fort also housed a stone commissary and hospital.' It's only rubble and scant ruins today. How is this the headquarters for our Army?"

"The old 'fort' is on private property. You'll see," Chase said as they pulled onto a long dirt drive that ended in a ramshackle shotgun house that didn't look much sturdier than the empty shacks they'd seen outside Wheeless.

A tall man dressed in black fatigues emerged from the structure, which hardly seemed big enough to house him. Wen examined the hulking man, who she'd later learn was about the same height as Chase, six-two, but seemed quite a bit taller. Dark hair buzzed in an out-of-date flat-top, and three-day stubble completed the soldier-of-fortune persona he'd apparently cultivated.

"I'm Blitz," the man said in a voice that belonged to a rodeo announcer. "Welcome to the Camp." He held out his hand. Chase took it.

"That's a good nick name for a guy in your line of work," Wen said. "What's your real name?"

"Don't have one."

"Okay, mystery man, impress us."

He winked at Wen, perhaps trying to soften her up. It did the opposite.

"It doesn't look like much," Chase said, surveying the area. "Is that tumbleweed?" he asked as several tired shrubs rolled by.

"Yep," Blitz said. "And all this nothingness, by design, fits the mission. *We don't exist* kind of thing."

"But there's an army I paid for somewhere around here, right?"

"Sure enough. You're standing on it."

Tess Federgreen, head of the ultra-secret Corporate Intelligence Security Section—or CISS—was ready for a break. CISS, arguably the most powerful clandestine agency in the world (and the least known), had been formed as a joint operation of the CIA, NSA, and FBI, with an unusual mandate to prevent war between corporations. Every week there seemed to be twice as much pressure as the week before. "It's insane," Tess said, almost daily.

"I won't bother you unless the world starts to melt down," Linda, Tess's deputy, said as she handed her a secure tablet with the latest briefings.

"It's already started to meltdown," Tess muttered, narrowing her green eyes.

"Maybe it'll slow down a little," Linda said.

"Ha. If only . . . "

"At least Taos is still Taos," Linda said, speaking of the New Mexico town that was Tess's favorite spot on earth; a place where she escaped as often as possible to dance, to take in the art, to hike the dusty trails, eat green chilis, or, in the winter, to ski. Fortunately, there had been an unusual amount of early season snow this year.

Tess glanced up at the giant photo prints of Northern New Mexico. "I need Taos time."

"Too bad Michael Hearne won't be in town," Linda

said, knowing Tess was a huge fan of the singer, a former Taos resident.

"At least I've got his new album," Tess said. "And Don Richmond and the Rifters are playing at the Sagebrush, so at least I can dance."

Linda looked down at the buzzing phone in her hand. "It's the president."

Tess didn't *want* to take the call, but the president of the United States was the closest thing she had to a boss. She sighed and held out her hand.

Linda left the room, not because she wasn't allowed to hear the call, but because she had a million things to do, and she knew the call would put Tess in a bad mood. The threat of nuclear war tended to do that to people.

Cranson was annoyed to be back at the plantation house. He had hoped to never see the place again.

"We know where she's going," Belfort told Cranson. "A vacation at a little ski resort in Taos, New Mexico."

"Skiing?" Cranson asked, as if it was a gift. "How convenient."

"I want it done on the slopes. We need it to look accidental. I'm thinking an avalanche would be nice."

"In November?"

"They've had early heavy snows. Conditions there are always a little dicey," he said.

"What about her security?"

"Four CISS agents. They might as well just perish along with her. Heroes . . . that kind of thing."

Cranson nodded. "I understand."

"You'll need to get there early, make sure everything's ready."

"It shouldn't be a problem."

"You'll have the element of surprise, and, of course, numbers are on your side."

"Four CISS agents? It's as if they *want* her dead."

"Perhaps they do," Belfort said.

He gave Cranson the details of Tess's itinerary, and the name of a local contact who could help. "Be careful what you do with your computer," Belfort said. "That virus is pretty dangerous."

ANC - Always News Channel - Top Story

"Stu Lemon reporting. Our top story at this hour: The NoLiv virus has now been reported in more than seventy-three countries. As you may have seen in our earlier coverage, this is not acting like past computer viruses. There are documented cases of data distortion, with as many as sixty thousand bank accounts already affected. Barn Winslow, from TransNational Bank, explains."

"Thanks for having me, Stu. So far, our firewalls are holding. We've taken precautions by bringing our network offline and switching our customers to telebanking. However, most of the other banks have experienced infections. We've never seen anything like this before. The virus actually targets these accounts and withdraws almost everything, down to a few cents."

"That must be difficult for people, to suddenly find what is basically a zero balance. Are the banks able to correct the deficit and restore the balances?"

"It's not that simple. The virus somehow makes these transactions look legitimate, so tracing them has proven challenging."

"Meaning the banks have not had success yet."

"Correct."

"And where is the money going?"
"We are working with the Federal Reserve and law enforcement agencies to determine that."
"Could this be what's behind this virus? The money?"
"I'm a banker, so I'd have to answer yes, it's always about the money."

Chapter Ten

Blitz led them down into the basement of the ramshackle house.

Chase glanced around the tight space, cluttered with stacks of old books, dusty shelves filled with odds and ends, including at least two stripped lawnmower engines. A workbench served as a bike rack for several old bicycles in need of repair. A washing machine and dryer piled with laundry seemed recent additions, but next to them was a long-faded red bookshelf jammed with worn copies of National Geographic. Chase glanced at the dates—most were from the 40s and 50s.

"Looks like it's time to do a load of wash," Blitz said, laughing. "We just don't want dirty laundry piling up, you know what I mean?" He pushed the old rotating setting dial on the washing machine, and the entire wall, including the plumbing pipes, rotated in a nearly silent motion.

"Impressive feat of engineering," Chase said.

"I've always loved secret passages. You know, like in those old mystery movies when a bookshelf reveals a secret room?" Blitz pointed to the three-foot opening revealed behind the dryer.

They walked into a small space lit blue by LED lighting.

"Stairs down," Blitz said, leading the way.

"Are you sure we can trust this guy?" Wen whispered.

"For now," Chase replied.

"Not quite the vote of confidence I was hoping for."

They descended the steps. Twenty seconds later, they were at the bottom facing a steel door with a biometric reader on the wall next to it.

"Right behind you," Blitz said, pressing his palm to the pad. The heavy door slid open. On the other side, a short corridor led to a series of doors. After another palm scan, one revealed an expansive room that resembled the control room in the Destino, except bigger—*much* bigger.

"Nice," Chase said, wanting to get inside and look around.

"Later." Blitz motioned him a bit further down the hall. "First, you need to see the *truly* remarkable side of our operations."

This time no scan was required. Blitz entered a simple ten-digit code and a gigantic garage door lifted.

"Wow," Chase said, attempting to take in the vast space. It had to be as big as six football fields.

"Largest underground training facility in the world."

"That you know of," Wen corrected.

"True," Blitz agreed, "and since facilities like this are often underground for a reason, like because they're intended to be secret, who knows . . . But I love the sound of 'largest in the world'."

"It *is* big," Wen amended. The massive "arena" had been built to resemble the above-ground world.

"Let's take a walk," Blitz said, starting a slow jog

through the faux forest. Eventually the "trees" thinned, and they were in a small "town", and soon wandered through an urban setting where *skyscrapers* touched the top of the twenty-eight-foot-high ceilings. "This is where we train the most elite special operatives in the world," Blitz explained, glancing at Wen as if to see if she was going to allow his claim to go unchallenged. When she said nothing, he turned to Chase. "This is where your money is going."

"I didn't pay to build this facility, did I?" Chase asked, thinking it might have cost more than his entire 1.2-billion-dollar net worth.

"Nah, your money just helps keep it operational. We've got additional contracts."

"With Tess Federgreen?" Chase asked.

"I can't confirm any affiliation with past or active clients. You understand."

"Yeah," Chase said, but Tess had been the one to connect Chase with Blitz, so it went without saying that CISS was a large and important user of them.

"What about the army?" Wen asked.

"There are currently three hundred and six men and seventeen women on site. We've got an undetermined number of others in the field right now."

"Undetermined?" Chase asked.

"Let's just say it's more than we've got here. But they're not all fighters. Some are intel gatherers, some are knockers."

"Knockers?" Wen echoed questioningly.

"That's what we call the ones who utilize deception and other means to damage enemy operations and assets. We do a little bit of psych-ops. From what I see, the shadow people do psych-ops as their specialty, or one of them."

"They're pretty good at assassination, too," Chase said.

Blitz nodded. "Yeah, but you two are still here today, so they can't be *that* good, right?"

"We might be better," Wen said.

"Yeah, I read the files." Blitz cleared his throat. "Thanks to the data Grimes' provided, we've got seventy-eight of their shadow operatives under some sort of surveillance or watch."

"Have they been planted yet?" Chase asked, referring to an enhanced GPS tag the Astronaut and Dez had developed.

"About a third of them," Blitz said. "That's a tough business, but we'll get them done."

"Any idea how many more to find?"

"Currently, could be north of five hundred, but the Circuit seems to have an endless supply of money, which means an endless supply of shadow people."

Chapter Eleven

Haris Tane had spent the day working phones. "Regulators are the scum of the earth," he'd said so many times, he'd considered getting it printed on tee-shirts.

But Regulators weren't even supposed to *exist*. They were an awful rumor among the shadow people and other killers he employed.

"Do you really believe there's a Darth Vader?" an associate asked him, almost mockingly. Vader was allegedly the code name of the person who ran the Regulators.

"Anything is possible," Tane had responded.

The man laughed and texted him a Yoda emoji, but Tane had been battling the mystical Regulators for years, even without ever actually seeing a single one of them. None of it seemed funny to him.

Whenever Tane dwelled on the Regulators, which was as little as possible, but more than he cared to admit, he thought of the Skyggers. He recalled a similar conversation he'd had decades earlier with another man, after he'd first heard whispers about the Skyggers, who were, he would soon learn, a group of extremely sophisticated stealth agents. The old man he'd gone to, known as *the maestro*, had taken Tane into his confidence on many other matters, and now it seemed he was ready to share the biggest secret of all.

"Skyggers may or may not exist," the white-haired man, who exuded so much wealth and power that even now, years after his death, Tane still felt inferior in comparison, had said before continuing in a gravelly whisper, "That question will never have an answer, and this is how it always will be."

"But what do they do?"

The maestro had squinted his eyes behind the rimless spectacles he always wore, and looked to the heavens as if the answers may have resided only there. "They change the world."

"Change?"

"Improve," the maestro had clarified, and then explained that the Skyggers were perhaps, "The most important players in the affairs of men. Little has occurred during the last five decades that they have not touched."

"But how?"

"There is an invisible force at the center of most major news stories. Skyggers are that force."

"How is that possible?" Tane had pressed. "Is the media in on it?"

"The media is not what you think," the maestro said in an amused tone. "You only think they are journalists, but they are carefully controlled and manipulated. They spread propaganda, not facts."

"Whose propaganda?"

The old man had smiled as if he might laugh, as if it was an incredibly silly question for anyone to ask, and that Tane asking it was even more ludicrous. "Ours."

That was the day Tane had discovered how the world

really worked. All the corruptions and schemes of which he'd previously been aware, suddenly seemed trivial. The maestro told him that a long time ago, the tasks had been handled by the CIA and other secret government agencies. "But of course, the clumsy bureaucratic handling of such things proved too unreliable."

"Who started the Skyggers?" he'd asked.

The maestro placed a single finger to his lips and shook his head slowly. "There is no before and no after."

Since the Maestro's death in 2017, the Skyggers reported directly to Tane. He was now the maestro, although it pained him to hear himself addressed as such. To him, there would only ever be one maestro.

The first thing Tane had found about the Skyggers was they were ultra-elite. There were never more than twenty-four of them, and they operated more like IT-Squads than shadow people. They moved in the periphery, making things happen, carefully orchestrating events that would have ripple effects lasting years, decades even. Killing was a rare and small aspect of their work.

Skyggers use was relatively rare, and they never worked alone. There were just two forms of deployment. A *Skygger Gloom* meant three agents were involved. They took part in situations such as mass shootings, riots, demonstrations, and sudden causes and movements that seemed to instantly fill the airwaves and the consciousness of a population. A *Skygger End*, when the full twenty-four operatives were in play, was extremely rare. The last time there had been a Skygger End had been sixteen years prior to Tane taking control. He himself had never actually ordered an End.

However, he had put multiple Skygger Glooms in simultaneous operation, including during recent turmoil following the 2020 US presidential election. There had been a lot of investigations into those events, but he wasn't worried. His people controlled most of them.

He remembered talking to the maestro after 9/11, asking the old man if he was worried about one of the Skyggers talking.

"We pay the Skyggers so much money they couldn't possibly be disloyal." He had looked into the distance for a moment, before continuing. "Each is regularly subjected to polygraphs, ocular, and fMRI brain scans for lie detection. They are also constantly monitored and AI assessed. These agents all come from classified agencies, the best of the best. But the biggest deterrent of all is they, better than anyone, know what we are capable of. Each Skygger is certain that if anything occurs outside of the secrecy, he or she will be dead in minutes."

"Have we ever lost one?"

"No. These people are like knights of the round table. They don't even know how to act beyond the realm and devotion to the crown."

"And you are the king?"

"Or the man with the most gold," he'd said, then laughed. "I suppose it's the same thing."

ANC News Bulletin

Government officials are asking that the public refrain from withdrawing money from banks for the next two weeks. This is a temporary measure meant to stop our financial institutions from being overwhelmed, as the NoLiv virus has swept through the banking industry with alarming speed.

The chair of the Federal Reserve has repeatedly stated, and reiterated hours ago, that your money is safe, and is fully insured by the FDIC. Samantha Lawson, the White House point person on the NoLiv virus, also issued a statement, saying, in part, "The money supply is not at risk. However, please conserve cash until this temporary situation is resolved."

In other news:
The Secret Service has confirmed an issue or incident occurred with the president's motorcade today in a rural, wooded area of Maryland when a vehicle in the motorcade caught fire. Although the cause is under investigation, preliminary indications are this was a mechanical issue, and the engine manufacturer is now involved in a review. The White House stresses that the presidential limousine was not involved. There were no injuries, nor any disruption to the president's schedule.

Chapter Twelve

Chase was happy to finally have an army to go up against the shadow people, but after reviewing the latest data, he realized it still wasn't big enough.

"Who are these people?" he asked, looking at the number of shadow people they'd already traced to the Circuit. "How did they amass all this?" The screens rolled with records of the seemingly endless resources at their disposal.

"By killing anyone in their way," Wen said.

Initially, Chase and Wen had been reluctant to use Blitz, but building their own army from scratch would have been far more expensive and time consuming. "We might have enough money," Chase had told Wen, "but we definitely don't have enough time."

Blitz finished giving them a tour of the underground camp, but avoided direct contact with any of the operatives.

"Probably not a good idea for us to meet them," Wen agreed.

Blitz explained that there were barracks at the other end of the facility, but that they rotated people out as soon as their training was complete. "We generally bring in experienced vets, so no one is here too long, but we make sure they're up on our S&M."

"S&M?" Chase echoed, raising a brow.

"Systems and methods."

Chase nodded. "What about loyalty?"

"Always a wildcard," Blitz acknowledged. "The Circuit can pay more."

"I don't think he understands quite how shadow people work," Wen said. "They won't pay more, they'll just kill more."

"Hope you're right."

"Me, too."

They wound up back in the control room.

"That's the man from the photo," Wen said, pointing to one of the screens.

Chase recalled looking at the images of the man with a Senator and the US Attorney General with Grimes in Iowa. "What happened to him?"

"We found him like that," Blitz said. "A bullet in his head just before we got there."

After another two days of reviewing plans and operations with Blitz, they checked in with Tess.

"We need to meet," she told them in a clipped tone. "In person."

"Is that really necessary?" Wen asked, surprised. "We're dead, remember?"

"Being dead is the only thing keeping us alive," Chase added.

"I've got some information on the Circuit," Tess explained. "International money laundering, political connections…"

"And that warrants an in-person?" Wen asked.

"Not by itself, but when you hear the rest, you'll understand."

"Where? When?" Chase asked.

She told them a time and place in a cryptic response only they would be able to figure out. Taos. The next afternoon.

None of them knew she might be dead by then.

Back in the control room, Chase stared at the screens, the data tracks, the combat units, the targeted operations, and felt buried by the enormity of what they'd initiated.

We have an army… we're at war, he thought. *But who are we at war with?*

Yet he knew it wasn't a single explosive action that would ignite the conflict. This was going to be a tense game of patience while they obtained more information on the Circuit and their assets.

Tess had intimated that Blitz had built his organization and the underground camp working for clients such as the NSA and CIA for at least the last decade. That background made Chase optimistic that they could unravel the group behind the shadow people, but he wondered how soon.

"When will we have enough?" Chase asked.

"Look at this," Blitz said, showing charts detailing money trails. "Every day it gets bigger."

Chase had been experiencing the same with their research in the Destino, and so had the Astronaut, but he'd hoped Blitz, being tied into the NSA, would be making better progress.

"Too many resources are going into the Turkish situation," Chase said. "Government priorities are costing us."

"We cannot wait." Blitz frowned. "Soon we'll have enough to send them a message."

"That makes no sense," Wen said. "Why would we want to send them a message? Why would we give them any warning at all?"

"These people are not stupid," Chase said, echoing Wen's concerns. "We know who they employ. They pay the most, they get the best. The Circuit will try to pilfer our ranks, same as we're doing."

"Don't worry," Blitz said. "They won't get anything until we have enough information to take out the majority of their operatives at once. The message will be part of the offensive—calculated psych-ops."

"I still don't like it," Wen said.

"You pay the bills, but I get the kills." Blitz chuckled. "This isn't a mission, not a one-off. It ain't no smash and grab. It's different than anything you've ever done before. This is a *war*." He met her gaze, suddenly intense and humorless. "And in a war like this, there is no second chance."

Chapter Thirteen

The following day, Chase and Wen left the camp. After double checking all their computer systems and installing a shielding the Astronaut said would help against NoLiv, they continued the push into Circuit assets.

Driving until they received a ping that a critical operation was underway, Chase finally pulled over near the Cimarron Cliffs outside the historic village of Cimarron, New Mexico, an old western mining town on the eastern slopes of the Sangre de Cristo Mountains. However, he had to drive out of the canyon and on toward the town of Eagle Nest before a reliable signal could be found.

Inside the control room of the Destino, Chase and Wen watched the large monitor displaying a feed relayed from the camp.

"The operation is about to go down," Blitz's voice came over the feed. "He's a shadow person. We're running links on him now."

"I recognize him," Wen said. "See his tattoo? He's from Finale."

"Finale is a group of mercenaries, elite special forces from countries around the world," Chase told Blitz. "A kind of French Foreign Legion run out of Morocco."

"I know who they are," Blitz replied.

"This guy took out an escort with us when we were in Thailand, remember, Chase?" Wen asked. "The jungle? We were trying to reach Dr. Dunson, as part of that pharmaceutical—"

"Yeah," Chase said. "He only escaped because you thought they had killed me."

"Right."

"We have an ID on him. Steven Rogers," Blitz said. "We're going to see if we can turn him."

"In the *highly* unlikely event you're successful with that, I'd like to be the one to interrogate him," Wen said.

"That's our operative coming in now," Blitz warned. The camper, dressed in tennis whites, strolled onto the clay court like he did it every day. "Two more campers just outside the courts."

"What's the plan?" Chase asked.

"Our guy will let Rogers know he's not alone, and then he's going to have a little conversation with him, see if he'll help us out," Blitz said. "But I'm curious… why don't you think we can convince Rogers to come to our side?"

The camper sat on the bench next to Rogers as the shadow person was lacing up his Nikes.

"He's Finale," Wen said. "He eats and breathes loyalty."

"Staring death in the face can change a person," Blitz said.

Chasing Lies

It was obvious by the expression on his face that Rogers was not happy. "I'm having a little trouble with our audio," Blitz said.

"Hope it's not the virus," Wen mused.

"I don't think so. We should have it in a second."

"Their conversation seems to be getting animated," Chase said, as Rogers was flailing his arms.

"This is probably the part where our guy is mentioning money," Blitz said.

The camera angles suddenly went wonky, bringing jerking movements and chaotic blurs.

"Oh hell!" Blitz swore.

"What's happening?" Chase asked.

"Nothing good," Wen replied.

When the camera regained focus, there was a hole in Rogers' head, and his body had slid backwards against the fence.

"Give me something!" Blitz said.

The camper who'd been next to Rogers had rolled under the bench and was scrambling to get off the court.

"We're trying to find where the shot came from," another camper reported. "He's a damned ghost! There's no impression trace, nothing!"

Blitz checked his monitors. The impression trace gave a digital heat signal after a person left an area. "That could mean he's still there."

"Maybe it's not a him," Wen said.

But Wen was wrong. Luke, operating that day without his pal Leia, was already back at his car before the camper got off the tennis court.

An hour later, Cranson, who had monitors for all active shadow people, phoned Belfort.

"We just lost another one."

Belfort knew he meant one of their operatives. "Damn it, what's going *on*?" Belfort said. "That must be, what, nine now?"

"Actually it's eleven in the last three weeks, if you don't count Boggs."

They *weren't* counting Boggs, who had died in a drunk driving accident ten days earlier. Boggs had not been the one drinking. A car, driven by an intoxicated man, came into his lane. Boggs had died at the scene. The drunk driver, miraculously, had survived. At the time, Boggs was the third shadow person they'd lost in the recent string of deaths. Cranson still wasn't sure if it had been an isolated event, and they normally would've written it off has an accident, but since someone out there seemed to be removing their operatives one-by-one on an almost daily basis, he was keeping the possibility that Boggs had been a victim of an intentional hit rather than the accidental one. Belfort, on the other hand, saw conspiracy everywhere.

"Of course we're counting Boggs, and there's little doubt that we have Grimes to thank for all this. Who else would have the information about our operatives and wants them dead?"

"Certainly seems to be the prime suspect, but I know Grimes, and he's too smart for this. He would've disappeared."

"He can't disappear from us," Belfort said.

"He also knows he can't kill all our operatives," Cranson added. "So why try? Why not just hide away?"

"Maybe it's not Grimes at all," Belfort theorized. "Maybe it's Chase and Wen."

Cranson was happy he wasn't facing Belfort, because he involuntarily rolled his eyes. He wanted to say, *not this again*, but instead played out the theory. "If they somehow *miraculously* survived that end-of-the-world blast that buried them, why not stay hidden? They'd finally be safe and free of us."

"Because they're just crazy enough to think they can take out all our operatives. The guy's got a billion dollars. That'll buy a *lot* of guns."

"Not enough," Cranson said, thinking of the portion of the Circuit's power that he was aware of, and it was enormous. "Not nearly enough."

ANC - Always News Channel - Breaking News

"KiKi Carlyle reporting. Breaking News at this hour: The president is urging calm as runs on banks have swept across the nation. The images you are seeing have not been on this scale since the early 1930s. Depositors lined up by the thousands outside banks around the country, but unlike the panics during the early years of the Great Depression, today customers also have access to their accounts via the internet.
"Or, rather, they did. Today, the president used his authority to shut down internet banking. The White House says this is a temporary move to protect the banking system, but thousands of depositors don't see it that way. Violence has been reported in seven cities as people have launched attacks on the bank buildings, and even on the bankers themselves when they can find them. Governors in New York and California, where the violence has been most widespread, have vowed to crack down. As you can see by this footage, National Guard troops have moved in to restore order."

Chapter Fourteen

Overnight, they'd parked the Destino in Angel Fire, a mountain town on the Enchanted Circle outside of Taos, so they wouldn't have to drive the big rig on the small roads leading through Taos Canyon. They'd arranged to borrow a Ford Mustang Shelby GT500SE, one of Chase's favorite American made vehicles, but at the last minute needed to switch to a Subaru Outback because of the snowy weather.

Wen looked at her ringing phone. "It's Grimes," she said, double checking the encryption.

"Listen," Grimes said when he heard the connection go through. "Our friends have a high priority removal plan in place for someone close to you."

Chase immediately thought of his brother, Boone, and of his mother. "Who?"

"The person you're on your way to meet."

Chase mouthed Tess's name to Wen. Her eyes widened.

"How soon?" Chase asked.

"It's in play now, a big operation. I don't know how much time you have, but it's at your destination."

"We're still at least ninety minutes from there," Chase said, pushing on the accelerator. "We'll see how quickly we can move. Meantime, find out all you can."

Wen contacted the Astronaut and asked him to try to reach Tess' deputy and warn them. They wouldn't find out until later that her assistant was in a suddenly called intelligence meeting about the nuclear threat from Turkey. She didn't get the message in time.

As usual, whenever they were in a new area, Wen read and researched. "Wish we had time to explore Taos," Wen said. It was a familiar refrain. The two of them had visited many beautiful places, but were usually too busy dodging bullets to enjoy the area. "Listen to this, from the Taos Pueblo website, 'The ancestors of the Taos people lived in this valley long before Columbus discovered America, and hundreds of years before Europe emerged from the Dark Ages.'" She looked out the window, checking for trouble, wondering if the snow would stop. "The buildings were probably constructed more than a thousand years ago. It says the first Spanish explorers arrived in 1540 and believed that the Pueblo was one of the fabled golden cities of Cibola. 'The pueblo is the oldest continuously inhabited community in the United States.'"

"Maybe we'll have time later today."

"The town is filled with galleries. It's been an art colony for decades, and there's lots of history."

"We'll come back one day."

They both knew it was unlikely.

"'The American flag is flown above the Taos Plaza twenty-four-seven,'" she went on. "Apparently during the

American Civil War, Confederate sympathizers attempted to steal the flag. So Kit Carson, a Union officer, stationed guards to protect the flag. Ever since, the flag has remained flying twenty-four hours a day."

"Same Kit Carson who ordered Camp Nichols to be built?"

"Yes," Wen said.

"Hope that's a good sign," Chase said, thinking of Blitz and the formation of their private army to take on the shadow people, wondering how big the fight would get.

Chase pushed the speed limit as much as he could with the slick roads. By the time highway 64 through the canyon turned into Kit Carson Road, a stretch filled with art galleries, the Astronaut had gotten back to them. "As you know, getting through to CISS, which doesn't officially exist, is almost impossible," he began. "The three direct lines we have to Tess, her deputy, and one other, have all gone silent."

"You mean there's no way to warn her?" Chase yelled as he took a right onto Paseo del Pueblo Norte.

"We're heading up to the ski valley right now," Wen told the Astronaut. "Find a way to get to her!"

The Taos Ski Valley's base sat on one of the highest municipalities in the US, with an elevation of 9,207 feet, although the highest part within village limits was 12,581 feet. The world class ski resort was watched over by Wheeler Peak, and skirted by the Pueblo lands, which included sacred Blue Lake. The lake and surrounding wilderness were part of vast tracts of land returned to the Pueblo people by former President Nixon.

"How do you know she's at the ski valley?" the Astronaut asked.

"Whenever she comes to Taos, if there's snow, she's skiing," Chase said. "Our meeting with her isn't until five at the Taos Inn. Judging by the falling snow, it's a powder day, so that's a guarantee she's up there."

"The mountains..." Wen said softly. "That's a great place for them to get her."

"She'll have security with her."

"Not enough of them," Wen said. "Those mountains are like a vast canvass, and they can paint a hundred ways to die on them!"

Real Truth - Internet Fact Based News

Fact-based news source on the Internet.
Posted by JI Right
Don't believe what they are saying in the mainstream media, or especially what the government is saying.
These runs on banks are only the beginning. The government is moving to block transactions in cryptocurrencies and gold prices are being kept artificially low by inflating the amount of paper gold available. All that against a backdrop of these new "temporary" regulations that people cannot use banks, cannot access their money.
The violence is a real threat to the elites. We expect them to shut down these protests within hours.
The NoLiv virus has apparently destroyed banking records. It has been distorting data, changing bank balances, charging small fees, etc. This cannot be fixed.
The virus lies.

Chapter Fifteen

Tess felt the exhilaration of the day, the crisp air, the warm sun. She loved the mountains, and Taos Ski Valley was her favorite. When one of her security detail, who wasn't used to the double-black diamond runs, complained, Tess laughed and then gave him the well-worn line, "Taos is a four letter word . . . for steep!"

The agent thought back on the map he'd studied and some of the names of the ski runs: *Snakedance, Inferno, Lower Inferno,* and *Psychopath*. "Is this a ski resort, or a torture chamber?" he muttered under his breath.

They'd just skied *Walkyries Chute* and worked their way back up to the *Highline Ridge*. The agent was relieved to learn the next run was dubbed "Main Street." *Sounds simple enough*, he thought.

"I'm glad conditions are too rough for them to open the lift," Tess said. "Kachina has only had a lift for a few seasons. Before that, we always hiked the ridge to get to the run."

Lucky us. The icy wind pummeled them, fully exposed on the narrow trail winding along the ridgeline.

"Do you see what the sun does to the crystals in the snow?" Tess asked, almost no strain in her voice.

"Make it colder?" the agent asked breathlessly.

"It plays the light. Ski anywhere else in the world, and you won't see the rays bend like this. The light here, the way it is, the *magic* of it—it changes the appearance of everything. Do you see how *vivid* it all looks?"

The agent glanced up ahead, seeing Kachina Peak, their destination, still farther off than he'd like. Beyond that was Wheeler, at 13,167 feet, New Mexico's highest mountain. They were in the southern most subrange of the Rocky Mountains, the Sangre de Cristos.

"Don't you love the Sangres?" Tess asked, still oblivious that anyone could be anything but happy to be here.

"Blood of Christ," the man said, repeating the translated version of the mountains' name. "Another pleasant image."

Tess didn't hear him; she was absorbed, dazzled anew by it all. Taos always took her away from the stress and the pressure of everything Washington. The turmoil of her life had never been worse, never more pressing, yet all that was different up on the slopes.

The day was glorious. Fresh snow had fallen all night, and although the white stuff was still coming down in town, where they were, very high up, the sky was blue.

"Powder day," Tess said, for the fifth time, as they finally reached the summit.

She surveyed the peaks ringing the top of the world like a crown of white, speckled with green ponderosas heavy with snow.

The drop was intimidating even to an experienced skier

like Tess. The agents exchanged concerned glances. They were all skiers, but not at her level.

Tess missed their apprehension, her mind, as always, moving fast. She was thinking ahead about seeing Don Richmond and the Rifters play that night, and had heard a rumor that her favorite singer, Michael Hearne, was in town and might show up on stage with them. She was also looking forward to stopping in to see her favorite photographer, Geraint Smith, and picking up another of his signed photo prints for her collection, probably two. His photos of Taos filled her offices.

However, all those thoughts were instantly relegated to memory. Right now she was one with the mountain. Her breath was controlled, eyes focused. *Up here, closer to the sun, magic happens.* The sun reflected in the snow, the deep blue sky like a drape opening against the high peaks. It all seemed like something from her imagination.

Tess pushed off. At first it felt as if she'd jumped from an airplane, something she'd done several times. Then her skis hit the powder and she was floating, soaring, flying in a dream. Down. Speed. Hundreds of feet blurred past in a seductive descent.

An indeterminable amount of time later, the distant sound of thunder tried to wake her from the dream.

The noise immediately turned horrific as it reverberated from the cliffs and peaks, now above her. *Boom, boom, boom, BOOM!*

Weeks' worth of early snow came crashing down with the fury and vengeance of an angry God. Tess knew she was in trouble as she screamed to the wind, "Avalanche!"

ANC - Always News Channel - Breaking News

Chasing Lies

"KiKi Carlyle reporting. Breaking News at this hour: We've just learned that Senator Robert Hale's personal and official computers, including those in his senate office, have tested positive for the NoLiv virus. Hale is the Chairman of the Senate Armed Services Committee, and sits on the Intelligence Committee. He has been working closely with the President on the situation with Turkey.
"'We don't believe there has been any breach of classified data,'" the senator's spokeswoman said.
"The senator's office also announced that new computers were brought in immediately, and are currently being kept off all networks."

Chapter Sixteen

Luke held his position standing on the top of one of the tallest towers in Dubai. The luxury suite inside stretched out in all directions. He estimated the cost of the space to have exceeded fifty million dollars. He usually was good at gauging such things. This time he guessed low by thirty million.

Once again, Leia had drawn the short straw, in the lead because of those nerves of steel. She was playing the hostess. "It's against the rules," he said in her ear.

She was still several floors below in another part of the suite, and chose to ignore his comment.

He'd had the more difficult entrance. She would walk in with the target, but he didn't have that luxury of being a beautiful woman.

Her silence might have worried him, except she was wearing a microchip linked to a monitoring AI which told him that she was still upright. He also knew she was not responding because they had had this argument about the rules several times.

Chasing Lies

This was the job they never should have taken. Every part of it was wrong. *We shouldn't be here*, he thought. He didn't want to say it out loud. It was too late anyway, they were in it, no need to make things worse. Leia knew how he felt. She agreed it was screwed up, but she believed they had no choice.

Why do they want him dead?

The Regulators had multiple backers; they were the paymasters. Sometimes Luke called them generals, and the first rule was you *never* killed a backer.

Just before they'd dropped into Dubai, Luke and Leia had their final argument.

"We can't do this," he'd said for the twentieth time.

"*The* general gave this order," she said, emphasizing *the* because it had come from the most important backer, a ten star general among five star generals. "He's the supreme allied commander!"

"Darth Vader," Luke said, stating the backer's code name. It was no accident that they called him Vader, as his power and wealth could have built a Death Star. "But why?"

"He told you why."

"No, I asked him if things had changed, if this was an exception."

"And he told you: 'Both. This is the first exception because things have changed.'"

"But that's not a reason, and when I pushed for more, he told me he didn't see why I needed that information. And I said, 'Because *I'm* the one breaking the damn rule.' *My* head's out there on the chopping block."

"The backers have disagreements among themselves."

"That's some disagreement," Luke scoffed. "If I get in a disagreement with my spouse, I don't have someone kill them."

"You're not married."

He waved a hand. "Whatever, that's not the *point*. I'm not a backer."

"Backers play by different rules than the rest of us," she said evenly. "You should know that by now."

"So they're having some territorial disputes with each other? Because if we're walking into the middle of some Mafia-like gangland war zone, I need to know."

"Vader has always told us what we needed to know."

"I don't know about *that*," he said.

"He's never sent us into a situation we didn't get out of."

"This could be the one."

As he waited for Leia and the target to arrive, he remembered his words and wondered if this *was* their final job. Beyond that was the question of if anyone would believe the headlines that one of the world's wealthiest men had jumped from one of the tallest buildings in the world.

We're about to find out.

As expected, the man's security detail remained in the foyer as he walked alone with Leia into the back rooms. The site had been carefully selected. They could have killed him anywhere in the world. He traveled a lot, had other residences, offices, but Dubai was chosen because it would send a message to the other backers. Even if the Dubai officials and general public believed that, for some reason, a man with everything would throw it all away, the other backers would know that somebody had declared war, and they would all wonder if they were next.

The target came into the room and pointed to the infinity pool.

"Hello, Leia," Luke said into her ear.

Leia ignored him again and gazed at the infinity pool. She smiled as if she couldn't wait to be naked in the water.

As soon as Leia and the Target reached the edge of the pool, Luke emerged from the water and caught the backer by the legs, using momentum and surprise to force him over the edge, sending the billionaire plunging down more than twenty-seven hundred feet.

Real Truth - Internet Fact Based News

Posted by JI Right
Are you kidding me? Senator Hale's computers are hacked by a malicious virus that we still don't know who is behind. Tell me why the government doesn't have a major investigation into the origins of this virus. Do they already know? Perhaps they already know.
Back on point. They say no breach of Hale's data. False. We have secured some of the data that was "not" leaked.
Apparently, the CIA has evidence that the Turkish military is already in possession of the missing Nukes. No surprise there. That these missiles are already capable of hitting any target in Europe, or the Middle East, also no surprise. However, the next revelation is communications from the CIA to Senator Hale that the US spy satellites have tracked movements and targeting. The coding shows that US military bases in Germany and British bases in the UK are dialed in.
Let's see how the Pentagon addresses this information. How long do you think it'll take the spin masters in the White House to discredit this?

Chapter Seventeen

Tess crouched and tucked. *It's a race for my life,* she thought. *A race I will likely lose.*

She tore down the mountain far faster than she ever had before. *But the snow is faster...*

Knowing she could never out race it, her only chance might be to outmaneuver it. Trying to concentrate every breath and muscle on staying vertical, Tess still found it impossible not to speculate. Her instincts and experience told her: *A mountain full of skiers... those explosions were not avalanche prevention, they were an attack—an attack on me.*

She spotted a contour in the land, and guessed it might absorb more snow. *If I can just make it there.*

Somehow, Tess managed to slide off to the edge of the avalanche's path. But getting any further would require an angled jump with no margin, a dangerous maneuver even under perfect conditions.

The snow barreled down faster; she could feel the vibration as if her body was flying through a thunder cloud.

An excellent skier, she had no choice but to make the

leap. The first bullets flew inches from her, tearing into a giant tree about ten feet away from her.

They triggered the avalanche because they want it to look like an accident, she thought. *But they also want to be sure my death gets done.*

She compressed her body even lower, racing the raging avalanche and bullets at the same time. The tumbling mass of debris and snow slid at speeds approaching two hundred miles an hour.

The only hope is the edge.

Even in her dizzying flight to escape, a list of suspects formed in her furious mind. It could have been a long one, considering her line of work, but it quickly narrowed down to three people.

The burn in her legs threatened to bring her down. Whipping winds created by the avalanche sent a bitter cold chill and spraying snow into her stinging face. She veered to the edge. Losing her grip, it was time to jump.

More bullets. The incoming rounds forced her to deviate just enough that at the exact moment she hurtled into the air, the slide's fringe caught her skis, twisted her the wrong way, and sent her into the deluge.

The wall of snow pushed from behind, forcing her against the mountain, then slammed her into the hard winter ground.

It pinned her skis-first. A split-second later, she couldn't move. Everything was white and cold. The avalanche seemed alive, breathing, moving, moaning, carrying her along in the rolling barrage.

"Help!" she screamed, but all that came out was a freezing, choking cry. The snow smothered her under the depths of frozen powder. The human body, three times denser than snow, sank quickly. *Buried alive.*

The loud white turmoil quickly transformed into an opaque darkness, closing in on her goggles and taking away the only point of reference she had for any kind of understanding of life. The crushing and twisting took her down further as the snow built on top of her and then encased her in something similar to quick dry cement, only much, much colder. It closed its wintry hand around her neck and shoved her face first into oblivion.

Unable to figure what direction the surface was, or even to orientate herself at all, Tess tried to think.

Must breathe.

But there already wasn't enough air. All she could feel was pressure, as if the entire mountain was moving on top of her. The crushing weight of it was excruciating.

Too. Much. Snow.

Tess knew she was dead.

Chase and Wen were outside the avalanche's path when it began. "Avalanche!" Chase yelled. "*That's* how they're going to kill her. The shadow people triggered it."

"There!" Wen pointed at its intended target. They already knew it was too late to do anything for Tess from where they were.

"Tess is never going to get out of that!"

"She might if she makes it across that." Wen, a far better skier than Chase, pointed at a ravine. "That's going to slow the—" Gunshots interrupted her. Wen actually saw the bark spray from the tree as they hit. "Keep going!" Wen screamed, even though there was absolutely no chance Tess would hear her.

"Look!"

They watched the entirety of her security detail go under the torrent of snow, engulfed in what must have been hundreds of tons of the freezing white stuff.

"It's over!"

"No!" Chase yelled as they watched Tess Federgreen buried by the avalanche. The snow kept coming, as if there was a raging, never-ending river of it. "It's like someone opened up the mountain and dumped it on her!"

"She's not coming back," Wen breathed.

"No," Chase agreed.

"We can't help her anymore," Wen said. "But we can get the people who did it." She pointed ahead to several skiers on an opposing ridge line. Looking up at the silhouetted figures, Chase could clearly see their guns.

Chapter Eighteen

From Dubai's tallest building, the condemned billionaire fell at more than four hundred feet per second, meaning he would impact with the concrete of the plaza below at a speed of two hundred seventy miles per hour. It also meant that the target would clearly beat Luke and Leia to the street. However, the two assassins would be down and out, via a high-speed private elevator, before anyone realized who the smeared remains of human were.

"It's not against the rules," Leia said as they rode the elevator down.

"But it *is*," Luke argued as he finished changing into dry clothes.

"There are new rules."

"Maybe, or maybe we're just a couple of patsies, and now we're going to get taken out either to cover up who really did this, or as retribution *for* doing it."

The two of them exited the elevator into the opulent lobby without eliciting so much as a glance from any of the security staff.

"They don't need to cover up who did it," Leia said as they walked into the still very warm evening air. "Vader's not like the other backers. He believes he's untouchable. Vader *knows* the others will know it was him, and he doesn't care."

"So you think we're fine?" he asked as they mingled in the traffic without ever looking over at the gathering crowd around the body.

"Yeah, we're fine. At least until the rules change again."

Luke sighed. "Clash of the titans."

"It's going to mean more jobs for us."

Chase hit a mogul, soaring into the air as blowing snow blasted his face. He came down hard thirty feet lower and raced toward where Tess had been buried. Hoping to reach her in time, he ignored the dangers of the avalanche, the mountain, and the people who had turned it all against Tess.

Further up the mountain, Wen spotted three of the shadow assassins seeking to verify the kill. *They're heading to finish Tess off. They'll be on top of Chase in seconds.* Wen rocketed toward them while attempting to line up a shot. Flying over a drop an average skier would have avoided, Wen went airborne, allowing her to steady her gun. She pulled the trigger, and an instant later, an ex-SEAL named Wyle kept skiing downhill even as his head exploded.

The woman skier next to him lost focus and crashed into a giant ponderosa, dying instantly. The third, a former Army Ranger and seasoned killer named Bronco, found cover and returned fire.

I can't get a clear shot, she thought, but fired anyway,

attempting to keep the man pinned down until she could get closer.

Bronco also continued shooting while speaking into his radio, alerting all the agents on the Mountain that they had company.

Wen, knowing Chase was safe for the moment, skied into a wooded tract across from Bronco. But she knew they were outnumbered and running out of time to escape.

Tess is already dead. We need to get off this mountain.

She grabbed a small explosive from her backpack and readied its digital fuse.

Bronco, standing behind a tree, zoomed his scope in on the bastard who'd shot Wyle. The two of them had been a team *for a thousand years*. Wyle had saved Bronco six times, but he'd never had the chance to return the favor. *And now I never will, because this SOB just blew Wyle's head off.* He looked through the scope, fired. *Damned if it isn't a woman. A woman I know. It's that Chinese bitch!*

Bronco had been on four missions to kill Chase and Wen. Each time they'd escaped, but only after she'd killed most of his team.

Four times, seventeen dead buddies, and that evil witch is still out there.

He grabbed his radio.

She was supposed to have died in an explosion, but Belfort still had people looking. *Oh, Belfort knew she hadn't died, and now she just killed Wyle and Kat.* He was *sure* it was Wen, but he looked through the scope again anyway. Long ago, he'd memorized every inch of her face. *There's no doubt.*

He took another shot, missed again, and the next time he looked, she was gone.

"She won't get far," Bronco muttered through gritted teeth. He transmitted the scope's image to every other shadow person in the ski valley. "Wen Sung just killed Wyle," he said on a full broadcast. She was a big payday, everyone on the mountain knew it. Ten million dollars for her, another ten for killing Chase, and Bronco had a feeling Belfort would throw a bonus on top of that.

Tess Federgreen was buried under twenty feet of snow. No one gave a damn about her anymore, not with twenty million bucks on the line, but Bronco didn't care about the money. *That bitch killed Wyle. Now she's going to die.*

ANC - Always News Channel - News Update

"Stu Lemon reporting. Our top stories at this hour: Samantha Lawson, the White House point person on the NoLiv virus, confirmed minutes ago that the virus is now infecting cell phones. Smart phones from all manufacturers have been infected. Most of those companies have issued security patches. However, at this time, the virus has mutated and found a way around the patches. Remember, this is not like viruses of the past. This is an AI-based mutation, so it can, and does, transform.
"Responding to questions about the worsening banking crisis, Lawson referred us to the Federal Reserve chairman, but added that more currency was being rushed into circulation in order to supplement the shortages caused by the bank closures. He said, 'We'll get through this if everyone remains calm, does their part, and listens to government directives.'
"The administration is also touting progress with the deepening nuclear standoff with Turkey as the world braces for war. 'The United Nations has convened an emergency meeting of the Security Council,'

the Secretary of State told reporters. 'Turkish representatives, who initially said they would not attend, have now agreed to take part.' These last-minute talks come as the fears of a preemptive strike reach a fever pitch. This could be our last chance to avoid war."

Chapter Nineteen

Bronco layered and entered the coordinates, then hit the distribute command which would project paths to intercept Wen for each of them. Whoever was closest would have the best chance and be green-lighted as priority above the others. "I don't care who gets the money, I just want her dead!"

He reveled in their advantage not just in numbers, but that they knew she'd be coming *down* the mountain because there was no way to go higher.

Wasterman and Stein aren't the closest, he said to himself, checking the positioning, *but they'll come looking for her, come looking for the money.* Those two were the most lethal shadow people on the mountain, and perhaps the greediest. *They'll drive her right into my hands.*

Bronco swapped magazines in his KRISS Vector submachine gun. He thought about how many of his friends she'd killed in the past. He knew how dangerous she was, and wished he'd get the chance to strangle her, to watch her die slowly, gasping for her last breath.

But she's the best... she's proven that too many times. She's certainly better than me... I'm not too proud to admit that. But I'll be waiting.

He knew he wouldn't get the chance to choke her to death. It would be a bullet that killed her, he just hoped it would be his. *But even if it isn't, I'll stick an extra one in her for Wyle.*

Suddenly, word came across the radio that Wasterman and Stein had Wen in their sites. Multiple gunshots echoed through the frigid air.

"Confirm kill," Bronco radioed. "*Confirm kill?*"

"Negative, negative," someone responded. "Wasterman and Stein dead. She's heading down toward you."

Bronco cursed. Two more friends gone. Part of him was glad she'd gotten away, yet he was still more than a little afraid. *Now maybe I'll get the shot.*

Bronco viewed the mountain in the viv-reader attached to his wrist. *There's only one way she can go.* The day before, when he'd help plant the explosives they'd used to trigger the avalanche, he had studied the terrain. *There's a drop off over there, too deep and dangerous. Of course, she's probably an expert skier—this bitch is an expert* everything—*but it's suicide on that side of the mountain. She has to come right past me.*

Chase tore off his goggles as he scooped and clawed at the snow, frantically digging, but he couldn't even be sure where she was. There had been too much distance between them, and too much snow to move.

He heard shooting higher up, but no bullets came his way. Not yet. But he was armed. They had come expecting to intercept assassins, and now he was furious at their failure. *Sorry Tess, we let you down.* He kept digging.

Chase looked around, trying to figure out if he was in the right place. *I can't believe how much the landscape changed after the avalanche went through...*

The gunfire grew closer.

Chase leapt into the hole he had been making. From inside the snowy foxhole, he looked for his targets and opened up with his MP7.

Two skiers with guns went down. *I guess they didn't think I was armed. They don't know who I am.* With the two of them dead, he went back to digging, knowing more would come, but also knowing Wen would come too.

Chase called in for help, Ski Patrol, 911, and had the Astronaut contacting CISS. All he could think of was Tess trapped beneath the snow. *How long can she survive under there?* he wondered.

Rechecking the terrain, Chase realized he might have been digging in the wrong place and got himself to a nearby section of trees. *So many trees were brought down.* Feeling around a tangled stand of ponderosa pines that resembled a snowy beaver dam, he noticed a thinner section on the other side, and remembered seeing her land around there. Quickly, he went to work. The new site had the extra benefit of being somewhat sheltered from the shadow people.

Wen saw three more shadows heading toward where Chase was and knew he wouldn't be able to see them until it was too late. She cut across at an angle that would cost her precious momentum in her downhill escape, but it was the only chance to catch them. Now she needed to jump.

In mid-flight, another Circuit agent appeared. Wen twisted, spinning sideways as bullets zinged past. Another skied below, aiming up at her, but she used her every advantage and cut him down before roughly landing on the opposing slope.

Now ahead of the men she'd seen, they came in pursuit as the bullets flew behind her, but they missed their chance.

You're already dead, she thought. *You just don't know it yet.*

She caught a hump, sailed into the air again, this time doing a back flip end over end, her skis pointing out, before coming down directly behind them, machine-gun blazing, bullets ripping into both men.

Chapter Twenty

Cranson, walking through a small marina on the Florida Gulf Coast, studied the latest reports. There had been a new sighting—not of Wen and Chase, because there had not been a credible one of those since the explosion at the nuclear facility—but numerous leads and visuals of Shelby and Grimes. Those two were high priority, high pay day hits that required his attention.

Although he did not believe Chase and Wen were alive, he knew that if they *were*, Shelby and Grimes would know. So even though he wanted them dead, he wanted them alive first.

"I need to find these two, rough them up a little, and question them," he muttered, reading that they'd been seen in the Midwest.

Cranson was extra curious. He didn't just need to know if there was a chance Chase and Wen had survived, he wanted to know why Shelby and Grimes had given up everything to help them. "They invited a death sentence upon themselves," he whispered, looking out to sea, knowing this was just the type of place that Grimes would like.

Cranson had known Grimes well, even considered him a friend, if such a thing could be possible among hitmen. The two of them had worked many jobs together, 'lived and died together', as they used to say. The pair had seen quite a few of their *friends* and associates die, most at the hands of Chase and Wen—the *majority* killed by Wen.

Like Bronco, Cranson secretly hoped Wen was still alive so he could kill her himself. Revenge wasn't something he generally delved into, but he'd learned enough about her and seen too much of her handiwork. He knew that if she was alive, he would never sleep soundly again. Sooner or later she'd come looking for him and add his name to the list of the dead.

"She's dead," he muttered, trying to assure himself. But Belfort's paranoia had been nagging at him, and Cranson had proven many times the only way to know for sure someone was really dead was to do it yourself. You needed to watch them breathe their last breath, watch them bleed out.

His phone rang, bringing his worst nightmare to life.

The caller's voice came through a series of relays, ensuring encryption. "This is Bronc. We have a problem."

"In Taos?" Cranson asked, knowing he was in Taos. He'd sent him there to kill Tess Federgreen. "Has the song played?"

"Yeah, that one's over," Cranson said, making it clear Tess was dead. "But we got a big flustercuck here."

Cranson, knowing Bronco to be a hard, cold man not prone to drama, braced for the news.

"I've seen a couple ghosts on the mountain."

Cranson clenched his jaw. He'd killed a lot of people. Seeing ghosts, or at least feeling the presence of one's victims, all the lives you'd taken, was one of the hazards of the game. But something inside of him knew it wasn't just any ghost, it was *the* ghosts. "Who?" he asked, desperately hoping he was wrong.

"That Chinese witch. I swear somehow the gates of hell opened and that evil scourge walked out."

"Are you *sure*? I mean one thousand percent dead *sure*?"

"She killed Wyle and Kat, and at least four others. I haven't heard from Tanger or Snark. Ask *them* if it's her!" Bronco said angrily, as if just thinking about Wen was painful.

Cranson cursed under his breath. Fortunately, he'd taken precautions, not thinking Chase and Wen might show up to save Tess, although now it seemed so obvious. They had serious connections to her, and if they were going to rise from the dead, that's why they would do it.

However, that didn't seem plausible a few days ago when the plans were made. He'd been most worried about Grimes penetrating the old teams and selling the tip to CISS.

"I just sent you a scope image," Bronco said.

"I see it, but the image isn't clear enough. Get a machine on her. I want a positive ID." The machine, technically a CloseMac-100, was an AI camera ID apparatus they used to identify Tess. It didn't just use facial features that were typically employed by airports. The CloseMac was far more sophisticated, utilizing all kinds of data points such as height, motion and movements, proportions, and more. With just a portion of a face, they could get a confirmed identification of a subject.

"I'll do better than that," Bronco growled. "I'm going to bring you her head!"

Bronco's radio crackled again. "Chase Malone positive ID. He's on the mountain."

Chase and Wen generally wore vIDs, a virtual Image Deviation system Chase and the Astronaut had created to fool the algorithms that powered facial recognition cameras. The ingenious spray-on application covered a subject's face with hundreds of nano micro-processors, each thinner than a human hair. The translucent gold specks were virtually undetectable to the naked eye. Unfortunately, the combination of cold temperatures and the reflecting snow made the ingenious invention unusable.

"Get the machine on him, too," Cranson, who was now monitoring all transmissions in Taos Ski Valley, growled into Bronco's ear.

"Zooming now," someone said. "Eighty-eight point seven percent certainty that it is Chase Malone. Positive ID."

Bronco didn't need the machine to tell him Chase was there. Chase and Wen were always together, and there was no doubt in his mind it was Chase.

"Kill him!" Bronco said into the radio, then lined up for another shot at Wen.

Come on you witch, come and die.

Chapter Twenty-One

Wen held the explosive, knowing the man who'd shot at her earlier from below would be down there waiting, estimating that as she broke over the rise, she'd be exposed again. *There's nowhere to go,* she thought, looking at the cliff to her left. *I might make the jump, but then I'll never be able to get back to Chase.*

Her skis sliced through the snow, now heavy over the slide area. Four new pursuers came down after her.

They must know who I am. They wouldn't go to this much trouble just to kill a potential witness.

She tucked, pushing herself down the mountain like a bobsled on ice.

The shadows fired repeatedly, but at those speeds, their aim was wildly off. At the last second, Wen came over the rise. Knowing she'd be meeting a bullet, she counted two beats, crouched, and twisted slightly, anticipating when he would take the shot, but not knowing from where, or the angle. She took the maneuver as if sailing into the blind, flipping a coin, betting her life.

The bullet hit her backpack, and now she knew where he was. She unloaded her machine gun as she roared over a fly, shooting in his direction. She didn't think she had the range, and certainly doubted the accuracy to take him out, but it would slow him, and more importantly, pin him down. Forcing him absent, the screen would allow her enough time to get by, make it into the trees herself. From up above, she'd surveyed and chartered her course. Now she guessed the distance enroute to where Tess was buried and Chase was digging. A second later she was back in range, and picked up his signal.

"Get out of there!" she barked through the in-ear.

"Still . . . digging!" he replied breathlessly. "I've got to save her."

"She's dead," Wen said, counting seconds. "And we've been made. They know who we are, and there are shadows all over the mountain."

"I'm . . . still . . . dig-ing!" he repeated.

"No time. Now that Tess is done, they're coming for us."

"I've . . . got to . . . try . . . to save . . . her."

"You've got to save yourself! Think of Tu, think of me. It's too late for her."

Bronco didn't need to see where his shot hit to know he'd missed. The returning machine gun fire told him she was still alive. Amidst the flying ice and snow, he dove onto the ground, thinking he'd been hit, yet knowing at the same time she wasn't close enough. The legend of her, the trouble she wrought, his own long experiences battling her, the countless bitter losses of friends suffered at her hands, it had all jaded him to thinking of her as a mythical outlaw sorceress.

Then the explosion came. The fury of hell erupted all around him. His ears rang, and he couldn't feel his right arm above the elbow.

Spitting out a mouthful of snow, he rolled back up, using his rifle as a crutch. Desperate to get her, he shot into the air blind. But there was nothing, as if she had vanished like some kind of snow dancer. He scoured the mountain.

How does she do it?

Pushing through the thick snow, the cold numbing his feet, Bronco stood up with more difficulty than expected and fired again, trying to summon her with his rifle as if it might be her language. "The mountains are getting to you Bronco," he muttered as he planted his poles and shoved off down the mountain, wondering where the others were. Reports of sightings on different parts of the mountain hit his radio.

Chase and Wen are down below, waiting.

After Wen lobbed the explosive at Bronco, she'd pivoted slightly, taking her weight and momentum to the left, catching air while soaring nearly twenty feet before dropping into a channel, one that in the spring might have been filled with snow melt and runoff. She'd stayed low with her knees tightly bent, pushing forward fast, hoping she was out of sight from the shooter, not sure how long she could ride that section, believing it would get her at least closer to where Chase was. She stole a glance behind her. Waited. Saw nothing. Figuring the gunner would've been back there by now, believing no one could see her from above, she raced on toward Chase.

ANC - Always News Channel - BREAKING NEWS

Samantha Lawson, the White House point person on the NoLiv virus, just announced that the president's Operation Digital Rocket has produced results. MetaFind and SEEEENall, two of the world's largest tech companies, have teamed up to produce Remedy, an antivirus program to stop NoLiv.

Tech behemoth MemoShot, and online retail giant AweSum, are both still working on their own antivirus program to combat NoLiv. "Today, we take the first step in destroying the virus that has cost us so much," Lawson said. "Remedy has an effective rate of 98% in eradicating NoLiv from all three major computer operating systems and protecting against reinfection."

We're also told the president will be addressing the nation tonight, although it is unclear if he will be talking about NoLiv, the Nuclear standoff with Turkey, or both.

Chapter Twenty-Two

Cranson heard irritation in Belfort's voice as he answered with, "What is it?"

"They're alive."

The silence that followed was not unexpected, but the length of it—thirty-eight seconds according to Cranson's timer—was.

When Belfort finally spoke, he sounded like a different person. "Chase and Wen?"

"Yes."

"I *told you* it was impossible to kill these two agents of Satan! They are *immortal*."

"They're in Taos."

"Of course they are." He let out a humorless laugh. "Interfering with the assignment. Killing our people."

"Yes."

"The only good news is this time, I'll get to watch them die."

Cranson wasn't sure how Belfort's outburst that they

were impossible to kill—*immortal,* even—reconciled with his claim that he would get to watch them die, and he wondered just how such an event would come to pass since Belfort never went in the field. "Yeah," he said, thinking of nothing else to say.

"Who else knows?" Belfort asked, sounding suddenly less confident. "We need to keep this from *them.*"

"All the agents we had in Taos."

"Chase and Wen are there. Aren't all our agents already dead?"

"Not *all.*"

"Get more people into the field."

"I've deployed a deathbot."

"Just one?" Belfort asked, as if Cranson had said he sent them a dozen roses. "Have you learned nothing about these two?"

"I'm moving more, but that was the only one in the area." The bot was actually an AICH-3P, which stood for AI controlled humanoid robot with enhanced real time Perspective, Predictive models, and Power regeneration, but that was a mouthful, and an AICH-3P didn't sound very lethal, so they just called them deathbots. "If they can evade the deathbot, maybe they *are* immortal, but we have two dozen more agents on site, and more en route. I don't think they're going to be able to evade all our agents *and* the deathbot."

Belfort laughed, an angry sound, and then continued a little too long, like in inmate in an asylum does. Cranson thought he was just making a point, but wasn't sure if he might finally be losing it. "We need to know where they're going next," Belfort eventually said, his laughter subsiding.

"They aren't *going* anywhere next," Cranson said. "They're never going to leave Taos."

"Let's pretend you're *wrong*," Belfort said, sounding as if he might explode. "Let's pretend you don't know what the hell you're talking about, and that they haven't eluded us a *thousand* other times over the past few years. And let's just say for a moment that they *do* leave Taos, that this time *isn't* different. Where. In. The. *Hell*. Do you think they'll be going?"

Cranson had no idea where, nor how he could ascertain their destination, but Belfort wanted an answer, so he said the first thing that entered his mind. "Georgia."

"Georgia?" Belfort repeated, as if he'd never heard the word before.

"I think they'll be coming for you," Cranson said, building his theory on the fly. "Someone is picking off our operatives one by one. A lot of people out there are asking too many questions about the people who work for us, and *to* people that work for us. I don't think Wen Sung and Chase Malone are running anymore. I think they're chasing now, and they have one big target . . . and it's painted on your back."

Belfort's eyes opened wide for an instant before narrowing into slits. His hands clenched like claws, as if the air around him were suddenly toxic. "If they're coming for me, then we've finally got them. Do you really believe they can find me?"

Cranson knew that his boss believed he had created a persona, an illusion of himself, so tightly engineered and protected that his true identity or whereabouts could never be discovered. It was an impressive construct, yet there were too many ways in this digital age to penetrate even the highest firewall. "Chase Malone is one of the world's leading AI experts. He has more than a billion dollars at his disposal. I do believe that sooner or later, he will find a way to find you."

Belfort looked around at the walls of the opulent mansion, knowing he would be walking out the door within the hour, but wondering if there was already somebody waiting on the other side. "Find them first."

Chapter Twenty-Three

A screeching broke the silence just before the bullets came. Wen didn't waste time thinking or even looking. Knowing her only friend on the mountain was still far below, she began firing as she twisted and turned. Whoever was up there with her, trying to kill her, was going to die.

Yet, seeing the source of the attack chilled her more than the snow ever could: a red-eyed, white robot on skis.

Wen knew of the existence of such combat bots—autonomous, AI driven robotic warriors were extreme examples of military technology—but she'd never imagined one of them could *ski*.

Years of training had taught her to instantly survey and identify any weakness of a new enemy. *The knees.*

She unloaded twenty rounds into its legs, but the bullets ricocheted away.

It's still coming...

Its red eyes were glowing like an evil science fiction villain. Wen guessed the bot's white armor had been fashioned from a titanium composite alloy, making it nearly impervious to normal gunfire.

Wen crossed diagonally into the trees. The killer ski-bot followed.

She dove down, rolling in a separation move that seemed to confuse her pursuer. Now, with a bit of distance and some cover, she stopped, drew out her last digital explosive, and waited. As the ski-bot came into range, she resisted, knowing she could not afford to miss. Counting its approach—*four. . . three. . . two...*—she flung the device.

The d.e.d. landed perfectly, right between the evil robot's skis, directly under its torso, then detonated. The bot was thrown several feet before it tumbled back down and rolled. It finally stopped nearly thirty feet down the slope from her.

She watched it for a second to be sure it was destroyed. To her horror, it moved. Slowly at first, then springing up with frightening agility.

She searched for another route to escape, but then saw the bot do something far more terrifying.

It began to ski *uphill*.

Those red eyes still blazing, it was coming for her as if in a perfect trajectory.

It's like it has a tracking beacon.

Rapid-fire bullets kept coming from some extension of its white metallic arms. Wen knew she was no match for this futuristic monster. She only hoped she could get down in time to warn Chase before it killed him, too.

A man wandered alone along a bamboo-lined trail while a

speaker floated near his shoulder. "They call me Darth Vader," he said.

"They call *someone* Darth Vader. They don't know about you, or the connection to the Regulators," the little speaker responded. "So they don't know *who* they are calling Darth Vader."

The man frowned. "Still, they know someone is out there."

"Yes, and that is unfortunate."

The man preferred being anonymous. He often said, "Winning a war is much easier if one's enemies don't know who they are fighting." As he strolled through the bamboo forest, its tall, slender trees swayed. He paused a moment to listen, not to the speaker, which remained as silent as a dragon fly, but to the breeze. *The wind through bamboo is the voice of God*, he thought.

Darth Vader was not a religious man. Not in the conventional sense, anyway. Yet he believed in something greater than himself, and that belief allowed him to make the decisions that would otherwise steal his sleep.

"Kill the Senator," he said to the speaker.

"Today?"

"Yes."

"Covert or overt?"

Vader thought about the question. He had considered all the options during the previous two days. *Should the senator's death appear accidental, or had the situation arrived at a point where an assassination was needed to shake things up? To instill some fear? Either way, the senator had to die, and he had to die before he could cast his vote.*

"Covert," he said. "The people who will need to know will know it was not of natural causes, but no need to alarm the general public . . . not with what's about to happen. There'll soon be plenty more for them to panic about."

Chapter Twenty-Four

Wen fired a burst into the trees above her, releasing dozens of cubic feet of snow. Using the white screen created by the deluge, she bolted through the saplings and raced downhill. Twenty or thirty yards into her escape, bullets splintered her skis; remarkably, a round even snapped one of her poles. Wen somersaulted, cascading into a snowbank, falling backwards. She fought the heavy snow, rolled, and crawled out. More bullets came.

Knowing the sci-fi *Terminator* would be there in a second, Wen dove down into the oblivion. On the other side the bank, she went into a sideways slide through the deep tracks of snow. *Chase!* she thought, finally catching a glimpse of a silhouetted person bent over digging.

The robot tracked her. Bullets sent snow and ice flying inches away as she hit a slick spot and careened lower. Having no idea what condition her gun was in, she tried to hold it above, but during her uncontrolled tumble through the powder, slush had packed into the barrel. Now, closer to

Chase, she saw how the slope dropped off in another direction.

He must have seen me. Flailing her arms and digging her feet in, she tried to slow her spill. *If he comes after me, he might not be able to escape either.* Wen turned to see if she had any options remaining and realized she was sliding toward the edge. *I either go over, or that red-eyed monster gets me.*

She flipped onto her back. While sledding headfirst, she cleared her MP7 submachine gun as well as she could, and prepared to fire.

Flying down the slope at unstoppable speeds toward the sharp edge, not knowing if the drop off was five feet or fifty, Wen's eyes took in the winter panorama, searching for something to cling to, for anything at all.

The bullets kept coming. The bot grew closer and the edge beckoned.

"There it is!" she yelled, maneuvering toward a stand of ponderosa pines skirted in a natural buildup of fresh snow.

Her feet went wide and caught a branch. Her head was already over. Wen used every muscle and the leverage of the terrain to pull herself up in time to see the killer bot aiming its weaponized arm at her, knowing a red dot was bouncing around her face.

The ski-bot had managed to stop. It had her. *I've been dead before*, she thought, firing meaningless bullets at the machine.

Why hasn't he fired back? she wondered. In an instant she realized, *Its AI program probably wants perfect alignment for the kill shot.* She began weaving and bobbing like a prize-fighter, still dangling dangerously close to going over.

Wen saw the monster's eyes dim and flicker, telling her that its processors were draining power to calculate and anticipate her moves. Its predictive models would know what she was going to do even before she did, and then it would take the perfect shot to end her life.

There was nowhere to go except down, to take a dive off the cliff, and she'd run out of time even for that.

The bot's eyes suddenly went white. It took a moment for her brain to understand.

Snow!

The robot's arms clawed at its head, attempting to clear the packed snow from its focal lenses. It could not shoot without viewing its target. One beady red eye reappeared, but another round of snow flew in and blocked it again. Now Wen saw from where. Chase was relentlessly pelting the multimillion-dollar state-of-the-art sophisticated killer robot with simple snowballs.

It seems to be working. Snowballs were stopping its deadly assault.

Wen managed to get up, staggering forward, releasing the broken skis from her boots and climbing to where the bot struggled with the childish attack. She threw herself into its composite body, trying to tackle the menace. Its weight and force surprised her.

I don't have the strength...

Chase piled on, smashing one more large snowball into its face. Together, they shoved it down the slope, its arms and legs struggling to correct its inverted position and stop its slide. There was not enough runway. Sparks emitted in the final inches, just before it plummeted over the edge.

Wen followed its trail down, stopping short to see her nemesis piled nearly twenty feet below, its legs sticking out of the snowdrift.

Chase grabbed her. "Come on, I need your help."

"What?" she asked, wanting to hug and kiss him.

"Digging."

She followed him through the powder. "We need to get

out of here before more bots show up." They crossed onto an avalanche trail of packed snow and debris.

"I found Tess."

"Is she alive?"

"I don't know yet. I've only reached her arms."

ANC - Always News Channel - Top Story

"Stu Lemon reporting. Our top story at this hour: We're just learning that Congressman Al Lewis, whose opposition to US military involvement in the Middle East was legendary, has died. He was the most vocal opponent against the Administration's Turkish policy, always advocating peaceful diplomacy to resolve the situation. Congressman Lewis had, only weeks ago, visited the former NATO ally and voiced skepticism that Turkey's president actually intended to seize the nuclear missiles.

"Wait, we've just been given an update. Apparently the Congressman died as a result of his pacemaker failing. Within the past ninety minutes, researchers at Stanford University have confirmed that the NoLiv virus has infected computer controlled medical equipment. If confirmed, the Congressman would be the fifth victim of NoLiv related medical equipment failure.

"In Virus news: Planners today have implemented new regulations. Samantha Lawson, the White House point person on the NoLiv virus, announced further measures to stop the spread, including masking. Each computer must be masked with anti-fabric. The RFID shielding material will block pirated WIFI signals from transmitting the virus from one user to another, like a Faraday cage. If these masks are not available, then device distancing will be required, meaning only one computer per household or office can be in use at one time."

Chapter Twenty-Five

Whitley, a tall, gorgeous woman who could have been a high fashion model, connected a few cables. Pulled back, her dark hair seemed a little severe, but Belfort liked it. He had been hoping for years to see it down, and there was reason to hope. She had always been friendly to him—*very* friendly.

"How's his mood today?" Belfort asked nervously.

"Same as always." She winked. Her shoulder-less silk top and short leather skirt drove him crazy. He wanted her to stay after the meeting. She would, but only long enough to pack up the gear, flirt a few lines, and then disappear.

"Yes," Belfort said. "He's always quite even."

She smiled. "That's a good way to describe him." Her arm brushed his as she left the room. "Good luck."

Belfort stood before the large monitor now carrying a live image of Haris Tane, the man he worked for—one of the men, anyway, there were quite a few. Belfort didn't know the exact number of bosses, but he had vague ideas. In fact, he knew too much about them, although he'd never met any in person. It was always Whitley who hooked up the monitors, wherever he was, when a "meeting" was required. Otherwise it was all done via phone.

Over the years, he'd tried to learn about the people who paid him so much, who allowed him to stay in such luxury. At the same time, he also tried to avoid uncovering too much; such was the paradox of working for the Circuit. Belfort knew what these people did to their enemies. Anyone who got in their way or threatened them was removed in one brutal way or another. He knew because he was the one in charge of that department, or at least one of the departments. Somewhere along the line, he'd also figured out that there were others like him who designed the ends of their enemies. The Circuit loved redundancy. Everything was planned and backed-up by contingencies three deep. Nothing was left to chance.

"We've had a little trouble," Belfort said.

Tane stood. His expensive suit and perfect haircut made him look younger than he was. The wealthy, self-assured man was tanned with clear eyes and a distinguished air, a typical and successful tycoon. He was all those things, but different, too. Tane was a manipulator of events, which was one of the reasons why Chase and Wen bothered him so much. They had often prevented things from going the way he wanted.

"Apparently they did not die in that blast," Belfort admitted.

"Yes, you seem to have miscalculated . . . again."

"Actually, that wasn't my operation. Chase and Wen

Chasing Lies

were on a suicide mission that, against all odds, they happened to survive."

"Yes," Tane said, "but you assessed the situation and determined they had *not* survived."

"I'm not making excuses, but you had the same data. The government made the same determination. No one thought *anybody* could survive. I don't know *how* they managed to get out alive." When Tane didn't reply immediately, Belfort added, "They are quite impressive in that regard."

Tane had not told Belfort that he had wanted the facility they'd "died" in destroyed, or at least would have if he had known about it. So, for once, Tane was pleased with Chase and Wen's actions. "I'm not surprised they came though. Their resilience and resourcefulness are two of the reasons we've tried to recruit them."

"It's also no surprise they would have no part in dealing with a group like the Circuit."

"No," Tane said sharply. "But you *do* work for us. And in spite of your failures with these two, I'm going to give you another chance." Tane stared at Belfort for a moment. "Another, another, another chance, and so on, to correct the situation. Listen to me. You make sure this time . . . once and for all, *remove* Chase and Wen from this earth."

"I will."

"Do you understand what is at stake?"

"Yes."

"No you don't, or you'd be wetting your pants right now."

Belfort fired off a laugh. "I have a special team assembled. They will not fail."

"I've heard this before," Tane said gruffly. "This *another chance* is your last. Is that clear?"

Belfort looked at Tane. This was the death sentence he had been avoiding for a long time.

Whitley appeared again. "You look tired," she said as she went to work dismantling the video equipment. "Can I get you a drink?"

"No thanks," he replied, still trying to shake Tane. "How long have you worked for the Circuit?"

"A long time."

"Do you do this for others . . . I mean, like me?"

"I do what they say," she said, closing her briefcase with all the special connectors that ensured encryption and no recordings. "But you're my favorite."

"I am?" he asked, pleasantly surprised, but he'd always suspected.

"Yes." She walked over to Belfort and wrapped her arms around him. It was a seductive embrace, the kind that normally lead to something else. He could feel her warm breath on his cheek, her head resting on his shoulder.

"You need to know something," she whispered in his ear. "If Chase and Wen are still alive in four days, you won't be. And I really wouldn't want that to happen."

She broke the embrace. Their faces remained inches apart.

He looked horrified.

"Don't worry," she said. "Just do your job, and everything will be fine." She kissed him, long, hot, passionately. "Don't let our first kiss be our last."

Chapter Twenty-Six

Chase and Wen reached the hole he'd been digging.

"Quite the excavation," Wen said, impressed by the volume of snow he'd moved, then she saw the arm. "She's totally buried, how could she…"

Chase, already digging, didn't bother answering. "Help me!" he yelled.

Wen squeezed in next to him and began scooping out snow. They quickly realized that although the position of her arm made it look as if she were upright, she was actually on her side, meaning they'd be able to expose her much faster.

They carefully pulled her out of the hole.

Wen checked her pulse. "She's still alive!"

Chase sighed in relief, although he knew that didn't necessarily mean she would live, or have brain function, or be able to walk again, or a hundred other things. But there was a pulse, and that meant there was a *chance*.

A moment later, Taos Ski Patrol arrived—two red-jacketed skiers. Then a woman and a dog on a snowmobile arrived.

The three patrollers appeared to be in their twenties, and they all immediately held up their hands.

"No," Wen said, realizing they had spotted their machine guns. "We're here protecting her." She pointed to Tess. "She's an important government official. There are agents here to kill her who we believe triggered the avalanche."

"Are they still out there?" one of them asked.

"I think some are."

"Can you take her out of here on that?" Chase asked, pointing to the snowmobile.

One of the skiers, still obviously nervous of their weapons, knelt next to Tess, then spoke into a walkie-talkie. The woman also decided to ignore her fears and began administering CPR.

"She needs a helicopter," the man told Chase after relaying GPS coordinates to base.

The avalanche dog, trained to find buried people, began working the area. In less than a minute, it located another victim, likely one of her security detail.

Wen and Chase slung their guns over their backs and began helping them dig for the skier.

At the same time, further up the mountain, Ski Patrol started organizing a probe line, a standard protocol where rescuers form a line across the debris field and systematically work their way down the slope using probe poles—prepositioned nearby for emergencies. They poked into the snow in hopes of locating any other buried skiers.

The sound of an approaching chopper jarred Wen away from her digging. Training warned her of a threat. Reflexes took over. She pointed her gun skyward.

"That's a *rescue* helicopter!" one of the men yelled.

"Sorry," Wen said, lowering her gun.

They quickly got Tess loaded. Chase and Wen started to climb in after her.

"You can't get on," a ski patrol said.

"We need to be on that bird," she said, holding up her MP7 again.

The man backed up, his hands held high. "Sure thing."

It was snowing heavily when they landed at Holy Cross Hospital in Taos. A trauma team was waiting.

While Wen guarded Tess, Chase contacted the Astronaut, who was finally able to get ahold of Tess's deputy.

CISS promised a full-scale response. "Any shadow people left in New Mexico," Linda, her deputy, said, "are going to discover a new definition for the word 'wrath.'"

Within hours, Tess was stabilized, and they were told she would live. By late afternoon, FBI agents relieved them of their guard duties, but Chase and Wen remained at Holy Cross, watching for trouble, waiting for what they knew would come. Surprisingly, by early evening, Tess was stable enough to talk.

She smiled slightly, painfully, when they walked in. "Thank you," she said hoarsely, a tear in her eye.

"You did the hard part," Chase said.

She shook her head. "A few more minutes and . . . "

"The Circuit put a hit on you. The snow probably kept you alive," Wen said.

"Until you could kill enough of them."

Wen nodded.

"You blew your cover to save me," Tess said. "Word's out you two are alive."

Chase sighed. "Would have happened sooner or later."

"Later would have been better," Tess said. "Harder to fight them when they know you're coming."

Chase shrugged, like it was nothing, but they all knew their biggest advantage, the one thing that gave them a chance of discovering who was behind the Circuit and the shadow people, had been lost when they were identified on the slopes of Kachina Peak in the Taos Ski Valley. "Too bad your vacation got cut short," he said.

"I was going to have to go back early anyway. Between the virus and the situation in Turkey, there's too much risk."

"Vacation is risky, too," Wen said.

"I wasn't just here to ski and dance." Tess closed her eyes for a moment. "In your quest, there are two people who can help you more than I can. One of them, a guy called PeacePipe, lives here in Taos. I was going to meet him this afternoon. He's a crazy, off-grid revolutionary. Lives in an Earthship."

"Sounds like our type of person."

"He's really no one's type, but he can help you. I'll have Linda text you his contact info."

"And the other?" Wen asked. "Is that person in Taos, too?"

"No, San Diego. Ed Underhill." Her eyes searched the room, as if uttering his name might bring an onslaught of trouble. "He's the opposite of PeacePipe. Pragmatic, patriotic. Intelligence is his life, and he knows where all the secrets are buried."

"Why will he help us?" Chase asked.

"Because I asked him to."

Chase nodded.

"I owe you my life. If there's ever anything you need," Tess said, sounding as sweet and soft as Chase had ever heard her.

"There is one thing," Chase said.

She nodded slowly, obviously knowing what he meant. "No promises."

Real Truth - Internet Fact Based News

Posted by JI Right
A congressman's pacemaker failed . . . the one vote that could derail war . . . the virus did this . . . and we are to believe this is an accident. Five medical equipment deaths, and one was the key opponent of the president's policies. Convenient.

Let's talk about social media giant MetaFind, and the king of search, SEEEENall, coming together to play savior. Do we really know what Remedy, the so-called antivirus program, is? They say tests show it stops NoLiv, but the virus is AI generated, and experts tell us the AI will just mutate around the virus, causing a long list of variants. Yet the White House makes these claims. How can they be so sure? We have no way of knowing long-term effects. Yet we are all supposed to install this onto our computers, our phones, whatever they say. MemoShot and AweSum are both still working on antivirus programs. And the always proprietary Anchor has stated they will create an app to protect their phones, computers, tablets, and watches. If Anchor doesn't trust its fellow tech companies, why should we?

Chapter Twenty-Seven

Chase and Wen decided to stay the night in Taos. On Tess's recommendation, they got a room at the Sagebrush Hotel, a historic Taos landmark, constructed in 1929 to serve guests traveling between New York and Arizona. Over the years, Tess, sounding as if she owned the place, had told them many notables had stayed there, such as Georgia O'Keeffe, Ansel Adams, Marlon Brando, Gene Hackman, Paul Newman, Robert Redford, Arnold Schwarzenegger, and President Gerald Ford.

"We're here for three reasons," Wen, who liked to always have a defined objective, said as they drove north on Paseo del Pueblo.

"To help protect Tess," Chase said. "To meet with PeacePipe. And the third is . . . ?"

"To trap the shadow people who will be coming to finish her off . . . and to find us."

"Sounds fun."

"It will be." She shifted through a pile of guns and

ammo on the floor of the front seat, pulling up her favorite, an MP7, and shoving in a magazine holding forty rounds.

"What do you think of this PeacePipe guy?" Wen asked.

"Tess calls him a *real Taos character*, but didn't give us much more on why he's worth our time."

As they drove, snow on adobe buildings blending with the last light of a winter sunset breaking through the remaining clouds, created a classic Taos mood.

"I feel like we're driving inside one of those enchanting little snow globes," Wen said. The flurries had been increasing. "Turn there."

Chase checked the rearview mirror, thinking she'd seen a shadow person, but it was Farolitos lanterns, paper bags with a little sand and a single candle, lining Ledoux Street and adorning walkways.

"It's magic," she whispered. "All these glowing bags reminds me of home, of the Lantern Festival. It marks the end of Chinese New Year."

Luminarias, small piñon bonfires, were lit every thirty feet or so along the narrow road, adding to the atmosphere.

"It definitely feels like we've entered another realm," Chase said. "Too bad there are killers inside this beautiful fantasy world with us."

Wen told Chase about the meeting spot, the streets leading to it, the surrounding buildings. She also spoke of the legendary past of the place, having researched it, always wanting to know everything about wherever they were. He turned right on Ranchitos Road and headed to the historic district and Taos Plaza. They found a parking spot off

Camino de la Placita, near Our Lady of Guadalupe Church.

The snow picked up as they crossed the already slick street, unaware that they were being watched.

She gave Chase a few extra unnecessary details, knowing he liked the trivia.

"The *Alley* occupies the oldest building in Taos," Wen said.

"Isn't Taos one of the oldest towns in the United States?"

"Yes. Pueblo Indians constructed the original building in the 1500s. It served as an outpost along the Chihuahua Trail."

"Sounds cool, but why are we meeting there?"

"I don't know. I guess PeacePipe likes it." She looked over at him. "Want to hear more?"

"Yeah."

"Along the way it was partially destroyed and occupied by the Spanish government, and later repaired and rebuilt. In 1846, it became the office of the first US Territorial Governor of New Mexico, who was assassinated in the following year."

"Doesn't bode well for us."

"Fast forward through many incarnations until 1997, when it became The Alley Cantina. Some of the earliest walls that still remain partially formed the original Plaza of Taos."

"Looking forward to seeing it."

"Some say it's haunted."

"Great, shadow people *and* ghosts . . . "

Chase thought of the history Wen had just told him as they passed under the adobe archway that led to The Alley.

Wen was thinking about the angles, the tight access, the limited escape routes.

The sound of hot Spanish guitar and sizzling Latin percussion greeted them as they paid the cover charge and entered the centuries' old place. It took them a minute to find a table; only a couple were available, both far from the stage.

Even though smoking was no longer allowed, the place smelled of stale cigarettes from decades of nicotine. The scents of beer and fried food did a decent job covering it.

"Want to dance?" Chase asked.

Wen gave him a quizzical look.

"Good music."

"They're Manzanares," she said as the lead singer's soulful vocals and the band's fiery sound filled the room. "It's fronted by two brothers, Michael and David, from New Mexico."

He wasn't surprised she also knew about the band. She'd probably done a background check on them. "They definitely have a little Santana thing going, maybe some Gipsy Kings influence." One of the brothers broke into a Flamenco-fused Middle Eastern guitar riff.

"Wow!" Chase exclaimed, impressed. "I'm glad this guy decided to meet here."

But Wen didn't like it. "Too many places for shadow people to hide and not enough ways out."

Chapter Twenty-Eight

Manzanares had the whole place vibrating. Dancers crowded the small area in front of the stage.

A man with brown leathery skin, wrapped in a beautiful Mexican blanket, worn like a poncho, stepped inside the crowded bar. He tipped his beige felt cowboy hat, its silver and turquoise band catching the light from the stage and glittering. He scanned the room for a moment until his eyes settled on them. He sauntered across the room like he owned the place and they were the intruders.

"I know it's you," he said without preamble, "'cause I know everyone here, everyone in Taos, and you don't belong here."

Chase glanced at Wen and nodded, not surprised this man was PeacePipe.

"How do you decide who belongs in Taos?" Chase asked.

"Ain't me that decides. It's the Mountain that does or doesn't."

"Oh-kay, then." Chase looked at Wen again, as if they

might be wasting their time with this crazy guy, as if they might want to leave, but he liked the music, and he was too tired to drive. "Tess said you could help us."

"Yeah, probably," he replied, smiling at a server who handed him a beer he'd never ordered. "NoLiv is not as simple as it appears."

Chase turned to Wen again, confused. "We're not really interested in the virus. We're trying to find some people."

He looked at Chase as if he were an idiot. "It's the same thing, Sammy."

"Who's Sammy?" Chase asked, even more confused.

"Oh, the virus is real," PeacePipe said, ignoring Chase's question. "It just isn't dangerous like they said. They tried to convince everyone that it would destroy their computers. The media created so much fear. But it's the *cure* that carries the true danger."

Chase nodded. "And this is connected to the Circuit?"

"Once they installed Remedy," PeacePipe continued, as if Chase wasn't there, "it made their computers susceptible to anything the authorities wanted to do. Whether it be another virus, or, more likely, just taking control."

"We really haven't looked at the virus," Chase said. "Our attention has been elsewhere."

"Foolish mortal," he said, laughing. "While you've been ding-ling-ing around with a game of hide and seek, there's been a takeover going on, and the people, with all their fear indexes pushed, have unwittingly given bad actors control over their lives, their systems, phones, computers, and the microphones and cameras in all those devices." He reached for a cigarette and then put it back. "It's impossible to eradicate."

Wen studied two men in black sweaters across the room who bothered her, but she wasn't sure why.

"Not without getting a new computer," Chase said, now caught up in the conversation.

"Ha, even if the manufacturers haven't pre-installed NoLiv, any new systems people purchase will now be infected almost instantly by any exchange between them and an infected computer." He reached for another cigarette, and this time put it unlit in his mouth. "And since almost seventy percent of the people around the world have already put Remedy on their computer, there are an incredible amount of infected systems out there. It's all by design. It's a crusade against freedom, don't you see? They've made it so it can't *be* avoided."

"Are you saying the Circuit is behind this?"

"You wearing a wire?" PeacePipe pushed across the table, knocking over his untouched beer, and patted Chase's chest.

The men in sweaters glanced over.

"No," Chase said, as Wen clutched a pistol under her coat. "No wire. We're trying to find the people behind the Circuit."

He looked at Chase with narrowed eyes. "Why?"

"We want to break them."

PeacePipe retreated back across the table. "You don't *look* like a stupid man, but maybe you are one."

"Can you help us or not?" Chase, exasperated, couldn't understand how Tess had ever connected with this fringe-nut, or why she imagined he could help them.

"The Circuit is behind the virus."

"What's their plan?"

"To take advantage of the situation."

The waitress appeared, wiped up the spill, and handed PeacePipe another beer. "Fries?" she asked him.

"Por favor," he replied.

"You two still don't want any food?" she asked, having served them soda waters before PeacePipe arrived.

"No thanks," Chase said.

Wen watched the men in the black sweaters.

"It's hard to imagine they could have foreseen how well their propaganda machines would work," PeacePipe continued once the server had gone. "Or how many people would so easily fall in line."

Chase, still not sure he believed the conspiracy theory, just shrugged.

"They knew," PeacePipe said defiantly. "They'd done so many experiments that it was obvious they could take advantage."

"What about the people who are resisting?" Chase nodded to PeacePipe as if to include him. "They call them conspiracy theorists."

"They are at risk," PeacePipe said. "They are at *grave* risk. Because now the perpetrators of this fantastic hoax, those in power who want absolute control, now they know exactly who the resistors are, and where these *troublemakers* live."

Two bullets ripped into PeacePipe's chest. By the time his head smacked the table, Chase and Wen were already on the floor, looking for the source of the hit. The band went silent, its music replaced by a chorus of screams and the echoes of near-constant gunfire.

ANC - Always News Channel - Top Story

"Zane Waterman reporting. Our top story at this hour: The mandates that the president announced during his speech have been implemented immediately. Although multiple lawsuits have been filed, it is expected they will take months or even years to work through the courts.

"All government workers, contractors, and companies employing more than one thousand people must install Remedy, the antivirus to NoLiv, on all computers—business and personal. This order includes phones and tablets, since coinciding with the president's speech, MetaFind and SEEEENall has announced a version of Remedy available for phones and tablets. Penalties for not complying with the president's executive order include being denied access to the Internet, losing your job, or restrictions being placed on access to other services.

"Unpatriotic protests have already been reported in a dozen cities. Authorities are authorizing law enforcement to deal with the nonconformists, declaring them 'threats to stability' and in some cases 'domestic terrorists.'"

Chapter Twenty-Nine

Wen shot one of the black sweaters before the other ran out the door. Chase was already pursuing him, but as soon as the cold, dark air hit him, he knew it was too late. Within the panicked mob of Alley patrons fleeing the violence, he spotted at least six shadow people.

"It's a set-up," Chase said, speaking to his shoulder, as he ran down Teresina Lane toward the plaza. "Where are you?"

Wen heard him through the in-ear comm. "I'm out the back, near where we parked. Killers everywhere!"

Bullets ricocheted off the street and adobe wall. "No kidding!" Chase cried, returning fire.

Snow covered everything, making even running challenging. The centuries' old plaza, lined with smooth adobe buildings adorned with orange lights for the season, shimmered under a fresh dusting of snow.

"There might be too many," Wen said. "I'll try to get to you."

At the center of the square, a towering fifty-five-foot-tall

Christmas tree glowed with colorful lights and decorative ornaments. Chase ran toward it. The festive scene belied the reality of assassins and flying bullets.

"We should have brought our army!" Chase hissed into his shoulder.

The other large trees, permanent residents of the Plaza, created a glowing fantasy world, with their trunks and winter-bare branches fully wrapped in purple or blue lights.

"We need to get back to the hospital," Chase said, suddenly worried the invasion might have reached Tess.

The red, Christmas themed, glowing spots and floodlights took on an eerie hue after the bloodbath that had erupted in the quiet historic center.

"I think that's where they want to send us!" Wen replied, still dodging scared locals while trying to discern enemies from friendlies.

Chase found temporary cover in the Plaza's gazebo. His smart watch indicated an incoming call from Grimes. "I'm kind of in a situation right now," Chase whispered as he took the call.

"I know," Grimes said. "We're here."

"Where?"

"Taos."

"What are you doing in Taos?" Chase asked.

"Saving you. *Again*," Grimes said. "We just killed three shadows on Bent Street. The town is filling up with them, and they aren't just here for Tess Federgreen."

"Yeah, we figured that out already."

"They know you two are alive," Grimes said. "I hope Tess was worth it, because Belfort is going to unload on you in the worst possible way."

Chase saw two groups approaching. Rather than fight a losing battle, he dashed out the other side of the gazebo, across the street, and climbed the front of the Hotel La Fonda, grabbing vigas protruding from the adobe and then using the lit La Fonda sign to pull himself up to the roof. Now thirty feet above the Plaza, he began picking off the unaware shadow people.

"One good thing," Grimes said breathlessly as he jogged toward the Plaza. "Remember when you wanted to know just how many Shadow People the Circuit has? You're about to find out."

"Thanks," Chase deadpanned. "But we didn't need you to come all the way out here to tell us they would be sending people. We knew that as soon as they made us on the mountain."

"Oh, we didn't come here to tell you anything," Grimes shot back. "We came because you don't have enough weapons for what's about to hit."

"We stayed in Taos because we *knew* they would show up," Chase said. "This isn't about running anymore, or even staying alive. It's about ending the shadow people."

A group of drones appeared above him.

Chase flashed the lumen device the Astronaut had given them. The massive beam not only illuminated the sky, blinding the drones' cameras, it also sent a GPS scattering signal.

"Exposing the shadows to the light," Chase said, as seven drones crashed onto the roofs and pavement below.

"Belfort will send hundreds," Grimes continued. "Maybe thousands."

"That's why we're building an army." Chase leaped across an alley onto the roof of an art gallery. "The shadow wars."

"Almost to the plaza," Grimes said. "Where do you need us?"

Wen, who'd been listening to Chase's half of the conversation in between taking out half a dozen more shadows, was now on the roof of the opposite side of the plaza. She stopped on top of the old courthouse. Always preferring the high ground, she directed her troops. "Chase, tell Grimes and Shelby to head to the intersection at Kit Carson. He can execute a mass there if he surprises them."

"Got it," Chase said, conveying the order. "I'll get on the other side of it."

Wen's vantage point did not afford her a view of Juan Largo Lane, where nearly thirty shadows were waiting behind World Cup Cafe.

The four of them were unknowingly headed directly toward the massacre.

Chapter Thirty

The falling snow, heavy now, temporarily hushed the Taos Plaza, as if it were a wintery postcard. The smell of piñon fires burning up Kit Carson Road blended with the scent of roasting chiles.

Chase, Wen, Shelby, and Grimes all crept closer to the concentration of shadow people waiting in the cold shadows of Largo Lane.

Sirens broke the silence as New Mexico State troopers and Town of Taos Police convened from different directions.

Wen dropped flat on the roof of the building overlooking Largo. Chase was across the corner of the Plaza on the roof of The Gorge Bar and Grill, and could now see enough of the shadow people to know the police were about to get slaughtered. "Grimes, get a diversion going, now!"

Grimes and Shelby were not far off, in a courtyard bordering a parking area. "Like what?"

"Shoot!"

Grimes opened fire into the air. It was the best they could do, hoping to divert some of the police away. Chase didn't know what else to try.

It didn't help much. Gunfire erupted. Seventeen minutes later, the only cops left alive were too severely injured to offer any protection.

Chase and Grimes ran up Kit Carson Road, unsure where Shelby and Wen were now. Chase used his last two rounds to pick off a stray shadow person. The man fell into a lumiaria still burning on the sidewalk. He stumbled to his feet, fully engulfed in flames, and lunged at Chase. Before Chase could react, Grimes grabbed him.

"Never fight a dead man!"

Chase turned back and saw the man roll into the snowy gutter. "I'm out of ammo," Chase said.

"Me, too."

"We need to find some cover."

"This way," Grimes said, turning onto Dragoon Lane.

"How do you know where this goes?" Chase asked.

"I don't, but it's dark and out of the way."

"So are shadows!"

Wen had wound up in the courtyard of the Historic Taos Inn, deep in a shootout with shadow people who had taken position on the other side of Paseo del Pueblo on the treed grounds of Pat Woodall Fine Art. As the bullets volleyed across the street, another group of shadows had gotten inside the Gallery and were setting up a communications center.

Shelby, trapped on Martyrs Lane, didn't like being surrounded by killers on a street named for someone dying for a cause. She couldn't reach any of the others for help.

"I guess I'll just have to shoot my way out," she

muttered as she broke into a small adobe apartment that she thought would provide the best chance of surviving after judging the adobe walls to be ten to fourteen inches thick.

Chase and Wen's comms had also failed. They did not know where the other was. At that point, it didn't matter. They were still outnumbered, with the dark snowy night closing in on them.

The man some called Darth Vader sat in the middle of a dimly lit circular room, surrounded by floor-to-ceiling screens projecting satellite images from multiple points around the globe. One of them was a little high desert town in New Mexico.

"Mess in Taos," a woman said, glancing at a tablet, then back to the big view.

"Yes," Vader replied. The grainy, green-hued images from Taos were blotted with bright points. The luminarias, seasonal street fires, were finally starting to burn down.

"What do you want to do with it?" She changed screens on her tablet, waiting for the command she believed he was about to give.

"I can't do everything to fight this war," he said, sounding more frustrated than the situation should have called for.

"They're going to die."

"Is that really a problem?"

"You've said in the past that you thought it might be."

"That was before."

"Before?" she echoed.

"The Skyggers deployment."

"There have been plenty of Skyggers in the past few years... why is this one any different?"

"They're playing the End Game."

She gasped. "Are you sure?" But it was a silly question. He was always sure of everything. It was why he was who he was.

"Do you have any idea why the devil is so feared?" he asked absently, then continued without waiting for her to respond. "The devil's most dangerous deed was to convince humanity that he was not real."

"Is he real?" she asked, knowing Vader was not a religious man.

"He is, and his earthly name is Haris Tane."

She nodded. One of Vader's obsessions. There were ten or twenty people around which the work of her boss revolved; those who came in and out of his orbit were the ones who he believed were sending humanity to a frightening future. "Then Taos?"

"Give them help," he said in a resigned voice, as if agreeing to put down a beloved pet.

The woman tapped the screen of her tablet, knowing her finger had just killed at least twenty people.

Real Truth - Internet Fact Based News

Posted by JI Right

Urgent post — ACTION REQUIRED!
REAL TRUTH has been de-platformed. MetaFind has shut down our social media pages, and our video channel LookThru, which is owned by search giant SEEEENall, has also been shut down. Other social media sites have followed MetaFind's lead and either slapped warning labels on our post, taken them down all together, or otherwise

censored us through editing. It seems the establishment wants no dissenting opinions about NoLiv or the situation in Turkey. We could be walking straight into World War III, and they don't want anyone to debate it.

Follow us through our website and sign up for our mailing list. Or there may be no other way to see our posts.

Chapter Thirty-One

A few blocks from the Taos Plaza, in a corner of Kit Carson Park, which housed a small historic cemetery, Grimes and Chase huddled in the darkness.

"What are we going to do now?" Chase asked Grimes as the falling snow intensified.

"Staying here is a good idea," Grimes replied.

"We're in the *cemetery*," Chase said, tapping an old tombstone.

"Yeah, well, better to be in a graveyard alive than to be in one dead."

"Wen . . . *Wen?*" Chase tried, talking into his shoulder. "Communications is still down. I don't know what's wrong with this stuff."

"They jammed it," Grimes said. "It's got nothing to do with the grade of your equipment. Nobody's cell phones are working on this end of town either."

"We've got to go find Wen."

"Listen, hero, if anybody can take care of themselves, it's Wen."

"But—"

"She doesn't need *us* running around out there with no weapons."

"They may have also run out of ammo," Chase argued. "There's been a lot of shooting going on . . . maybe everyone's run out of ammunition."

Grimes looked back at him like he was stupid. "Shadow people *never* run out."

"True," Chase amended. "There's a lot of dead cops on the streets. We might be able to strip their weapons."

"Yeah, let's go looking for a needle in a haystack while the barn's on fire."

"I don't believe it," Chase said. "We're sitting behind Kit Carson's grave."

"Dude was a bad dude." Grimes looked at the inscription, barely visible on the snowy night. "1868. Been dead a while."

"Yeah, well, he's kind of been haunting me, but maybe this is a good sign."

Bright lights flooded in on them.

"What the—"

"Don't move!" a gruff voice yelled

"We've got you dead nailed," another added from behind them.

"Move and die, Grimes!" a third barked from the other side of the little cemetery.

Red dots appeared on Chase and Grimes, dancing between their faces and chests.

"Doesn't seem to be a very good sign after all," Grimes whispered through gritted teeth.

"The only reason you're not dead yet, Mumford Grimes, is because Belfort prefers to have a chat with you. But it's not required for the payout, so it's your choice."

"Is that you, Rockland?" Grimes asked.

"Yeah."

"I thought we were friends," Grimes said.

"My only friend is the ten million bucks I get for bringing you in."

Grimes sighed. "Sounds about right."

"Toss out your weapons, slowly."

"We're out of ammunition."

"I don't mind them empty."

"Here you go," Grimes said, throwing his Uzi.

Chase thought of keeping his, since he had not specifically been asked for it, but decided that might not be the best way to prolong his life.

"I want that little Eagle you're always packing," Rockland demanded.

"It's empty, too."

"And we've established I don't mind them empty."

"It's sentimental," Grimes shot back.

"So is the speech I'm going to give at your funeral if you don't surrender that pistol, now!"

Grimes pitched it out toward Rockland.

"You know what else I'd like, right?"

"A new brain, tin man?" Grimes quipped.

"Still a funny boy, I see. The knives. I think you call them East and West."

"You're not afraid of a couple knives when you've got five machine guns pointed at me, are you?"

"I'll tell you what I am—I'm tired of talking to you. You're trying these stalling tactics hoping your girlfriend, Shelby, can get here, but that's not how this movie is going to end. You're not the hero, and this sure as hell ain't Hollywood, so put me in a good mood and hand over East and West *very* carefully, or I'm going to have one of those machine guns cut you in half."

Grimes pulled up his pant legs, revealing two, long, custom-made knives that went from his knees to just above his ankles, held on by over-strong magnets.

He lobbed them out underhanded. "Take good care of these. They're sentimental, too."

"Oh yeah, I know. *Real sentimental.* You killed Wrangler with those."

"Wrangler was trying to kill *me*," Grimes said. "I thought it would be a better idea if I didn't let him do that."

"He was a friend of mine," Rockland said.

"I thought you only had ten million friends."

"I will soon." He turned to Chase. "What about you, billionaire? Got any more weapons I need to know about?"

Chase thought of his multi tool. The blade didn't have a name like East or West, but it was sharp, and could do damage in Chase's practiced hand. "No," he replied. "But I can give you a lot more than ten million to let us go. How about twenty million?"

"I don't think so," Rockland snarled. "Grimes, you better tell your rich friend here that he could offer me ten *billion* and I wouldn't take it. The fine people who are paying me are not the kind of folks you want to piss off."

"You could disappear with twenty million," Grimes said.

Rockland scoffed. "Like *you* did? Hell, I might as well be wearing a suicide vest. And how about that advice coming from one of the two people dumb enough to challenge the Circuit, the other being your pretty, but wildly misguided girlfriend. And she'll be dead soon, too."

Out of the darkness surrounding the glow from Rockland's lights, the sudden burst of machine gun fire sent Chase and Grimes slamming onto the ground as if they'd been hit. It took Chase a surreal second to realize he had not been.

"He was right," he heard Shelby say. "I am a bit misguided, but he was wrong about my demise. Turns out it was him who would be dead soon."

Grimes got to his feet, surveying the five dead bodies around him in the illuminated shadows of their dropped spotlights. "Nice work," he said, looking up at Shelby and Wen.

"Too bad," Shelby said. "I always liked Rockland."

"Me, too," Grimes said. "Tough business."

"Maybe it's just me," Chase said to Grimes, "but I'm not a fan of people who are trying to kill me."

"Killing is always tough," Wen said. "No matter who's doing the dying."

ANC - Always News Channel - Top Story

"Stu Lemon reporting. Our top story at this hour: The NoLiv virus is wreaking havoc with supply chains, leading to shortages. According to experts, this should be a short-term problem. Bill Doorset, who made his fortune in the computer industry before turning to philanthropy, explains, 'The virus is infecting logistics companies at a much higher rate than other businesses.' Why is that, Bill?"

"Nice to be with you, Stu. We don't know yet, but researchers speculate that this is one of the anomalies of the virus, part of what makes it so dangerous."

"Is Remedy helping stop the spread to those firms?"

"Yes, but there have been snap-over cases where the virus has infiltrated the systems in spite of installed Remedy."

"What percentage of cases?"

"We don't have that data yet, but engineers are developing secondary installs, plug-ins, which will make up for the deteriorating code."

"So, to be fully protected, the recommendation now is Remedy and a plug-in?"

"Remedy and two plug-ins."

"Oh, two?"

"Yes. MetaFind and SEEEENall have been working around the clock to stay ahead of the virus and the new variants."

"What about MemoShot, a company you know intimately. How are their efforts coming?"

"As you know, I am no longer involved in the company I founded, but they are close to coming up with a one-time install to combat the NoLiv virus."

"One and done, that sounds simple."

"Nothing is simple about stopping NoLiv. Remember, this is an AI based virus. We've never faced anything like this."

"So people need to install Remedy and the plug-ins right away."

"It's our only hope to return to normal."

Chapter Thirty-Two

Two men sat across from each other, each on an ice blue leather couch. The marble floor shone with a similar blue tint. The light wood of the polished table between them was filled with electronic devices that could have been the latest prototypes from a top smart phone maker.

By all appearances, the men could have been in a penthouse suite, but instead, their high stakes meeting was taking place onboard an Airbus ACJ320neo private jet.

"What's the plan?" Timothy Blanc asked, checking his Patek Philippe Titanium watch. Blanc was a pale, skeletally thin man.

"We're going to remove the obstacles," Haris Tane replied. His eyes matched the leather couches.

"I don't mean what are we going to do about Chase Malone and Wen Sung. It's Belfort I'm worried about."

"He seems to be handling things."

"The man has made a lot of mistakes."

Tane shrugged. "Belfort is still the best we have. There's a lot of history."

Blanc made a sour face. "Too much history."

"I had a long, hard talk with him, if you know what I mean," Tane said, sipping a club soda. "I don't think there'll be any other problems, but just in case, I've called in a Skygger Gloom."

Blanc's gray eyes widened. "So you *are* worried."

The doctors at Holy Cross Hospital in Taos did not think Tess was ready to leave the hospital. Tess thought differently. She'd called in three IT-Squads, each consisting of nine agents. The elite CISS units were largely made up of hand-picked former special forces. Originally the IT-Squads belonged to the NSA, but that had recently changed, and Tess had assumed full authority.

Although IT-Squad agents *were* armed with HK MP5N 9mm submachine guns and HK Mk 23 SOCOM .45 ACP pistols, their preferred tools were the highest tech contained in the US intelligence community's arsenal. These IT-Squads' primary purpose was obtaining and disseminating the most powerful and dangerous weapon—information. Today, they had another mission—protecting Tess, getting her back to CISS's Vienna, Virginia headquarters.

Normally, IT-Squads worked on small, covert, targeted objectives, and getting Tess safely out of Holy Cross Hospital and evacuating her from Taos would have been a simple task. However, nothing was normal anymore. The IT-Squad commander had called in FBI SWAT units and CATs (the Secret Service Counter Assault Team). The CATs toted SR-16 carbine assault rifles and traveled with other heavy artillery.

"We will not lose her," the SWAT Commander said, as

he reviewed the FBI deployments around the hospital and fanning out across Weimer and Estes Roads and to Highway 68, Paseo Del Cañon.

A government nurse, who'd been flown in to escort Tess home, wheeled her down the hallway. Paintings and prints from local Taos artists lined the walls of the small hospital.

One of her legs was in a full cast, the other one up to her knee, an arm in another. Tess wore a neck brace, and her broken ribs were still bandaged.

"You look like you were in a car wreck," the IT-Squad leader said to her.

"I was in a collision with a mountain," she replied, her voice strained, the pain in it obvious.

"I heard a couple of mountains actually fell on you."

"That's what it felt like."

Another IT-Squad agent jogged toward them. "We need to get her out the back entrance."

"Report," the leader asked, as the nurse spun the wheelchair.

"We took out two snipers," the agent said, turning to Tess. "One had a line on your room's window, the other was targeting the entrance. He had a clear shot."

"How did they get this close?" Tess snapped, then moaned and coughed.

"FBI is in a heavy sweep. If there's more, we'll find them. Secret Service had CAT positioned along the motorcade's exit route."

"I won't be in a car!" she said, as if they'd suggested she ride a donkey through town.

"No, of course not. The plan is to helicopter you to the Taos airport. We have a plane waiting to fly you to Kirtland," he said, referring to the Air Force base in Albuquerque, New Mexico.

They rushed to the back entrance. "This is not the most secure," one of the agents said as he threw open the doors.

The chopper landed as close to the building as possible. Tess was happy to see it was a Sikorsky HH-60 Pave Hawk with two M134 miniguns and a pair of .50 caliber heavy machine guns.

Two orderlies appeared and helped Tess onboard, strapping her into a light gurney. The IT-Squad leader and nurse followed.

As soon as they were in the air, the leader received a message from the SWAT commander. "We've got drones incoming," the leader said across the headsets.

"Drones?" Tess said. "Ours or theirs?"

"Not ours! Two waves. Twenty-eight combat drones in each wave."

"Divert!" Tess said, wincing in pain. "Do *not* go to the Taos Airport. Take us straight to Kirtland."

The leader broke in, "Third wave incoming! Brace, brace!"

Chapter Thirty-Three

Grimes, Shelby, Chase, and Wen had spent the remainder of the cold, snowy night sleeping by a warm kiva fireplace at the Taos Pueblo. It turned out that Shelby knew an artist there. Lost to the world, protected by the spirits of a thousand years of brave warriors, shielded by Taos Mountain, cradled by the earthen walls and incredible silence, they slept deeply, as if drugged. Even Wen, although she woke every ninety minutes like clockwork to assess the flames.

No one had seen the paramilitary forces drop into the dark streets via HALO jump. The high altitude/low opening parachuting technique delivered thirty stealth special-op support troops, who quickly cleared the town of the remaining shadow people.

Chasing Lies

In the early dawn hours, as flurries continued to fall, they parted ways. Shelby's friend drove her and Grimes to the Airport. Another reliable man from the Pueblo ferried Chase and Wen to the Destino in Angel Fire.

As they separated, Chase told Grimes, "I guess that's another time you saved me."

"Nah, it was Shelby and Wen who saved us."

"Sure, they fired the shots, but it was your big mouth that kept Rockland talking long enough."

Grimes laughed in spite of himself. "I guess you're right about that."

As the big rig rolled down Interstate 25 and made the connection to I-40 West, Wen called to check on Tu.

Hours later, at another remote truck stop, this one in Arizona, they made their first stop since leaving Taos. The Destino blended in as if it were just another semi hauling a load of imported goods from China.

Chase looked over at Wen. "Are we sure this is okay?"

"The Astronaut said the message was from CISS," she said, repeating what he already knew. "It obviously came from Tess."

"We could be meeting another PeacePipe."

"That wasn't a waste of time."

"No, but . . ."

"There's our meet," Wen said. "Is that . . . Chase, look who we're meeting!"

Chase leaped out of the truck and ran toward the man, who jogged to Chase. The two of them stared at each other for a moment, then threw themselves into a bear hug that might have included a few tears.

"They told me you were dead," Mars said. Mars, Chase's oldest friend, was supposed to be serving a long prison sentence. Seeing him free, out on the street without any armed guards watching him, seemed alien to Chase.

"Yeah, sorry about that," Chase said. "We sort of *were* dead, though."

Mars nodded knowingly. "It was almost worth it though, for the elation I got when I found out it wasn't true."

Chase smiled. "I'll bet."

"Part of me never really believed it anyway."

"I'm glad you didn't," Chase said. "Because I was pretty sure we were dead, down at the bottom that shaft, buried under all that rubble. I didn't think we were going to get out."

"Yeah, I can't imagine."

"It's times like that when you realize who matters, who you're going to miss, wonder how they'll take the news. There are a handful of people on my list, and you're one of them, brother."

Mars nodded. "I know what you're saying. My list is even smaller than yours."

Wen joined them. "Good to see you, Mars." She hugged the man who'd once saved her life.

"You're as beautiful as ever," he said.

"Thanks, charmer, but you look tired. Are you okay?"

"Prison guards woke me in the night, told me to pack my stuff. Gave me fifteen minutes. They hustled me out with no explanation of what was going on. After a couple car rides, they put me on a military plane. We were in the air, still didn't know where we were going or what was happening. Finally, they handed me a phone. It was Tess."

Chase and Wen exchanged a glance.

"Yeah, not who I was expecting, either," Mars continued. "She told me that I'm basically out on a permanent writ until a pardon comes through. I asked her if it was real, if it would really come. She told me to count on it. So, here I am."

"She came through," Chase said, mostly to himself. In the hospital, Tess had understood exactly what Chase was asking for.

"So do the shadow people know you've been resurrected?" Mars asked.

"Unfortunately."

"Then I guess it's time to restart the decoying?" The decoying method had been developed to create false sightings of Chase and Wen around the world by utilizing AI and surveillance cameras.

"Probably a good idea," Chase said. "But I could use you for something more important."

"Name it."

"I need you to run an army."

Mars raised an eyebrow. "Whose army?"

"We're not running from the shadow people anymore," Chase told him. "This time, they're running from us."

"How's that going to work?"

"Like I said, we put together an army."

"How *big* an army?"

"A couple thousand . . . so far. But after last night, I know we're going to need more… a lot more."

Chapter Thirty-Four

Scores of autonomous mini combat drones swarmed over Taos, overwhelming the Sikorsky Hawk helicopter carrying Tess.

"Take it down," the leader said as the drones swarmed.

"Negative," the chopper's pilot said as he took evasive actions, banking low, fast, and nearly sideways across the parking lot.

Three missiles hit the Walmart. The chopper was already over the high school as fire erupted in the parts of the Walmart that hadn't been hit in the initial blasts.

A drone kamikazed into the side of the Sikorsky, sending them into a momentary spin, but the pilot recovered and kept the bird in the air. Limping along, they made it to the Mabel Dodge Luhan House.

"Down!" the leader shouted as more drones massed.

"Watch it!" Tess yelled. The chopper careened toward the third-floor solarium at the historic site. The pilot pulled up and missed crashing into it by inches.

The property was bordered by Pueblo lands, which

included many open fields where they could set down. "We'd be sitting ducks," the leader said. "Do not land."

"We're not much safer up here," the pilot countered.

"At least we're a moving target."

The drones had regrouped into an attack formation. The pilot barely made a maneuver to escape three missiles, which sailed past and destroyed a wedge-shaped metal building next door to the KTAOS Solar Center, a radio station and music venue.

Tess saw the structure destroyed, leaving what was once an art gallery looking like a huge, crushed, smoldering tin can. The station, KTAO, was broadcasting pre-recorded programming, so no live reports of what was happening were on the air.

"Down, down!" Tess yelled. "Before they shoot us down!"

The pilot managed a hard landing into the vast fields behind the venue, which were part of the more than one hundred eleven thousand acres belonging to the Taos Pueblo. The sky, filled with attack drones, appeared horrific, biblical, as if a million giant locusts were descending to destroy the earth.

Mars looked around at the interior of the Destino. "A team of mercenaries, a secret underground base, a mobile command center that looks like the bridge of the USS Enterprise... you don't have an Iron Man suit, do you, Stark?"

"No, but that's a clever idea," Chase said. "I'll ask the Astronaut to build one for me."

Mars reviewed the details of the army, who they'd all

taken to calling *campers*, since they'd been trained and housed at the subterranean facility at Camp Nichols. "A lot of mercenaries is one thing," the former inmate said. "*Smart* mercenaries are even better, especially in a war like this."

Blitz had arranged for a team of three operatives to drive the Destino in eight-hour rotations. Since the cab had two sleeping compartments, and the small private bedroom in the trailer accommodated Chase and Wen, they could now drive twenty-four hours a day. The three drivers were also combat vets, which added to their protection.

Chase liked to believe Wen slept her entire shift, but was never quite sure. While the driver pushed toward San Diego, Chase explained their grand plan to Mars, including what they'd learned about the group behind the shadows.

"So you're hunting shadow people at the same time you're hunting Circuit assets?" Mars asked.

"Exactly," Chase said. "And the AI programs are doing most of the work on both fronts, but when we find shadow people, we need personnel on the ground to either bring them to our side—"

"Or remove them," Mars finished.

Chase nodded. "The campers can handle that, but on the financial side, we need brilliant criminal minds to move on the Circuit."

"I see," Mars said, smiling. "You want me to do some recruitment."

"Right."

"How many players you looking for?"

"As many as you can get."

"What kind of numbers you throwing? I'll work for free, but the kinds of people you want . . . "

"Whatever it takes."

"Then consider it done."

One of the pilots of the Airbus ACJ320neo private jet interrupted the two men. "We'll be landing in a few minutes."

Blanc waited until the pilot returned to the cockpit. "I'd like to know, just how worried are you about Belfort?"

"You should know by now," Tane said. "I never worry. I prepare."

"He screwed up the business in Taos. It might be time."

"Skygger will handle this."

"Who is the Skygger for? Belfort, or Chase and Wen?"

"If Belfort fails, one unit will paper him, and another unit will end Malone and Sung."

"Why didn't we do that before?" Blanc asked.

"We don't use Skyggers to solve problems. We use them to create them."

"And yet, now . . . "

Tane shook his head. "Times have changed. Nukes are in play, a virus is sweeping the world, economies are shaking, power is shifting."

"Still."

"Look at it this way: Belfort, Chase, and Wen have enormous potential to aid our rivals. Therefore, if they are removed, we are creating a problem for those that oppose us."

"Vader," Blanc said.

"Yes, but events will soon turn against him as well."

Chapter Thirty-Five

Two people clad in black and white camouflage, who'd arrived in Taos via HALO jump hours before, surveyed the area by satellite imagery on their handhelds. They moved invisibly through the snow-covered fields north of town. Tess's chopper had flown low overhead, but they'd already known it was coming, as well as the drones. The handhelds had AI. Its programs tapped the sat's sky view and projected the Sikorsky's path and probable destruction.

One of the men called in a SOUP, or *status-order-update-procedure*. After giving the coordinates, he looked back into the airspace above them.

"Is there time?" the other, a woman, asked.

"It's almost instantaneous."

Moments later, the drones fell out of the sky, crashing onto rooftops, cars, and into the street.

"What just happened?" the pilot asked, getting the Sikorsky Hawk helicopter airborne again.

"I hope that was some help from above," Tess said, unsure how the drones had all dropped at once, but having her suspicions. She thought of the one person who might be able to help, who might be able to save her life: Holt Gatewood.

Three minutes later, they landed again, this time at the airport, where she was safely transferred to a waiting plane.

Behind a snow-covered chamisa, the two operatives, cloaked in white and black camo, watched it all happen on their handhelds, then reported in.

"Close out," Darth Vader told them. "That was more than the mission." Sitting in the middle of his circular room, he studied the floor-to-ceiling monitors, absorbing satellite images from around the globe, and decided where to send them next. He looked at his assistant. "Make the arrangements for Turkey."

For years, Tess had a difficult time liking Holt Gatewood, the administrator of HITE, short for Hidden Information and Technology Exchange, a government entity so classified that most US presidents usually didn't learn about it unless they got a second term. HITE, sometimes referred to as the *'invisible agency'* by the few who knew of its existence, had been established after World War II to handle captured Nazi secrets and technology, as well as more controversial materials such as metaphysical data and artifacts. If a UFO of extraterrestrial origin really *did* crash in Roswell, New Mexico, during the summer of 1947, HITE would have wound up with the wreckage and whatever it may have contained. But almost no one knew if they *did* have something like that or not, or what other extraordinary things they might hold.

Although the agency's name included *Exchange*, which made it sound like other government departments and corporations might have some access to HITE's information, and even if that may have been part of the initial intent, it rarely happened. Instead, a select committee made up of top US intelligence leaders—with security clearances *much* higher than that of the President of the United States—decided who, where, when, and *if* the information or assets would be released. Mostly, though, it was HITE's administrator who held the keys, the power. He could ignite huge shifts of wealth by introducing new technologies—be it weapons, computers, satellites, pharmaceuticals, or things no one had dreamed up yet.

Tess called her deputy from the air and instructed her to track Gatewood down. By the time they reached the airbase, Linda reported that she had thus far been unable to reach him.

"I hope he hasn't been targeted, too," Tess said, thinking of the president, then her own assassination attempts. Tess recalled how she had learned to like the man she sometimes referred to as "the Godfather," since she considered HITE as close to the mafia as existed in the US Intelligence community, and he required absolute loyalty from all. The don-like reputation was solidified by Gatewood's attention to his appearance. He kept his thinning black hair perfectly trimmed to make it appear as thick as possible. Graying at the temples was part of his "look," as was the tan that never faded, which he maintained year-round by spending his weekends in the Caribbean, Bahamas, or some other warm destination. He favored perfectly tailored suits and polished Cucinellis, maybe attire more befitting a business tycoon than a government worker, but HITE was not a "normal" federal agency, and its director's secret eight figure salary reflected that.

She smiled at the thought of him now, how he carried himself with the confidence of a Caesar, as if, with the flick of his finger, empires could fall. *It may not be much of an exaggeration,* she thought, while waiting for Linda to call again.

She and Gatewood had worked together on many extremely delicate crises. They were two of the three members of CHAD, and in the acronym-loving town of Washington, it was perhaps the least spoken of of all the government alphabet agencies. Just knowing it stood for CISS, HITE, and DARPA meant you had the highest security clearances, but it did not mean you had any idea what CHAD *did*, or even what CISS or HITE *were*.

"Gatewood saved Chase and Wen," she mumbled to herself while waiting for her next plane ride, the one that would take her back to DC. *He's saved the world a few times, too. With my help, of course.*

She couldn't wait to get to Mission Control, her command center inside CISS headquarters in Vienna, Virginia, the place she felt safest of all.

He can save me, too.

Chapter Thirty-Six

The Destino rolled down Interstate-8 toward San Diego. A phone and car were arranged for Mars. They would drop him along the way.

Wen checked the monitors displaying views from the exterior cameras. Every vehicle was fed into the SEER system, along with a facial ID of every driver and passenger, while an AI reviewed threat assessments, air, and local environments, constantly correlated against enhanced algorithmic synchs.

"What about decoying?" Mars asked. Decoying worked by making false reports and sightings of Chase and Wen at random intervals across the globe. AI programs would generate a constant stream of bad information. Through credit card use, surveillance cameras linked to facial recognition data bases, and a number of other related methods, the sightings would flood in at critical times and overwhelm the shadow people and others who were seeking Chase and Wen. "Now that you're alive again, we should keep them guessing," he continued. "But it could be very difficult in the current climate. The virus is wreaking havoc on everything."

"Even with Remedy, it's not stopping systems from getting infected," Wen said. "It's just stopping them from crashing completely."

"Yeah," Chase said. "We've had a tough time keeping NoLiv from our systems. We've decided not to install Remedy. There are just too many unknowns about long-term effects." He thought about PeacePipe's warnings and wondered if he'd been shot because he really *did* know what he was talking about, instead of just taking bullets intended for Chase.

"I hear you."

Wen watched a van four cars back and debated its intentions.

"And we have to continually shut down SEER to keep the virus out."

"SEER?" Mars asked, being one of the few to know about Chase's ultra-secret program. "You've been using it to track the shadow people?"

"And the Circuit, but constantly shutting down everything to keep the virus out. It's like living in 1980 or something."

"You weren't alive in 1980."

"Thankfully, that's true." Chase smiled. "Anyway, I've got some workarounds."

Wen decided the van was okay. The AI agreed.

"Yeah, and what will you need my guys to do?" Mars asked.

"What criminals do," Chase said. "No offense."

"None taken," Mars replied, punching his arm.

"*Ow*," Chase whined overdramatically.

"Need some help, babe?" Wen asked, waving a gun in their direction.

"No thanks, babe," Mars shot back. "I think I can handle him."

"I meant *Chase*," she said, smiling.

Mars winked at her. "Either way."

"Maybe some break-ins and other kinds of thefts," Chase said, ignoring the flirting. "Cyber-attacks, blackmail, extortion, arson, that type of thing."

"Arson?" Mars echoed skeptically.

"We need destruction of assets. No innocent people getting hurt, but I want to seize or destroy anything that gives them money—money they're using to pay shadows."

The system alerted that a black SUV eight vehicles back might pose a threat. It automatically ran the plates, coming up as Homeland Security. Wen kept an eye on it, but it passed without incident.

"You know our army is only good when we're defending something or killing other soldiers. My guys have lots of special skills. They can con the Circuit, sabotage, rob banks . . . All that money is coming from a big operation. We need to grind it to a halt."

"Bring it down one piece at a time," Chase agreed.

"My guys can do that, but they aren't all exactly trustworthy. I mean, some of them I would trust with my life, but most of them are … well, *criminals*."

Chase waved a hand. "I don't care about that. They can keep whatever they get, but if any are caught, and we can't find a way to get them out, they're on their own."

"They could be a liability—talk, roll on us, know what I mean?"

"If any do, by the time they tell what little they know, it'll be too late. Because they won't know anymore."

Wen checked the cameras again. This time it was a chopper. The system ID'd it as a traffic copter, but she wasn't sure, since she knew that if she wanted to get close to a target, stealing a traffic copter would be one way she might do it. But a few minutes later, it was gone.

"Message from Tu," Chase said.

"How's the boy doing?" Mars asked.

"He's developed a program of his own, with only a little help from the Astronaut."

"Quite a brain."

Chase nodded, sad that Tu had been subjected to prenatal DNA manipulations to enhance his intelligence, but happy he could use it for good. "He pored through all the data that SEER has generated and found a banking connection that goes all the way to the Federal Reserve. It might be something. He's tracking the money supply, treasury auctions, national debt fluctuations, government expenditures. It involves gross domestic product, foreign aid, the international monetary fund, and World Trade Organization and other global financial entities; expiration of options and stock market moves, the exchange rate, dollar against the Chinese Yuan, and a thousand other variables. It's some really elaborate equation that I don't comprehend. Even the Astronaut is quite impressed."

"And where's it lead?"

"We're hoping it will unveil the faces behind the Circuit."

"He'd have to be online to check it. What about the virus?"

"He's downloaded the sources of information, and other various items, and started correlating. When he *does* go online, he's got the same filter we've been using to circumvent the virus."

"The government says only Remedy works, that none of the old anti-virus methods will work against NoLiv."

"They lie."

ANC - Always News Channel - Top Story

"KiKi Carlyle reporting. Our top story at this hour: Samantha Lawson, the White House point person on the NoLiv virus, just finished a press conference where she stated that given the looming crisis in Turkey, combined with the virus, the President is considering implementing either the Insurrection Act, or the Posse Comitatus Act. The use of such emergency measures means that certain civil liberties may be suspended, including the right to be free from unreasonable searches and seizures, freedom of association, freedom of movement, and, in certain cases, freedom of speech. Additionally, the writ of habeas corpus—the right to a trial before imprisonment—may be suspended. Further, National Guard troops and other branches of the military may be used to enforce those restrictions and other Executive orders, such as the mandates to install Remedy and other cures for the NoLiv virus.

"Retired General Abe Sanatkous joins us via satellite from Washington. General, help us unpack this."

"Good to be with you, KiKi. Well, I applaud the president here. He's acting in his role as Commander in Chief. The United States is skirting as close to nuclear conflict as we've been since the Cuban Missile Crisis, while at the same time facing a critical domestic situation, with NoLiv as bad as anything we've dealt with since computers and the internet came to dominate our daily lives."

"NoLiv is a worldwide disaster."

"And globalization means the ramifications of it are magnified. I urge everyone to install Remedy. Don't listen to the naysayers. Remedy really does work."

"The demonstrators and resisters you just alluded to seem to be growing in number."

"This is because of foreign bad actors. Our enemies are using the virus to further divide us. They are taking advantage of our perceived weakness by spreading disinformation. We need to de-platform those helping them."

"Below is a list of websites where Remedy can be downloaded. We can beat this if everyone does their part."

Chapter Thirty-Seven

Tess finally reached Gatewood across an encrypted video feed.

"I heard about Taos," he said once they were connected. "I've been there a few times to visit Rummy."

Tess recalled meeting the late Defense Secretary, Donald Rumsfeld, at his home in Taos on a few occasions. "Yeah, well, this was no social call."

"Apparently not."

"You know who did this," she said almost pleadingly. "I need to know who."

"You, better than most, know it's a complicated world. I can't."

"Damn it, there's nothing complicated about the fact that they tried to kill me!"

"Actually, there is. Normally they don't reach this high. Generally someone in your position is already in bed with them."

"You know me better than that. I play straight."

"As straight as can be expected in our line of work."

"Yes," she conceded.

"Tess . . . " he said in a way that made her name sound like a request to stop.

"Who is it?" she pressed. "Tell me who ordered this."

"Tess . . . "

"Who!"

"You *know* who it is," he snapped.

His statement startled her, but she could not deny the accuracy of his claim. For years, Tess had her suspicions. She'd seen glimpses of something she didn't want to get too close to, something she couldn't quite define, because it was so dangerous it made her look away. His vague confirmation of this frightened and angered her. Most of the anger she felt was toward herself, for letting it go all this time. "I need names."

"You know I can't give you names."

"You can't, or you won't?"

In the tense, silent moments that followed, she realized her response sounded like a character in one of those cheap suspense thrillers she'd read as a girl growing up, the ones that had influenced her to want to be whatever it was she had become—a spymaster, an advisor to presidents, a preserver of democracy; but had the spymaster fallen prey to a puppet master? Was she really just doing the bidding of those who now sought to destroy her?

"Damn it," Gatewood's voice brought her back. "It's not that simple."

"Is the great Holt Gatewood afraid?" Her statement had been meant to be reverse psychology prodding, but as Tess uttered the words, she realized he *was* afraid. And if *he* was afraid, with his access to the future, with his ability to shape and destroy entire industries, then what of her?

"We should all be afraid," he said, confirming her thoughts.

"When we are most afraid is the time when courage is the most necessary."

He shook his head. "I can assure you this call is encrypted to such a level that it will never be revealed, and the room from which I'm speaking is likewise protected by technology that renders it impossible for anyone to eavesdrop. I am also using an experimental satellite technology to shield your current communications with me from any devices that might seek to intercept our words."

"I expected as much."

"The fact is they have decided they want you dead, and therefore, you are dead. I'm truly sorry. You know you're one of my favorite people."

She scoffed. "Really? Well, friends don't let friends get assassinated."

"I can think of no way to do anything to help you that does not end in my own death. And although that may sound like cowardice to you, I have my family to think of, my work. My work is no small matter."

"Of course it isn't." She knew they were in the middle of a war for the future. It'd been her work, too. "I fight on the same battlefield every day. Although I'm not privy to the technology and HITE aspects you deal with, I know the stakes and the players." It wasn't just companies and countries. Ironically, she knew it was a former director of HITE, and those he had recruited, who may have been the most dangerous of all.

"We're past the point—"

"You alone can make the difference in my life, in my death."

"You have no idea what you're up against."

"That's not true."

"Tess, they can change the world to destroy you."

"We've been friends." She hesitated, not really sure they *had* been friends.

He nodded, as if to concede that point.

"Save me, Holt. If you choose not to, then you're deciding to protect *them*, whoever they are, and they are not nice people. You and I, we're the good guys . . . you're a *good* man, Holt." Tess met his eyes. "But the people who want me dead are the forces of evil. They *must* be stopped."

"If you realize the magnitude of their power, you recognize the magnitude of their threat, and if I hope to live to defeat—"

"It reminds me of the famous poem by a German pastor. Do you know it?

First they came for the Communists
And I did not speak out
Because I was not a Communist
Then they came for the Socialists
And I did not speak out
Because I was not a Socialist
Then they came for the trade unionists
And I did not speak out
Because I was not a trade unionist
Then they came for the Jews
And I did not speak out
Because I was not a Jew
Then they came for me
And there was no one left
To speak out for me

"What will you do when they come for you?" Tess asked.

Holt shook his head. "I will try to figure out a way . . . before that happens."

"And if you can't? You'll realize then that I was one of the people who could've saved you."

He gave her a name. "That's all I can do. And I hope you realize I've just signed my own death warrant, so you better work fast, you better work good, and you better get them before they get me."

"Thank you," she said, calculating what the odds realistically were.

Later, she thought Gatewood must have believed she at least had a chance since he'd told her the name. But that hadn't been it at all. He'd told her because she'd been right when she said he was a good man. In the end, he had given her the name simply because he believed it was the right thing to do; not because Tess living or dying was ultimately all that important, but because someone needed to try to stop them, and she had a better opportunity than almost anyone else. Almost anyone, except for him.

Real Truth - Internet Fact Based News

Posted by JI Right

This is Real Truth coming to you from an undisclosed location. The powers that be, the technocrats, the billionaires who control the platforms, the media . . . us, have twice brought down our site. We've been removed from all search engines. They want us to be invisible.
What can you do to help, to counter this censorship, to resist the surveillance state?
Send links to these reports to your friends and relatives.
Check our website for a list of email providers and search engines that

do not track you or censor you, or otherwise control and manipulate data for their many agendas.

Now let's get right into it. Carnage on the streets in the tiny, picturesque town of Taos, New Mexico. We have reports from multiple eyewitnesses. There are dozens of police officers dead. We have footage of a missile hitting the local Walmart, which has been obliterated. Click here to see a live video, which clearly proves that this story was not accurately reported.

They are claiming it was gas lines that exploded. I guess we are to believe that same blast also killed the dozens of brave police officers more than a mile away.

None of this footage you're seeing is being reported on any other news sites.

Hey, mainstream media, why not? What happened there? Who is fighting who? And is it so dangerous that they do not want us to know?

Chapter Thirty-Eight

Tane and Blanc stood in one of the Circuit's private television studios, which could monitor and override every major network. From behind the glass, the two billionaires watched the feeds and footage from around the world.

"How long do you think we can keep this out of the media?" Blanc asked.

"Forever," Tane replied, as if it were a ridiculous question. "At least the media anybody cares about."

"Did you read the trackings?" Blanc asked, referring to a daily report which kept tabs on events and news stories being covered by alternative news outlets on the Internet.

"I don't have time to read the trackings. We've got hundreds of people on staff to handle that."

Even before the rise of the Internet, the maestro had employed a group to monitor and subscribe to all sources reporting with any kind of journalistic integrity. Once identified, the same group would work to discredit the source, throw obstacles in their way, or completely destroy them.

"They've got a big budget, but every day it seems

unsanctioned stories proliferate even more," Blanc said. "Some of these sites actually have a fairly good idea of what's really going on."

"Where are they getting this information?"

"Money. People talk."

"Money?" Tane scoffed. "That's our domain."

"Mostly."

"We should be able to put an end to that without it requiring any of my time, and then . . ." He paused to stare at one of the monitors. "What the hell is *that*?"

"Taos."

The footage coming from security cameras and a few bits of amateur footage provided to the local TV station showed the firefight between Chase's group and the shadow people. Other scenes showed Tess's escape.

"How did they get there? Who sent them?"

"Belfort, but there's more going on."

Tane knew he was right. Somebody else had been in Taos. "Damn Regulators."

"Hard to imagine anything else."

"Damn Vader."

"A lot of dead police officers."

"So?"

"The Real Truth website has added Taos to the list."

Tane frowned in confusion. "What list?"

"The list of shootings, massacres, unexplained deaths that aren't being covered in the mainstream media."

"Real Truth?"

"A fairly popular alternative site," Blanc explained. "We kicked them off LookThru, and their site no longer comes up in search results on SEEEENall, but it's got tens of millions of followers."

"Who's running it, and why the hell is he still alive?"

Blanc shrugged. "We haven't decided to end him yet."

"I just decided."

Blanc smiled. "He's no fool. We've been unable to locate him."

"Is he on *our* list?" Tane asked, referring to the Circuit's watchlist which covered millions of people worldwide considered to be troublemakers to some degree. Potential problems, they were ranked by categories with red being considered extremely dangerous; the only category worse was black, meaning marked for death. Black was the smallest part of the list, mainly because the Circuit was extremely efficient at killing the graduates from the red list. Chase Malone and Wen Sung had been on the black list longer than anyone.

"Real Truth is a hazy thing. We don't even know who he is for sure," Blanc said. "The guy doesn't post under his real name, and he doesn't ever show his face on video."

"We have ways. This shouldn't be that difficult."

"It wouldn't surprise me if we find out he's on the Regulator's payroll."

Tane shook his head. "One day I'm going to find Vader, and rid the world of his foul existence."

"One day . . ."

"And that . . . what's that story?" Normally there was someone else watching the feeds. They had a crew of censors who moved and killed stories, and even more producers who inserted new ones. However, with events heating up and his growing frustration with delays in finding Chase and Wen, among other rising issues, Tane had decided to come do it himself. He considered it one of the most important parts of their operations, critical to shaping opinion, controlling the narrative, defining the *truth*.

"All these stories to bury... so many people to discredit,"

Tane said. "And the other way around—people to bury, stories to discredit."

A man entered the studio. "You wanted to see me, sir?"

Tane nodded at one of his best hatchet men, a small, wiry man in charge of his largest team of fixers.

"Anybody comes up with anything on the virus, crosses the line, goes against the agenda on *any* topic, take them out. Understand?"

"Yes, sir."

"We're at a new level. I don't want *any* air getting in. Bring an onslaught, crush them with pedophile accusations, nail them as racists, link them to extremist groups, show them to be agents of Russia, put them on with Epstein, his plane, his island—do *whatever* it takes. Allow our opponents to gain no traction on anything."

"So no limits?"

"None," Tane confirmed.

"No mercy."

"Not even a trace of it."

Chapter Thirty-Nine

From the dusty outcropping on a jagged ridge line well above and away from a secret military base in eastern Turkey, Luke stared through high-power digital binoculars. "Is that . . . ?" he asked, as the focus automatically adjusted. "I believe those are Skyggers."

Leia, an eighth of a mile away, thought there had been a glitch with their comms. "Are you sure?" She wasn't surprised, though. She would have been more surprised if they *hadn't* been there, but it meant everything had suddenly grown more dangerous, more difficult, her and Luke's lives perhaps in more peril than ever before, and everyone else in the world was as well. "You could be wrong."

"I've got an image capture. I'm sending it."

"You'll never get a confirmation."

"You mean in time?

"At all," she said. "Skyggers aren't real, remember? They don't exist." Leia stared through her scope. She had a clear shot at the backs of two of them, but couldn't see the rest.

"If we get anything above thirty percent probable, I'm going to assume my assessment is correct. Five dollars?"

"I don't gamble."

"Ha! What are you doing now? What do you do every day?"

She already knew he was right, just didn't think they'd get any verification. "Why are they here?" she asked.

"Why wouldn't they be?"

"That's not what I mean," she said as three of them came into her view. "What are they doing *here*?"

"I'm betting the plan is to recover some nukes."

She couldn't tell if he was being sarcastic or not. "That's not what's Skyggers do," she said.

"You tell me, then. More likely they're planting evidence, or inciting those demonstrations going on in Istanbul."

"We're not anywhere near Istanbul."

"It doesn't mean they're not having influence." He zoomed in again. "Those men down there, they're not all Turkish."

She still couldn't see enough. "So?"

"I'm going to send them all in."

"We don't have *time* for this."

"We've got all the time in the world. At least until something happens."

Luke and Leia continued watching their targets, recording their movements, even their lips, which would be analyzed later to reveal their conversations.

"Those trucks aren't here by accident," Luke said.

"And they aren't normal rigs," Leia said.

"No," Luke agreed. "They're sophisticated, expensive rigs capable of moving sophisticated, expensive equipment."

"Did they bring the nukes here, or are they taking them out? That's the question."

"Or they're going to *get* the nukes."

"What? Our intel said the nukes are already here."

"How often has Intel been wrong?"

"Often, but this is—"

"Hold on," he said. "Response coming in. Thirty-seven percent probable this guy is Skygger."

"So that means…"

"Something funny is going on here that's not very funny at all."

"What about the people who aren't Turkish?" she asked.

"Nothing yet."

A handful of others had come and gone, but the core group they'd identified at the start remained the point of their focus. "The seven people we're watching, three Americans and four locals who may not be locals," Leia began. "If those three are Skyggers, then what exactly are the other four doing?"

"The other four," he said, reading the screen on his wrist, "are an interesting group. Two of them are Turkish, the other two are Iranians."

"The plot thickens," she said. "How far are we from the border?"

He knew she meant the border with Iran. "By roads or as the crow flies?" he asked, already searching the GPS.

"Since they have such fancy trucks, let's go by road."

"Two hundred seventy-two kilometers."

"I guess we have a pretty good idea then, why those Skyggers are here and why we're here."

"It was never about Turkey," Luke said.

"No, it's about Iran. But I bet you'll never see that on the news or in the Pentagon briefings."

"No, this is far more dangerous than a nuclear confrontation between the US and Turkey. We're watching the birth of World War III here."

ANC - Always News Channel - Top Story

"Stu Lemon reporting. Our top story at this hour: Reports of protests and non-compliance around anti-fabric masking and device distancing have drawn police to crackdown on resisters. The president has authorized prosecutors to seize assets and freeze bank accounts of the protestors. Some advisors have suggested that the executive orders could be used to take children from the parents of non-compliance citizens designated as threats to stability, or rebels. There is also confirmation at this hour that many online disinformation sites, pretending to be independent news services, are being removed from servers owned by AweSum.

"The president recently announced SEC sanctions on companies that continue to support and promote disinformation. It is widely agreed that the executive order can be used in litigation against passive corporate involvement, including hosting and advertising these dangerous entities. Industry watchers expect search giant SEEEENall to demonetize and ban advertising by the same offenders.

"Note that we cannot name the affected sites, as it would publicize and promote them, thereby putting us at risk of "nonconforming" with the new regulations."

Chapter Forty

A handsome, fit man opened the door, his black hair only flecked with gray, but his goatee mostly white. He moved a football-sized sailing ship carved from pine to his left hand, then extended his right arm to shake. Wood shavings, like crumbs, decorated his dark cashmere. "I guess you are my interruptions," Ed Underhill said. "Good to meet you. I'd offer you a seat, but you might stay longer."

The scents of fresh pine and coffee mixed with the slight smells of paint thinner and turpentine, wafting from the partially open door.

Chase laughed. "Wood carver, huh?"

"Sometimes. When people leave me alone long enough." He stepped aside. "Come in, I guess."

The exposed brick walls and openness of the place gave the feel of being in a New York City loft apartment, the kind renovated from an old factory, but instead of the Hudson River through the wide windows, the sweeping view was of the Pacific Ocean.

"Nice spot you got here," Chase commented.

"I like seeing the ocean while I work," Underhill said, resuming his work, shaving curls of soft wood off the ship's stern. "My father was a general in the Airforce, stationed all over the world, he loved the sea. That's probably where I got it. Sense of freedom."

"How long have you known Tess?" Wen asked.

"Forever. Back when I was in the game, we found common ground on many topics, both working different sides of certain challenges within the intelligence sphere. It used to matter, you know?" He looked at them. "A person, a group effort... you could make a difference."

"But you got out?"

"I escaped." He waved his hand around. "This isn't exactly a Langley-compliant office."

"You still work for them?"

He glared at her. "Are you writing a book?"

"We've been burned a lot."

"Who hasn't?" His expression looked as if the memory of a dozen betrayals suddenly caught in his throat. "I do occasional work for Tess, maybe a few others." He paused and studied them again. "Tess asked me to help you out, so I guess you're here on her dime."

Wen nodded. "We're trying to track down a group of people involved with an organization known as the Circuit."

Underhill stopped working on the elaborate wood ship and set down his carving knife. "Sorry, I can't help you."

"Yes, you can," Wen insisted.

He shot her a look, as if deciding whether to break his rule about not hitting women. "I don't think you really want to know about the Circuit."

"So you've heard of them?" Chase asked.

"Damn right, I've heard of them. They're a blight on

humanity. They're what's *wrong* with the world. I'd like to see them all head straight for hell."

"So then these are friends of yours?" Chase joked.

"Chase, people tell me I've got a good sense of humor, that I tell a good joke, a humorous story. I don't think there's too many things one *can't* make light of, but the Circuit is one of them. Understand?"

"I'm trying," Chase said. "We want to know who runs the Circuit. We want to find them."

Underhill shook his head. "I don't think that's a very good idea."

"Why not?"

"There's only two of you." He picked up his knife again, holding it as if ready to fight. "If you want to go after the Circuit, you need an army."

"We've got one."

Underhill tried to suppress a smile. "Really? How big is your army?"

Chase looked at Wen as if wondering if they should disclose such a significant fact to a man they hardly knew, and then answered anyway. "There's over a thousand highly-trained commandos."

Underhill laughed.

"Wait, I thought we weren't supposed to joke about the Circuit."

"The joke isn't about the Circuit," Underhill said. "It's about your army. A thousand John Wicks, along with a thousand Jason Bournes, wouldn't be enough. You have no idea what you're dealing with."

"That's what we're here *trying* to find out," Chase pressed.

"No," Underhill said. "Go tell Tess she gave you a bad lead."

Wen's eyes focused on his every facial muscle. "What are you afraid of?"

"You," he said, moving toward a larger carving, a ten-foot-high totem pole filled with angry faces. "I'm afraid of you." He began sanding some of the lower details, as if Chase and Wen were no longer there.

Wen walked over to him. "You're afraid of the Circuit."

"That is true, but I know enough that I can avoid their wrath. You two, on the other hand, I don't know, but I'll bet you know hardly anything about the Circuit, because no one alive knows much—"

"Besides you."

He looked at her as if she'd just thrown up on his shoes. "As I said, I know enough. And if I gave you anything, you two will just go out there, recklessly looking for the kings of the Circuit, get yourselves killed, and it will lead them back to me. I don't need to die today."

"Do we look reckless?" Wen asked, her death stare making it far less like a question than a threat.

"No, but you are." He closed his eyes for a moment. "Anyone crazy enough to want to track down the Circuit is more than reckless. They're fools."

"We are none of those things," Chase said. "However, the Circuit has been trying to kill us for more than two years, and the only way they will stop is if we find them."

Underhill squinted his eyes, nodding slowly. "Two years? And you're still alive? How is that possible?"

"Because we are not reckless," Wen said.

He walked over to Chase and shoved him.

"Hey!" Chase protested.

"You don't appear to be a ghost," Underhill said. "You claim to have avoided the Circuit assassins for more than two years?"

"Almost three," Chase muttered.

"Tell me how," he said, his voice sounding impressed, his expression skeptical.

"We're good at killing," Wen said.

"Better than they are?"

"Apparently," Chase answered.

"Are you sure it's the *Circuit* who's been trying to kill you? Because they usually don't miss their targets."

"We're positive," Wen said, losing patience.

He shook his head. "You really should be dead by now."

"And yet we are not."

"You will be . . . "

"Are you going to help us, or not?"

"You don't understand their power."

"Then ask yourself this, Mr. Underhill. Why does the Circuit send *hundreds* of shadow operatives to assassinate us?"

He smiled, realizing her point. "Because they fear *you*."

Real Truth - Internet Fact Based News

Posted by JI Right

Peaceful protestors are being called 'rioters' or even 'terrorists.' They are being listed, harassed, arrested. Many have lost their jobs. Some have even been threatened with having their children taken from them.
No one has been hurt, no injuries. What is going on?
Since when did Americans support, let alone cheer, censorship and government crackdowns on constitutional rights like the freedom to assemble, the freedom of speech?

Chasing Lies

Anti-war demonstrators questioning the administration's policies on Turkey have met with similar fates. This, after the mainstream media doesn't even cover the rallies. Perhaps this answers the question as to why, over the past decade, the local police departments have steadily been militarized. It's almost as if they were expecting uprisings.

And to that point, here is footage, shot from the cell phones of those on the scene, of people in line at banks being told to go home, or face arrest. Police in full military gear are actually shoving resisters to the ground. Intimidation, brutality . . . whose side are the authorities on? Not the innocent citizens, rather the corporate and banking factions that now control what was once a thriving democracy.

Prosperous, happy, free people do not revolt, and yet . . .

Chapter Forty-One

Underhill walked through what appeared to be a hallway which had been created by many totem poles and other large carvings. He stayed back there for a few minutes, rustling though boxes filled with chisels, files, rasps, and other carving tools. He returned with a small block of wood in his hand.

"Okay, I do have a contact, a man who runs the mechanical division of the Circuit. They are constructed of many parts."

"Thank you," Chase said, seeing the pain in his eyes.

"There's a place where he stays," Underhill continued. "He moves around all the time, as you might imagine someone in his line of work would."

"Where—"

"Los Angeles, a fabulous mansion. Not his. It belongs to someone else. That's partially how he remains untraceable. He always stays at someone else's home—and I use that word loosely. These are protected estates, secure penthouses in ultra-secure buildings." He didn't look at them as he whittled away at the block of wood. "Point is, not only are they difficult to locate, these places are even more difficult to get into. But I'll leave that to you."

"Is he there now?" Wen asked.

"I would have no way of knowing that. That kind of information would be extremely dangerous to possess. I would wager the odds are against it, but if he is, there would be extra security. If he isn't, maybe you'll get lucky and find something he's left behind."

"Seems a long shot."

"Everything is with the Circuit. Maybe just the mansion's address will provide another link in your search, your Quixotesque quest." He continued working the block of wood with his knife, Chase raising a brow, trying to figure out what was taking shape.

"What else can you tell us about the Circuit?"

"For them, it's a matter of control, and how they act upon that control. They easily destroy people, companies, even governments. They leave nowhere to hide. It's best not to open yourself to them, but since they already *have* decided to eliminate you—"

"We have nothing left to lose," Wen said.

"Except your life."

"You think we're crazy?"

"Yes," Underhill said dryly. "You shouldn't do this, but I pray you succeed."

"We will."

He nodded, as if she was one of his daughters who had just told him she could walk on water. "When the Circuit finds out that I helped you, because the Circuit finds *everything* out—"

"How could they?"

He smiled the way one does when dealing with idiots.

"The Circuit is everywhere, and they are looking for you. That means they will dig *so deep* they'll know more about your bowel movements than you do." His expert hands shaved more of the wood from the block. "Make no mistake, they will learn where you got your information, because that's one of the reasons they're so powerful and so dangerous—they have access to *all* of it. And the Circuit doesn't let their enemies live. They can erase your entire existence; that means you, everyone you've ever known, this place we're sitting in right now. If the Circuit finds out about this conversation, then this place won't exist anymore either."

"You're exaggerating," Wen said.

"Am I?" Underhill looked as if he might laugh. "Why don't you tell me why you're *really* so interested in the Circuit."

"We're afraid not of *them*," Chase said, "but of what they are doing."

Underhill scoffed. "There's a difference between being afraid, and being smart. I'm neither, but I know how the world actually works—not what they want you to think, but the real deal." He stopped, inspected the block, went at it a bit more aggressively, then continued his rant. "I read the signs, looking for trouble, looking for opportunities. I don't exactly know which one you are, trouble or opportunity, but since Tess sent you, I'm going to assume that you are smart and not afraid." He stared at Wen. "You claim you are not reckless. But when I give you this information, these leads, that's it. This is our last meeting."

"Agreed," Chase said.

Underhill handed him the block of wood, now shaped like a dagger with a tiny slot revealed in its handle. "It's a read-three," he said. "After the third viewing, the data will erase."

"Got it." Chase turned the wooden dagger until the micro card dropped out.

"I don't know who they are, or their ultimate objectives," Underhill said. "But what I *do* know is on there."

Chase shoved it in his pocket, then opened his tablet. "Can you do us another favor?"

Underhill's expression turned incredulous. "What? You want me to rob a bank, now?"

"I thought we weren't joking," Chase said.

"You asked for another favor. That wasn't a joke?"

Chase showed him photos of Belfort.

Underhill looked at Chase, impressed. "That's the guy. So you do know something. He's the one who heads the mechanical division. He's probably been responsible for thousands of deaths."

"Name's Belfort."

"That's not his real name," Underhill said.

"Do you know what is?"

"No. But he's not that high up in the organization."

"In a house of cards," Chase began, "if you knock out a single card on the bottom, the whole thing falls."

"The Circuit isn't a house of cards, it's like a fortress on another planet, something out of Star Wars . . . apparently there's a man connected to the Circuit who they call Darth Vader."

"Crazy egomaniacs," Wen said. "We're chasing characters from fiction. We're chasing lies."

"Final question," Chase asked. "What are you working on?"

"A ship," Underhill said, pointing over his shoulder. "I've got a fleet of them. All replicas of historic vessels."

"Not your carving, I meant in connection with the Circuit."

"I know what you meant."

Chase huffed in amusement. "You don't want to answer."

He stared at them for a long moment. "I've been working with some reporters. Not the entertainers and propagandists that fill the media's ranks today, but a few of the last remaining journalists."

"Why?"

"Ever hear of Operation Mockingbird?"

"Yeah. Back in the nineteen-fifties and sixties, the CIA infiltrated the US Media, until Senate hearings brought it to light in the early seventies and they shut it down."

"They never shut it down," Underhill said. "It only grew bigger."

"You mean the CIA still controls most of the media now?"

He shook his head. "No. *All* of it."

Chapter Forty-Two

Linda looked at her boss as the voice command wheelchair brought Tess into mission control. "Why didn't you tell me? I would've met you upstairs."

Tess smiled and winced at the same time. "Don't you have anything better to do?"

"You look—"

"I know, awful, like a truck hit me. But it wasn't a truck, it was a mountain."

"I was gonna say you don't look as bad as I thought you would."

"I don't like lies," Tess said. "Although I wrote the book on them." This time she smiled only with her eyes.

"The president is doing a dark briefing in three minutes from the situation room," Linda said. "We're linked in."

"Speaking of lies . . ." Tess said.

"Are you sure the president is lying?"

"Only when his lips are moving." She smiled again, but it quickly faded. "I always knew this day would come."

"What are we going to do?"

"The first task is staying alive."

"You've already done that."

"At least for the moment," Tess replied. "It's like playing chess. If we can stay alive long enough, the president won't be our problem anymore."

"Why not?" Linda asked. "He'll be removed from office?"

"From the planet."

Linda's face registered surprise. Then she pointed. "We're on in three, two, one."

Tess nodded.

The president's private briefing on Turkey and the virus took twenty-three minutes. He took no questions.

At the end of it, Tess rolled her eyes. "The man uttered not one syllable of truth."

"What now?"

"Better prepare for war."

"Nuclear war with Turkey?"

"I wish it were that easy."

Underhill showed Chase and Wen early communications that predated the founding of the major social media companies, search engines, and digital payment systems that showed the CIA and NSA were behind the initial funding and architecture of those firms. "It was all designed," he said, waving his carving knife. "No one is surprised where we are without privacy or uncensored dialogue. They led us here one *like* and one *search* at a time."

"Washington controls tech," Chase said. "I thought it was the other way around."

"Because that's what they want you to think. And your

own tech arrogance and bias helps make you extra blind to the reality."

Chase smiled. "Is that why you work out here now, instead of in DC?"

"I can work anywhere. The problem with DC is in our nation's capital, everyone is owned by one interest or another."

"You just said Washington owns tech, now you're saying *everyone* is owned . . . "

"There is a transitory Washington and a permanent Washington. The intelligence community runs things, don't ever doubt that. Intelligence is the top rung, then the Pentagon, then the army-ants of bureaucrats at State, and twenty other agencies."

"When did this corruption start?" Chase asked.

"It was baked in," Underhill said. "From the start, governments are corrupt. In a democracy, the citizens have the chance to keep that under control, but they must be vigilant. Americans were vigilant for a long time, until those in power figured out how to manipulate them. The media keeps them well distracted now, so they don't know where to look."

A call came in.

"I have to take this," Underhill said.

"Of course," Chase replied, surprised when Underhill put the call on speaker.

"I'm as good as dead," the man on the other end said, in a weak voice that sounded a little familiar to Chase. "The devastation of your reputation is due to the scandalization of your radicalization."

"PeacePipe, where are you?"

"Hospital. Took a few bullets too many."

"*PeacePipe?*" Chase exclaimed. "We thought you were

dead! We went back for you, but you were gone. No sign of you in the local hospital, or Albuquerque, either."

"They took me to Denver. Not sure why, not sure how."

"You're in Denver?" Chase asked.

"No longer," he said hoarsely. "They moved me to another place more secure."

"Who is 'they'?" Wen asked.

"Tess."

"Why?" Chase asked.

"They're still coming for me, man. They're coming for her, for you, they're coming for all of us!"

"Who?"

"The *Circuit*," he said. "And it's not their guns we need to fear, it's the NoLiv. The virus is part of it. They're boxing us in with the requirements. I'm sending you an important trace of programmer code . . . in case I don't make it . . . You'll see what I'm talking about. Once you see what the code does . . . where it leads . . . find the reporter Stone Boselovic."

"What do we do when we find him?" Wen asked.

"Get him to tell you his source, before . . . "

"Before what?"

"Before he winds up dead like me."

"I just received the code," Underhill said. "What do we use to open it?"

No response.

"PeacePipe? How do we open it?"

"PeacePipe?" Chase tried.

Wen checked the phone. "The line is dead." She ran to the front windows. "Maybe it's not on his end. They could be here!"

Underhill touched a button. Views from more than

twenty cameras lit up a row of screens Chase hadn't noticed before.

"We're clear," he said with the assurance of a person who'd run the same drill a thousand times before.

"How do you know PeacePipe?" Chase asked, not sure how such a radical and almost comical character like the guy they'd met in Taos could wind up in the same room with a straight-laced man like Underhill.

"I'm busy with the NoLiv virus, running it down, Peace-Pipe has a link into the underworld where some of the most valuable data lives. It filters down there. And a certain number of mischievous characters and malcontents reside in the cracks of society unnoticed by the powerful, or at least are not worried about. The Circuit seems to believe marginalized portions of the population pose no threat. They might be underestimating them."

Chase thought of PeacePipe. "Or not."

"PeacePipe and I also share a certain humor."

"Really?" Chase said. "What kind?"

"It's not your scene."

Wen laughed. "Then the Circuit, the CIA, and the virus intersect?"

Underhill nodded. "And hopefully the code he sent will explain it. If we can figure out how to get into it."

"Lucky for you, codes *are* my scene," Chase said. "Let's take a look."

Less than half an hour later, Chase got in. "It's worse than we thought," he said grimly. "Let's find Stone Boselovic before Belfort does."

ANC - Always News Channel - Breaking News

Word from the White House today that the president has signed an executive order mandating that companies with more than five hundred employees require all employees to install Remedy on their personal devices. Already several major companies have terminated thousands of employees for refusing to install Remedy.

Video sight LookThru, which is owned by search giant SEEEENall, as well as other video sites, MetaFind, and other social media companies, have continued taking down a vast number of videos that outrageously have been questioning the mandates and Remedy's effectiveness.

The online centers that test for the NoLiv virus have had record numbers of applications. Reports of the test sites crashing have been exaggerated according to tech and media experts. The government has begun setting up physical test centers in the large retail chains around the country. The first locations in Arizona, California, and Ohio have seen people lining up for hours to get an appointment. Complaints of false positives and cleared negatives still abound, but for the most part, the process has been going very smoothly.

All major tech companies have provided an app for easily testing your phone.

Opponents suggest that the testing centers have become breeding grounds for the virus. However, there is no proof of this.

Billionaire philanthropist, Bill Doorset, said today, "Nonconforming entities, which includes people, are simply dangerous. They present a clear danger to us all."

The Speaker of the House also chimed in on the controversy, saying that, "These nonconformists are a threat to our country."

Chasing Lies

Below is a list of websites where you can view and track the numbers of tests that have been given, as well as the number of positives and negatives posted. They break it down by country, state, county, device, and more. The number of people who have installed Remedy is also tracked.

The US government has agreed to provide stimulus checks so that people can replace their devices that were destroyed by the virus. Senator Allen, of California, announced today that he would sponsor the Resistors Inciters Social nonConformers (or RISC) Act, which will impose stiff fines of up to $100,000 per offense, and up to one year in prison to non-conformers who refuse to install Remedy, mask their devices, or who spread disinformation about the virus or Remedy.

Chapter Forty-Three

Los Angeles traffic always frustrated Chase, but riding in the back of the Destino somehow made it seem less bothersome. Although they did need to park several miles away from their destination, it meant they were able to use the two motorcycles stowed in the rear of the truck for the first time.

The Astronaut had found a window of time where the mansion's security personnel would be the lightest. The high-tech property relied heavily on a sophisticated electronic surveillance system. They had been able to neutralize it by utilizing a Tappan; the device used Wi-Fi to break into the cameras, and replace looped prior footage to conceal their presence. Floor sensors, beams, and sonic aggregatros were defeated by a swath of AI programs once the security defenses were infiltrated.

Chase recalled facing a similar situation when they had broken into a corrupt tech company executive's mansion in Illinois. He'd almost been caught. Instead, Wen had captured Shelby. "Reminds me of the guy's place from Bargo."

"That was different," Wen said. "Someone was waiting there to kill us."

Chase tilted his head as if to say, *Could be the same thing here.*

"The Astronaut is working on figuring out the ownership of this palace," Wen said. "But we know for sure this is not Belfort's mansion."

"Whoever's it is, sure has a lot of money," Chase said. "And this kind of money leaves a trail."

"This kind of money covers up the trail," Wen countered.

"But in the digital world, covering up a trail leaves a whole different kind of trail," Chase said. "We'll see what the Astronaut can come up with."

Inside, three sweeping staircases led to different wings of the home. Each wrapped around large boulders as six separate waterfalls cascaded down from upper floors, leaving the impression of being at the Grand Canyon's Havasu Falls. The turquoise pond at the base, surrounded by red rock pathways, appeared to be something created in nature, but was actually a regulation Olympic-sized swimming pool.

"Feels like we're in one of the seven wonders of the world," Chase said, looking up at the largest chandelier he'd ever seen, its twelve-foot diameter supporting terraced layers of tennis ball sized crystals. "This guy has *way* too much money on his hands."

"Says the billionaire," Wen said.

"Any idea how we're going to locate Belfort's room in this castle?"

Wen, not sure how they would do that, kept moving, not

realizing they had tripped an invisible beam of light belonging to a secondary security system connected to an analog coded communications hub. "First we have to be sure the home is secure, then—"

A message on her wrist interrupted her. She checked the ultra-sophisticated custom tablet, like a phone-sized watch, strapped to her arm.

The Astronaut's face appeared. "Internal security video of the mansion is archived. I got in and found a match to Belfort's photo, traced it to his most frequent movements, found his lair." He sent a floor plan with the room he'd identified marked.

"This looks like it," Chase said a few minutes later as they walked into a palatial bedroom hung with modern art, abstracts of muted colors, and furnished in custom, modern, angular pieces of various slick metals, polished woods, and shiny fabrics that were uncomfortable to look at. Chase couldn't imagine sitting or sleeping there. An office about the size of a squash court was attached to one end.

"You really think something's here?" Chase asked.

"A man like Belfort has many secrets to hide," the Astronaut said. "He can't place them in a bank's safety deposit box because, in the event of a death, the IRS would seal it. And, as he knows well, banks should never be trusted. Anything he might want to protect can't be in digital format only—too easy to find, to track, to destroy. So it must be physical, and he has to put it somewhere."

"But would he really leave something in a property he doesn't own?"

The Astronaut, monitoring the house, grounds, and surrounding area, noticed a blip on his screen.

"A place he doesn't own might be the best place, and he

could always retrieve it later," Wen said. "Or you could easily pay someone to come in and get it."

"Someone like us," Chase joked.

"Let's hope we can save him the trouble."

"It's not like Belfort's going to leave behind a computer or file cabinet," Chase said, looking at the slabs of glass of various translucent colors that seemed to make up all the furnishings. "If anything's here, it's going to be well hidden."

"We potentially have incoming personnel," the Astronaut's voice interrupted. "Our system-projected trajectory shows a vehicle."

Chase opened the small bag of tools they'd brought and pulled out a crowbar and a small portable saw. He and Wen began ripping into walls. Almost fifteen minutes later, after pulling up sections of the bamboo floor, Chase found an envelope. He quickly tore it open and showed the contents to Wen: a batch of photos and some pages.

"So who are these people?" Chase asked.

"You should leave," the Astronaut warned.

"Can't yet, there may be more." Wen looked at the photos. "He went to an awful lot of trouble for these snapshots of . . . ," she counted them, "eleven different people."

"Who are the eleven?" Chase asked. "And these papers, there's maybe twenty pages. Are these documents related to the people in the photos? Or something else he wanted to stash?"

Wen shook her head. "Why would he have this stuff here? These could just be on a thumb drive somewhere."

"Vehicle on the grounds," the Astronaut said insistently.

"He probably has the same stuff in digital form at another location—maybe fifty places—but he's smart enough to know that having a physical copy is still the ultimate security."

"We need to go," Wen said.

"Unfortunately, there's really no way to cover up the fact that we've been here."

"And he's going to know it was us."

"What?" Chase quipped. "Are you worried Belfort will get mad at us, maybe hire some people to kill us?"

Chapter Forty-Four

Shelby and Grimes moved on the house. The layout was no mystery to them. They had been there before.

The bedroom was dark, even though the sun had been up for hours. This was also no surprise. They knew the man sleeping in the king-sized waterbed always slept until two or three in the afternoon. They called him the Vampire. He was a shadow person, one of the closest to Belfort—and also an old friend of Shelby and Grimes.

"You okay with this?" Grimes asked before they went in. "Killing a friend?"

"We weren't friends," she said. "Associates. We all hung out because we worked together, because no one else knew our burden."

"All right." Grimes wasn't going to argue, he often said, *"People justify their demons because they're afraid to face them."*

Prior to waking him, they removed thirteen weapons from his immediate surroundings. There were probably more, maybe even one under the pillow, but they couldn't risk that. Grimes and Shelby both secretly hoped the man would pull a hidden gun and try to kill them. *Self-defense makes it easier to sleep at night.*

Once the man told them what they needed to know, they shot him. He'd known it was coming. There was no other way around it.

"He was a cold-blooded killer," Grimes said. "Sometimes they get what's coming."

Shelby nodded. "We're the same," she said quietly. "Just running faster."

Wen peered into the monitor on her wrist.

"Those aren't just local rent-a-cops," Wen said. "They're Vinton."

"Never heard of them," Chase said, looking out the window.

"Remember when we were interviewing firms to protect Tu? We went with Sepio," she said, speaking of the elite, private security force whose exorbitant fees matched their skill level. Sepio exclusively served billionaires. "Vinton was our second choice. They're a bit more combat oriented—*aggressively violent.*"

"Now I remember. They shoot first, ask questions later."

"Correct. They're engaged in all kinds of tactics."

"Maybe we should just get out of here. There must be a backdoor."

"Twenty-two exterior doors," she said.

"Great. I hardly think they can cover them all."

"We've still got to guess which one."

"At least they don't know we're still here."

An explosion of glass blew across them. Wen rolled away. Chase dove toward the doorway to the hall.

A man burst through a window, appearing like a terrifying shadow, dressed in tight black fatigues, a dark mask, and a black Kevlar helmet. Yet he was no shadow person.

"Vinton!" Wen yelled, sure he was one of the specialized, highly trained, highly paid killers, and that meant there would be nine more on site, with additional units on the way.

Wen fired three perfect shots, obliterating the man's face. "They know we're here now."

Two Vintons charged up the twin staircases. Wen pointed to the massive chandelier.

"A little cliché," Chase said. "Don't you think?"

"The steps don't seem to be an option," she said, climbing up to the railing.

"What if we don't make it?"

"Then you won't have to worry about them killing you."

Chase vaulted over the railing as Wen leaped from it. They hit the chandelier at the same time. The Vintons unloaded. Crystal shattered, a storm of glass raining down. The angle provided just enough cover.

"What now?" Chase asked, having climbed into the center section.

"There!" Wen pointed to the floor below, an ornate bridge on the other side.

"What if we don't make it?" he asked again.

"Same answer," she said, launching herself.

ANC - Always News Channel - Top Story

"Stu Lemon reporting. Our top story at this hour: CIA analysts have

uncovered a plot hatched by opposition leaders in Turkey to sell nukes in some kind of economic stimulus. It seems a crazy way to improve their prospects to me, but we have ANC contributor, former Director of National Intelligence, Logan Whiten, here to help us understand the implications of this bombshell development. Director Whiten, could the opposition really believe this is a good idea?"

"Stu, thanks for having me. There is evidence they are interested in selling some of the nukes to help their economy. Particularly during the virus time, Turkey, like so many countries, has been impacted negatively by the lockdowns imposed on tech devices during the NoLiv crisis."

"But selling nukes?"

"With the Turkish government declaring ownership of our nuclear weapons, the opposition seems to be in favor of this."

"What about calls for US Special Forces to be used to secure the nukes?"

"That is the purview of the Commander in Chief, and although I am in favor of an operation such as you describe, I would never publicly suggest what the President should do."

"All options on the table."

"Yes, all options must always be on the table."

"Thank you, Director."

Real Truth - Internet Fact Based News

Posted by JI Right

The tech giants, mainstream media, and a list of corrupt politicians accuse us of presenting disinformation. We could say Pot calling the Kettle black, but instead we offer the following facts:

The mainstream media has ignored these facts.
But being facts, they cannot be disputed.
Try.

1. The Turkish government continues to deny that they ever said they would be keeping the nukes.
2. Turkish opposition leaders claim they would not consider selling nukes. It's such a preposterous idea, they cannot believe anyone would even believe it.
3. Officials in Turkey claim to have evidence that the CIA is perpetrating a slow coup in their country. They have been trying to present this information to the United Nations, but those efforts are being blocked by the United States.
4. Turkish ambassador to the United States has asserted that Deep Fakes (that is, synthetic media where the original speaker's voice or image has been replaced in an undetectable manner) have been utilized to further the US CIA agenda.

Why is no one looking into this? We sit on the brink of nuclear confrontation. At the same time, huge portions of the worldwide economy are shut down by the virus, and yet the media operates in lockstep with the US government.

Chapter Forty-Five

Clearing the railing, Wen tucked and rolled. Even before she was fully turned around, her pair of MP7s were inflicting damage. While firing from behind, she took out two advancing Vintons. Chase landed awkwardly, bashing his shoulder into a brass and stainless hall table, then crunching his elbow against the paneled wall. The force and momentum of his landing also pushed the barrel of his Scorpion EVO submachine into his leg, cutting a gash. He suddenly felt as if he'd been dropped from a circus acrobatic squad as he managed to squirm out of the line of fire.

"You okay?" Wen asked, slipping her wrist under his shoulder and scooping him up off the marble floor, sweeping him along as they both ran, looking for a way out.

"Fine," he said, pointing to a door. "How about there?"

They ran into the room. Bright sun poured through the endless windows while strategic mirrors reflected the outside glare a hundred ways.

"Not the kind of place we want to have a fight," Wen

said. Hardly slowing, she the saw blood on his leg. "What's that?"

"Nothing," he said. "Self-inflicted."

Wen pushed open a glass door leading to a garden balcony overlooking koi ponds and lush landscaping. Without stopping, Wen went over the rail and disappeared.

"You've got four on the grounds," the Astronaut said into their ears. "You're dropping in on top of them."

A second later, Chase stopped, got his bearings, and looked over for Wen. He spotted her taking down two Vintons who'd made the mistake of being in her path. She'd used her knife, obviously trying not to attract attention.

Even before he could figure out how she'd gotten down so fast, he watched as she sent lethal throwing stars into two more approaching Vintons.

Unfortunately, one of them squeezed the trigger of his AK-47. The bullets easily missed Wen, but now everyone knew where they were.

"Three more, seventy feet and closing," the Astronaut warned.

Chase climbed down a tree branch extending from a Goldenrain Tree. Gunfire intensified. He hit the ground amid a hail of bullets from above. Shooters from the same balcony he had just left penned him in.

Three Vintons appeared on the path in front of him. Chase got two and, magically, Wen took out the third before disappearing deeper into the gardens.

"Run!" she said into his ear. "Sent heat upstairs."

Chase dove into a thick section of pampas grass and found a couple of mature Jacaranda trees to shield himself. Seconds later, the balcony exploded.

In the chaos, Chase worked his way through a small meadow ringed with citrus trees and dominated by hundreds of Tababuia, a brightly plumed plant in full blooming regalia. Beyond them, several flowering trees offered even more cover—until their bright pink and white petals exploded over him like confetti as Vintons fired machine guns his way, shredding the leaves and flora.

"Two objectives," Wen said into his earpiece. "Kill and escape."

Wen, with all her tactical experience, generally made those decisions—unless he in was in front of the action.

"I'd been hoping to escape and avoid the killing. They aren't shadow people," he replied. "These are just security guys doing their job."

"Not security, *Vintons*, trying to kill us!"

"And more Vintons incoming," the Astronaut said. "You two need to get out of there!"

Chase spotted a wood and stone pagoda which looked as if it had been imported from the grounds of a Japanese Temple. Crouching there, he counted. "Where are they?" he asked.

The sound of sporadic gunfire answered, but some were otherwise occupied with Wen. There had been some behind him who should have been there by now.

They've slowed their pursuit because their training and experience told them this was a place of danger, a place where they themselves would take cover, and lie in wait. He'd learned that from Wen. *They must know who they're after.*

The soft stone shattered, the painted wood splintering around him. The grainy taste of it filled his mouth and nostrils. He spun and dove into a strange, knee-deep sea of red and yellow flowers he'd never seen before.

"What just blew?" Wen asked.

"My cover," Chase responded. "I don't know what did it , but I know it's more firepower than we have."

"Go!" the Astronaut barked.

More gunshots told him Wen was farther away.

"Where are you?" he asked.

"R-un!" she responded in broken speech.

He couldn't. His camouflage, now only flowers, were traceable. *Die fighting.* He crawled and rolled as far as he could from his path, then on his back, opened fire into where he'd been, hoping they were now there. Two went down, two more went for cover. Up until that moment, seeing the blurring movements, he'd hoped there'd only been two back there. *Still two to kill.* He never thought there might be more.

Then he saw them. A *lot* more.

"Run!" she yelled again in his ear. Suddenly, all he heard was sustained gunfire.

Chapter Forty-Six

Chase watched what seemed like a platoon of black-clad Vintons fill the expansive grounds of the estate. "There are too many of them!" Chase yelled. "Where are they all coming from?"

Wen couldn't see Chase, but had eyes on sixteen Vintons. "I don't know, I can't raise the Astronaut!"

"Why would there be so many Vintons waiting here?"

"Somehow they knew we were coming."

"Then why not shadow people?"

"We don't have time to figure this out right now!"

Chase and Wen were in opposite corners of a seven-acre garden, shielded from pricey neighbors by a twelve-foot-high wall. Its security-minded contractors had made it impossible to scale, but Chase was an expert climber. *If I could just get there, I could get up it.* However, there were at least fifteen guns between him and there, and all he had left was his Beretta 9 mm pistol and about thirty rounds. Wen, acres away, still held two MP7 submachine guns with more than one hundred rounds, but she no longer possessed any heavy firepower, grenade launchers, or explosives.

She was hemmed in between a couple of boulders that looked like they had been there since the age of the dinosaurs, but had probably been brought in as part of the massive landscaping project only a decade or two before.

The Vintons began to move in on them. "We've been here before," Wen said. '*Here*' being a place and time where they were certain they were going to die.

"I'm not sure I recall being together when we were this down," Chase said. "I always knew you could rescue me."

"Or vice versa," Wen said.

Chase knew what Wen was thinking even before she said the dreaded words, even if he didn't disagree with them. "Let's take as many of them with us as we can."

"Yeah," he said.

"We're not done until we're dead!"

Wen counted. She calculated. Not knowing the Vintons' exact training protocols, it still wasn't difficult to figure how they would attack cornered prey. "How much do you have?"

"Maybe thirty," Chase said, having already checked his ammo. "Just the Berretta."

"I'll lead."

Before he could reply, she was out, running between fruit trees and flowering shrubs, shooting in short precision bursts.

The Vintons closest to him, momentarily distracted, made easy targets, but with a handgun, his aim wasn't as good as hers, and he hit two out of five before he had to dive behind a small retaining wall constructed of large granite chunks.

He knew they'd be on him any second. *Too many*, he repeated to himself, listening to Wen's fire fight on the other side of the property.

He took a deep breath, whispered a farewell she'd never hear, and rolled out of his hiding place, looking for Vintons, knowing he'd be dead in under a minute.

Then he saw the shadows. Not shadow people, *real* shadows, blocking out the sun. A small buzzing noise grew to sound like ten chainsaws running at the same time. Chase looked up. Twenty-six gray and blue elongated parachutes filled the sky, large fans spinning behind the *pilots*. The paramotors created an ominous scene, like more than two dozen giant vultures sweeping down.

"Campers!" Wen yelled in his ear.

The sky brigade began firing while still airborne.

"Blitz came through," Chase said as the camper's bullets ripped into the Vintons.

The surprising aerial assault destroyed the elite security operatives in less than two minutes. The campers landed only long enough to pick up Chase and Wen. Police sirens told them more trouble was coming. Jail was the last place they wanted to end up.

The campers flew them the brief distance to the Destino, and then disappeared. Chase and Wen cleared out of the area almost as quickly.

"You know what this means?" Chase asked, as they pulled onto I-5 South.

"We're still alive?" Wen said.

"True, and that's pretty wonderful," Chase said. "But I was thinking about it... this was the first real battle of the shadow war."

"We've been hitting them for months."

"Yes, but covertly. This time our army dropped out of the sky, engaged the enemy, and won."

"We feel like we won because we're alive, but we didn't win anything," Wen said. "They know."

"Yeah," he said quietly.

"We just went up to another level, and we're about to find out just how big the Circuit really is."

Chapter Forty-Seven

A few hours later, Chase and Wen arrived back in San Diego. Two men watched them from a distance as they approached Ed Underhill's building.

"I thought I told you that our last meeting was our last meeting," Underhill said as he opened the heavy door, his hair full of sawdust.

"We need more on the Circuit." Wen showed him the photos and pages of code.

"So you found something?" he said, surprised they'd gotten into the mansion and lived to tell about it. "Looks like more of the same code we got from PeacePipe."

Chase nodded. "It is. I have someone working on it." He decided not to tell Underhill about the Astronaut, but expected with his intelligence background, he knew about the savants, might even have known their Astronaut, Nash Graham. "Too much for me to do right now."

"But it's related?"

"Yeah, I broke down enough of it to know it's the same language."

"But it's endless. This must be most of it." Underhill worked his knife into the eye of the lion he was carving. "Where did Belfort get it? And why is he still alive?"

"Maybe these papers are all that's *keeping* him alive?" Chase said.

Underhill nodded, but Chase could tell he was bothered, that he didn't really believe that. "They don't know he has it."

Wen, glancing out one of the windows, said, "I don't want to speculate about Belfort right now. We don't even know if he's still alive. You have to give us everything you have on the Circuit. No holding back. We need to be ready for the next battle."

Underhill rubbed his chin, then went back to carving, this time concentrating on the mane.

Wen looked at Chase as if trying to decide which one of them should force Underhill to talk. Chase shrugged. Wen walked over to check the monitors; the screen on her wrist gave her similar views of the Destino. It all appeared clear, but that's not how she felt.

"Everything you need to know is going to be found in NoLiv," Underhill finally said. "The virus wasn't created accidentally."

"Do you have proof?" Chase asked.

Underhill nodded slowly. "There is a tenant form."

"What's that?" Wen asked.

"It's a mutation of code," Chase answered.

"Correct," Underhill said. "It's been tracked to an AI program that crossed with an online video game."

Chase shook his head. "No way."

"Right?" Underhill said, almost, but not quite smiling for a second. "You know enough about how things work to know that could never be." Underhill paused, staring at Chase. "Why haven't you already dug into this?"

"I've been a little too busy trying to stay alive, save the world, and track a bunch of monsters."

"All that goes through the virus." Underhill walked to his computer. "NoLiv is not just a computer virus."

"Okay, tell us," Wen said, now staring out to the ocean. "You say it's not an accident, then what is it?"

"They developed it, manufactured it, that's what they do. They wanted it to happen. It was intentional."

"Intentional?" Wen echoed. "Then where's the ransom, their demands? How do they benefit?"

"It's not the virus that they were interested in," Underhill explained. "The virus isn't anywhere near as dangerous as they say. Most people don't even know they have it. The cure is what they were after. The antivirus program they're getting everybody to install—"

"Remedy?"

"Yes, Remedy. What do you think that does?"

Wen frowned. "Stops the NoLiv virus from destroying your computer."

"Nobody's computer has actually been destroyed by the virus. It's a dummy attack, a false flag. But when they install Remedy . . . that's when the real trouble begins. Remedy takes control of any device it's installed on. Remedy is the *real* virus."

Chase looked at him, shocked for a moment, and couldn't help but smile at the brilliance of it, and the audacity of it. "They must have a lot of help. It's quite impressive when you consider the scale they've achieved."

"The largest computer virus in history is directly linked to the Circuit. That's our way in," Underhill said. "We use the virus to penetrate the Circuit's fortress."

"Wait, so they can access everyone's devices," Wen began. "How is that different than monitoring search histories and storing every phone call and email like the NSA already does?"

"They'll have complete control over everyone, by using their direct access into the computers and other devices. This means zero privacy. They can see anything and everything."

"Welcome to your nightmare," Wen said to Chase.

The men watching the building made a call, and listened carefully to the instructions they received.

"And everyone who has obediently installed Remedy, has, in effect, told the Circuit that they will believe anything the media and government tell them. They are the easiest to control. It will never end."

"And the ones who refused?" Wen asked, remembering PeacePipe's rant.

Underhill shrugged. "The Circuit will make sure they are pushed out. One by one, they will be de-platformed, unemployed, denied credit, or advancement of any kind. Soon, they will no longer exist."

"We're working on a counter-program," Chase said.

"For the virus?"

"For their whole system, but we're still missing pieces."

"Track the virus code," Underhill said. "Remember, I told you about the media takeover. Find that intersection, and you will find the Circuit."

A few minutes later, the men watched Chase and Wen leave.

Chapter Forty-Eight

Tane stood on a penthouse balcony, gazing across the river at a panoramic view of Washington, DC. *The most powerful city in the world,* he mused. *Only when I'm here.*

The man on the other end of the phone had, outrageously, put him on hold. When he came back on the line, seventy-three seconds had passed. Tane wanted them back.

"It's difficult," the FBI director said.

"Just *do it*," Tane snapped, in a burst of uncharacteristic impatience. It wasn't just the wasted time, he was irritated to be talking to the director of the FBI rather than the president of the United States. The POTUS would usually handle such matters for Tane. *As it should be.*

"We're spread very thin right now," the director explained. "I have resources deployed all over for the virus, manpower rounding up these anti-Remedy protestors. Additionally, we've got a division working with the social media platforms, following up on any posters dissenting from the government narratives, policies, and directives."

"None of that is *this* important!"

"The administration has been pushing us to discredit those groups and individuals who disagree with its policies . . . I would think you would be in lockstep with them, since—"

"You can cancel people, censor them, and destroy them later. Right now, this is what needs doing. So do it!"

"I've only got so many agents," he said. "There's no guarantee that we're going to find them in an area where I have side agents."

"Side agents?"

"Side agents being the ones who plant evidence or engage in other gray areas."

"I don't want evidence planted," Tane said coolly. "I want them dead."

"I understand. And that's a lot to ask."

"I wasn't really *asking*."

"It's just an expression," the director responded.

"You may not have someone there who will execute in that manner. However, there are ways."

"Yes sir, ways," the director echoed. "We can broadcast that they are armed and dangerous, that they pose an imminent threat, that they must be stopped, that they possess voice-activated detonators, things like that. Although we cannot issue shoot-to-kill orders, they can be created by default."

"I don't care how you do it, so long as it is done *today*."

"First we have to find them."

"That's not a problem. They're going to be in Las Vegas. I'll send you the details."

"Excellent. We have a unit of some of my most creative side agents there."

"Don't let me down, Director," Tane said, as if talking to an errant part-time employee—which is exactly what he was. Tane made a mental note to have him replaced as soon as Chase and Wen were dead, or in the morning, whichever came first. "Make this problem go away, or you and I are going to have a new problem. One you won't like nearly as much as this one."

Chase took a call from Grimes as the Destino headed toward the interstate. "We uncovered a location where Belfort has been known to work," Grimes said, hoping the information was worth the man's life they'd taken. He understood that leaving him alive would have been too risky, and he'd killed a lot of people . . . but in his unspoken admission, he wasn't used to killing people he *knew*.

"Tell me it's not in Los Angeles," Chase said.

"How do you feel about gambling?" Grimes asked.

"That's the story of our lives."

After the call, Chase checked in with the Astronaut and asked him to run down everything he could find on the Vegas address Grimes had just given them. "How's our virus coming?" Chase asked.

"Our team is already almost there," he said, speaking of the efforts to use the Circuit's own tactics on them by Tu, Dez (Chase's original business partner), his wife Bull (a notorious hacker), and a small group of trusted employees.

"Is the code helping?"

"The code is a substantial result," the Astronaut said, speaking of PeacePipe's code.

"And the new information we found in the mansion?"

"Belfort never should have had access to this."

"He must have thought it was insurance," Chase said.

"Instead, it's going to be his death sentence," Wen added.

"This new code, when fully broken down and merged in our AI algorithms will task, recover, and provide the ability to penetrate the core of the Circuit's operational system," the Astronaut explained.

"Really?" Chase said. "We got the Circuit's Holy Grail?"

"My systems are still tearing it down, but it is definitely a core code to a massive economic output, and contains definitions of treasury-level chains."

"Incredible! We're in!"

"Obtaining entrance is at least probable," the Astronaut responded. "Results from that point will vary depending on what we encounter inside."

Chase smiled. Getting to the treasury was the best way to bring down a kingdom.

"What about NoLiv's origin?" Wen asked later. "If we can show proof that the Circuit is responsible for the virus . . . "

"Think how much they're making, though," Chase said. "All those installations of Remedy. Governments around the world are paying for almost all of the private installs. Corporate installs cost even more. Not only are they expanding their control and obliterating privacy, they're making a fortune in the process."

"Fear is the most powerful weapon that can be used against people one doesn't wish to kill. Virus, virus, virus. They shut everything down, made people show complete obedience, allowed no dissenting opinions or debate." Wen shook her head. "I can't believe everyone went along so easily."

"The Circuit has figured out the same thing the government has long known. Fear is the easiest way to control a population."

Chapter Forty-Nine

Underhill, alone in a secret section of his studio, decided it was time to go all the way in his push to uncover the Circuit. He rattled off a verbal alphanumeric sequence, then followed the leads, opening digital doors he would normally avoid. *Extra precautions now.*

He enjoyed a certain amount of protection through his extensive contacts within the intelligence community, particularly when doing a favor for Tess. Even so, he was nervous.

He continued the voice commands, keeping his hands free to carve the lion he'd been working on for several days, a commission for a longtime client. He put the knife down. Checked his external cameras. Went back to carving. Stopped again after a few minutes. Checked the windows.

More single-sided conversations with the computer, although it answered in its way, doing its master's bidding. He sanded a little of the tail, even though it wasn't ready for that. It was mindless, almost meditative work. He checked the computer screen. The program was digging through apparent clues, millions of them, leading him to a place he wasn't sure he wanted to go.

Even before Chase and Wen showed up, he'd been putting the puzzle together, piece by piece, for years. His mind worked that way, seeing the connections in each job he took during all that time navigating through the intelligence gauntlet. Yet he tried equally hard to ignore it, to preserve his own safety, and that of his family and friends. The Circuit cared for nothing outside of their lust for power, obeyed no rules, knew no boundaries of decency and honor. He knew all that, and still he'd jumped in headfirst, trying to find a way to stop their theft of freedom, democracy, civilization itself.

Now here it was, unavoidable, staring him in the face. *Too much corruption to hide.*

"Download to linked screen, seven deep," he gave the voice commands. "To priority drive."

It was his habit to make critical backups, and this was a critical one. As soon as it was completed, he would label the physical drive, secure it, and then hide it with the others. *Redundancy... that keeps things straight.*

He proceeded only after the backup synched. "If you go deeper this time," he muttered, "there's no turning back."

The matrix coded grid he'd seen a thousand times raced across the screen like a million insects devouring something alive. *It's the moat around their castle... meant to protect, to keep trouble from entering.* This kind of digital fortress was deemed impenetrable. Just getting to it took skills few in the world possessed. *Let's see what you do with Saber.* The NSA tool usually penetrated, but after thirty or forty seconds, he could already tell it wasn't going to make it. Underhill considered leaving Saber running, just to see, but the longer it ran, the more risk it brought.

"Okay, let's see how you do with Shogun." He waited, giving this one a full two minutes. For a moment, it almost looked like Shogun might break through, but then it flatlined. One final weapon in his arsenal, this created for the stubborn ones, was rarely used partially because Saber and Shogun both rarely failed. It was unusual to face something this hardened, but the critical nature of what was behind those walls made it as vital to protect as it was to retrieve.

He took a deep breath before implementing Serpent. It only had a few uses before it would implode and become unusable. His finger hovered a millimeter above the button that would send Serpent. It could not be deployed without a physical biometric reading.

This is the point of no return.

He checked Shogun one more time. Nothing.

Ready.

The tense silence was shattered by an alarm. The high-pitched sound startled him; he almost pushed the button by accident. Instead, reflexes took over. Underhill scooped up the latest backup drive, grabbed a bag with others that had been previously moved off-site, and headed to a trap door. He didn't need to check the alarm to verify what the problem was, he already knew. *Every second counts.* If there'd been a mistake, he could recover from that later.

There are no mistakes.

The facial recognition scan instantly identified him and opened the door. He quickly descended the steps. There was a kill-switch halfway down that would give him one final chance to override the automation that would destroy the contents of every computer and digital storage he'd left behind. Next to it, a screen showed the camera's views.

"FBI... son of a gun," he said, moving further down the

stairs, leaving behind the coded switch, knowing it was about to end. Entering the subterranean level, his unpleasant escape route that he'd last rehearsed eight months earlier, took him into the sewers. By the time he exited into the back of a dry cleaner's half a block away, he'd had time to wonder why the FBI, why now. And he knew the answer.

Chase Malone.

But all the blame didn't fall on Chase.

I was too close to the Circuit, far too close. Serpent was about to cut into their defenses.

One more block, this one out in the open, but he was disguised now thanks to the pack he'd stored long ago at the dry cleaners.

It's up to Chase and Wen now. Tess might be able to help them out, unless she's been compromised. Either way, she's in real danger. Anyone who knows anything about the Circuit... no one is safe.

He reached a small van kept in a parking garage. Inside, he powered on the device that would verify the successful destruction of his data.

Damn it, some of it survived. They came with cyber experts. They were able to freeze it. His elaborate precautions, defenses, and rundown programs, the fully automated self-destruct sequences, they'd gotten past it all.

That gave him his answer. The Circuit knew who he was, and what he had found.

I'm a dead man.

ANC - Always News Channel - Top Story

"Zane Waterman reporting. Our top story at this hour: In response to protestors' and dissenters' claims that the Turkey situation is being

trumped up by the CIA and media, ANC contributor, and former Director of National Intelligence, Logan Whiten, is here to address these baseless allegations."

"Thanks, Zane. These people marching, clogging up social media, and making LookThru videos, don't deserve our time, and frankly, I'm disappointed that ANC and any of the other networks are giving them any airtime at all. I mean, come on. These kind of fringe conspiracy freaks think the earth is flat and the moon landing was faked."

"Of course, Director, but we like to look at both sides of the story."

"I respect the journalistic integrity of ANC, I really do, but these unpatriotic rabble-rousers are an ignorant bunch, and I think we all know who these . . . who they voted for in 2020."

"Yes, but to the claims, Director, that Turkey is denying—"

"Come on Zane, the United States Government does not recognize claims that have no credibility made by those who are tied to extremists and terrorists. Look, in this country, we have family members turning against family members, friends turning on friends, over their support for Remedy. Some say their machines were infected with NoLiv even after they installed Remedy. No one ever said they couldn't still get infected, but Remedy does a fine job of preventing these devices from becoming DOA. So there are those at work to divide our nation, to weaken us."

"And that relates to Turkey?"

"The Russians are claiming this is a false flag in order to destabilize their region. And China is warning that this is about oil from their region."

"And the virus interrupts operations, response, and situational conduct?"

"Turkey is moving more towards Russia and China. This move is being covered up by the laughable conspiracies directly attributable to Russian disinformation and hacking operations sanctioned and funded by the Kremlin."

Chasing Lies

"No truth to the Internet rumors then."
"Anyone who believes this nonsense being espoused by so-called truth and alternative news websites, should ask themselves a simple question: 'Whose side are you on?'"

Chapter Fifty

Belfort had trouble catching his breath for a moment. He'd been expecting to hear Chase and Wen were dead. Instead, he had just been told they had breached one of his secret residences. A place where he'd been sleeping only a week before.

"They were in Los Angeles?" Belfort barked. "They were in my damned Los Angeles mansion!?"

Cranson decided now was not a suitable time to point out that it wasn't *his* mansion. "Yes."

"How did they find out about Los Angeles?"

"We don't know."

"Only a few people know about Los Angeles, and you're one of them."

"True, but it wasn't me who told them."

Belfort glared back at him. "How do I know that?"

"With all due respect, if I'd given them Los Angeles, I would've already killed you."

Belfort wrinkled his face, as if this insulted *and* annoyed him, but in the end, he nodded. It was sound logic he could not argue with. "You run down everyone who knew about Los Angeles. Find out."

"You didn't have anything there, did you? Anything that would help them?"

"No," Belfort said, but he did, and he knew he did. But he sure wasn't going to tell Cranson or anyone else about his hidden insurance policies. Chase would not find them— *no one* could have found them. "I need to go to Los Angeles, see for myself."

"Not a good idea. Since they already know you were there, they could have it under surveillance now."

"I don't give a damn! If people are watching, then we'll kill the people watching."

Cranson said nothing.

Belfort stood back. "Okay, okay. Send someone in there. I won't go. I don't need any more aggravation. Just get someone in there, and show me film of every inch of the place. I want to see exactly what happened, exactly how they left it."

Cranson raised an eyebrow. "If you had nothing there, there isn't anything to worry about."

"Just give me the damn pictures!" Belfort looked over his shoulder, knowing if they found anything, he was doomed.

Thirty-two minutes later, Underhill was onboard an anonymous cabin cruiser, floating in international waters, skirting the Baja peninsula. The captain of the small vessel had served under his father in the US Navy. There was history. There was loyalty. This was part of a long in-place plan.

Waiting in Mexico was another friend and a new identity, a full set of the best papers available. Tess had arranged it years ago through a blind, meaning even she would not know who he was about to become.

He stood on deck, looking up at the sky, then out to sea, wondering if the Circuit would get to him before he made it to those papers. He had a little money set aside. Not enough for a lavish lifestyle, but if he was careful, and didn't drink too much *cerveza*, he might be able to make it stretch.

Underhill had a solid connection in Nicaragua from back in his agency days, a man who would kill for him, who actually *had* done just that decades earlier.

I'll stay in Nicaragua for a few years, maybe take a trip to Panama, but just a visit. Border crossings were the riskiest part of living on the run. He'd keep those to a minimum.

He had copies of the drives, data that would help Chase get into the Circuit, but after the FBI raid, that information would only be good for a few days at best, possibly only hours. He'd arranged for the originals to be at a safe place where Chase could get to them. Then he would destroy his copies. He did *not* want to get caught with those.

He'd also sent messages to Tess and Chase warning them about the FBI, but there'd been no time to confirm those had reached them. In fact, he doubted it.

Staring out at the ocean, lost in worries and plans, he suddenly saw a whale breach. The breathtaking sight gave him a surge of momentary hope.

Maybe, just maybe, Chase and Wen might get to the Circuit, possibly even figure out a way to destroy them . . .

He looked up at the empty sky.

No . . . that's never going to happen.

Chapter Fifty-One

The indicator on his wrist told Chase there was an incoming call from Mars. After saying a three-digit code, the video communications opened.

"What have you got?" Chase asked.

"Quite a lot, actually. Some of my well-paid friends have managed to secure extra openings into numerous Circuit holdings."

"How'd they pull that off?"

"That's what they do, man, but I can't say how. Anyway, based on what you gave us from SEER and some extra data from the Astronaut, we've identified thirty-two major corporations representing more than three trillion dollars."

"Amazing. What's the plan?"

"We're set to cripple them," Mars said confidently. "Too many details to go into now, but the full array of what we spoke about."

"Man, that's really fast work."

"My team is highly motivated," he said, sounding like a corporate executive.

Chase thought back on their conversation and wondered how Mars and his band of outlaws could have already gotten extortion, blackmail, sabotage, and related attacks in place across so many different arenas.

"We're talking about some of the top criminal minds in the country," Mars continued. "A hundred and sixty-three were released on furloughs, another almost two hundred were already out. Three hundred fifty-nine on the payroll with access to the most advanced tech arsenal ever assembled."

"I worry some of them are going to go to the Circuit."

"It's possible," Mars said. "But we're paying our guys a *lot*, and none of them know the Circuit as an identifiable target. They're simply given each corporate shake at a time. From there, they get the payday, and we promise them a piece of the action."

"How's that looking?"

"Foldable assets are out there, already coming in."

"Good, but the big stuff is yet to come."

"Yeah. I've pretty much got this laid out as a coordinated attack—we're calling it *Flash-Burn*. There are a lot of moving parts. Many of these stings can only take place within certain windows, but the Astronaut and Tu helped work out all the variables. We've matched criteria with parameters and come up with a pretty cool schedule. Beginning in eight hours, the dominoes start to fall."

"How long will it continue for?"

"Assuming they don't find ways to stop us—which is unlikely given how busy the whole fiasco is going to be keeping them—the final hit occurs about three hours after we start."

"That's a pretty tight bang of fireworks," Chase said.

Wen looked up from the monitors. "In their weakened

state, in that moment of distraction and confusion, Blitz will take out all the rest of the shadows we've identified, and hopefully we'll be going for Belfort and some of the other leaders."

"You've got names?"

"Not yet, but we're getting close. And maybe this operation will smoke some of them out."

"There are going to be a lot of ramifications to Flash-Burn," Mars said. "These are *major* corporations. According to the Astronaut's calculations, we may crash the economy. It could be a real mess."

"I'm not sure how we can avoid that," Chase said.

"I mean, the repercussions are going to hit a lot of good people, working class. Are we *sure* we want to do this? Is it all worth it?"

"Not if this was just about saving Wen and me, but it's the proof of what they control, what we've discovered. The Circuit is clearly trying to take over the world." As Chase heard his own words, it sounded cheap, almost laughable, and if he had not lived in the nightmare of the last few years, he might've thought he was overstating it. But he knew he wasn't. "If they haven't already taken it over."

"All right then," Mars said. "Let the chips fall where they may."

Chapter Fifty-Two

The Astronaut's image on Wen's wrist looked strained, the typically even expression of the old savant's youngish face was pinched into a kind of lost and angry look.

"What's wrong?" Wen asked.

"PeacePipe's code . . . it's missing a part."

"That's why we need to find Boselovic," Chase said, leaning in so the Astronaut could see him, happy someone else was driving the Destino so they could work in the trailer's command center.

"I found Boselovic."

"Great," Wen said. "Did you talk to him?"

"No," the Astronaut shook his head rapidly, like a child refusing to eat beets. "Boselovic is dead."

"Because he was about to publish a story," Chase theorized, shoulders slumping. "He knew what the code was."

"He's dead now," the Astronaut repeated.

"We understand," Wen said. "His profile said he was married. Can we talk to his wife? Maybe she knows—"

"She's dead, too. Boselovic and his wife are dead."

"Wow," Chase said. "He had a grown son."

"I know. I'm looking for him. He's in danger."

"Boselovic was close to his son," Chase added. "He may have told him, or his son may know how to figure out who the source of the code was. We have to find him."

"Underhill was right," the Astronaut said. "Boselovic is dead. The code you found from Belfort is definitely connected to what PeacePipe sent."

"An organization as big as the Circuit can't keep everything hidden," Chase said. "They can't control everyone."

"At least not yet," Wen said, thinking of the Communist government in China.

"We have to use that, find the cracks. Break it wide open."

"Boselovic is dead," the Astronaut said. "You stay alive, Wen. Stay alive."

"We will," she said, and almost added, "you, too," but decided that would upset him even more.

Tess put into play a plan she had hoped would never be needed, but always knew would come one day.

"Linda, you're going to have to cover for me."

"For what?" she asked, confused, seeing Tess packing a large canvas briefcase. "Where are you going?"

"I have to disappear for a while. The Circuit is making a major escalation. This isn't just a simple play, this is the End Game."

"What's that mean?"

"The world is on fire," Tess said. "It may be too late to stop it, and out of the ashes will come a new world order—one you won't be able to recognize, one you won't like."

"Because of Turkey? The virus? What?"

"They've made those maneuvers, they're using those events and false flags, to be a distraction so they can accomplish their real objective."

"The End Game?"

"Yes. When the illusion of freedom will finally be shattered, and with it, the last shreds of remaining individualism. We will all become servants of the state."

Vader paced the carpeted floor of the circular room, one of the places where he managed his chess match with Tane and the others of his ilk. The floor-to-ceiling screens were mostly dark, for the moment, except for those monitoring Washington, DC.

"He's still alive," a woman said, looking at an image of the president of the United States returning to the White House.

"For a little longer."

"They'll try again?"

"Mmm..." Vader nodded, distracted by something he was reading on a smaller screen.

"But I thought he was working with them?"

"Yes," he said absently, not looking up.

"Then why would they want to assassinate him, if he's helping?"

"Same reason they do anything—control."

"I know that, but how does killing him give them more control? They already control him. I would think he is a valuable asset to them."

Lost in what he was reading, he didn't immediately respond. "They are in the End Game," Vader finally said.

"Meaning they won't replace him? There won't be another president?"

"No, I suspect they'll appoint someone as president, at least for a while."

"Then why bother killing him?" she pressed.

He stopped reading, looked up, and found her eyes. "Because in the middle of a nuclear standoff, while the world is grappling with a vicious global computer virus, the violent death of a president will bring the one thing they most need to complete the End Game . . . complete and utter chaos."

Real Truth - Internet Fact Based News

Posted by JI Right

The government says you must install Remedy, although we have no way to know the long-term effects of this action. And it does not even seem to prevent the virus from infecting devices and computers at all. Now they say it never was supposed to, but it prevents them from being DOA. That's a lot of trouble for something that does almost nothing. Yet the restrictions, demands, and mandates say you must do the Remedy.

Consider what one prominent educator has to say:

"If you have to be persuaded, reminded, pressured, lied to, incentivized, coerced, bullied, socially shamed, guilt-tripped, threatened, punished, and criminalized . . . if all of this is considered necessary to gain your compliance — you can be absolutely certain that what is being promoted is not in your best interest."
— Professor Ian Watson of Rutgers University

Chapter Fifty-Three

The building looked very Vegas, although it was well off the strip. Eleven floors of mirrored brown topped with what appeared to be a green diamond jewel. A waterfall tumbled off one side. "It's almost beautiful," Wen said.

"Yeah, if it wasn't so ugly," Chase said. "In that ostentatious kind of way."

As an employee left the main entrance, Wen caught the door.

"Hey, you can't go in there without a keycard," the man said, flipping his up.

Wen grabbed it and shoved him back into the building. A second later, he was laying on the lobby floor.

Four security guards drew weapons. "Hold it right there!"

But Wen and Chase did not hold it, and an instant later, those four were also laying on the black tiles.

"How long will they be out?" Chase asked, having missed the explanation that Wickett, their new weapons expert, had given when he loaded up the Destino with all kinds of fancy new gadgets—including the powerful, fast-acting tranquilizing rounds.

"Depends on their weight, how many rounds penetrated, and where they took them," she replied while they pulled the five bodies across the shiny floor, dragging them into the empty security office.

"Roughly?"

"Ninety minutes, minimum."

"We'll be gone by then."

"We'd better be *long* gone."

Chase looked at one of the building's many cameras, relieved the Astronaut had remotely used Tappan to break into the cameras to loop prior footage. They were invisible. Quickly, he utilized a high-tech package of custom AI apps to defeat floor sensors, beams, and sonic aggregators.

"Elevator?" Wen asked.

"Better than the stairs."

The Astronaut, operating out of a small warehouse in a Texas border town, stood on an elevated section that was an exact replica of the Destino's trailer tech center. The Destino would instantly have access to all his data, and vice versa.

"Wen? Chase? Are you there?"

He'd picked up looming trouble, and was desperate to reach them. He looked again at the streams of feeds coming in from Las Vegas and pursed his lips, the workings of his overcharged mind grappling with a way to warn them.

"Wen, can you hear me?"

Chase and Wen exited the elevator on eleven, the top floor, feeling as if they'd just come through a portal to a tropical jungle.

The upper reaches of the building were encased in a four-story glass atrium that contained lush collections of exotic plants and trees. Small streams ran throughout.

"Belfort sure knows how to keep himself comfortable," Chase said as they crossed a tiny foot bridge, a two-foot-high waterfall running beneath them. "Why do they treat him so well?"

"He must be good at secret killings, and keeping secrets." Wen tapped her ear. "I can't reach the Astronaut."

Among the verdant vegetation and trickles of water—an oasis in the desert, as all views through the leaves and flora looked out over the sweeping desert surrounding Sin City—they barely noticed the last orange glow of the setting sun over the Spring Mountains.

"Maybe something in the building is interfering," Chase said, not sounding worried.

"Maybe." She looked back over her shoulder.

"Let's just get in and out quickly."

"Those must be the offices," Wen said, pointing at translucent cubes scattered through the "*forest*."

"I think you're right . . . I don't see any residential space. seems a waste to just have people working here," he said. "So beautiful."

"Like working in the jungle."

Two creeks merged to make a slightly bigger stream. The sound of water cascading over a rocky outcropping, then dropping four feet into a shallow pool, would have been a lovely distraction under any other circumstances

"Where do we go?" Chase asked.

"I don't know. Let's split up."

"Never a good idea," Chase mused. "You know in the movies, whenever they split up, that's when the killers come. Let's stick together, instead."

"You watch too many movies," she said.

Translucent staircases led through the foliage. Eventually, they made it to a high office, the one with the best view and the largest space.

"This must be Belfort's," Chase said.

"Looks like he's planning on coming back," Wen added, noticing it appeared more like a functioning office, one in which the occupant was away on vacation, as opposed to how they'd found his room in the mansion—stark, like an empty hotel room.

"Maybe he comes here often. Grimes did say he got this address from a particularly reliable source."

"No computers," she said.

"That would have been too easy."

"Let's find something fast," she said, trying unsuccessfully to reach the Astronaut again.

It didn't take long to complete their initial physical search. There were several file folders with actual files in them. One contained a list of hundreds of names and contact information for what, after crosschecking them with the names they already had, appeared to be a roster of shadow people.

The glass walls provided little space for hiding, and the tools of destruction that had helped in Los Angeles had no use here.

"Try FullView," Wen said. The special electronic imaging program, created by the Astronaut, could see behind things.

Chase was skeptical. Most everything, including the desk, was made of transparent glass. Yet, almost immediately, FullView found something.

"A hidden compartment," Chase said, looking behind the glass wall, trying to figure out how they had made it translucent. "It's like magic."

"What's in it?" Wen asked.

There was a pad to input a key code, but he opened it with a pry bar. "A *lot* of cash."

"That can come in handy."

"And a computer drive."

"A flash drive," she said, shaking her head. "There's always a flash drive."

"This isn't a flash drive, it's a hard drive. Twenty terabytes of data."

"Terabytes?" Wen looked down into the jungle again.

"That's the capacity, but I don't know what's on it."

"Let's take it and find out."

"And here I was just going to grab the money and leave the drive."

"This sure seems like some kind of insurance," Wen said, ignoring his poor attempt at humor and imagining all the Circuit's secrets that might be on the drive. "Anything else?"

"Just a gun."

"One can never have too many—"

Four loud pops, and suddenly the area below them was filling with smoke.

"Tear gas!" Wen shouted.

Chapter Fifty-Four

The atrium was filling with tear gas and colored smoke. "It was a trap!" Wen yelled.

"How do we get out?"

She tried connecting to the Astronaut again. Nothing. *That should have been a red flag*, she chided herself.

Their wrist tablets still had inputs. Twenty to thirty FBI agents were visible in various parts of the building, including at least fifteen wearing gas masks in the atrium.

Covering his mouth and nose, running into the trees, Chase's foot sloshed in a stream. "The water," he said. "Where's the water go?"

"The waterfall." They ran toward the wall. "Follow the water."

Mixed with the sounds of gunshots and shattering glass, they heard, "Chase Malone, Wen Sung, this is the FBI! We have a warrant for your arrest."

"Are they really FBI?" Chase panted as they continued running.

"Who cares? Whoever it is, they aren't friends of ours."

"All exits are blocked. Surrender now!"

They never stopped moving.

"You know the drill," the voice yelled again. "Weapons down, hands up, walk slowly to the elevator."

Chase shoved the hard drive and cash into his pack, doing his best to wrap the drive in a waterproof wetbag he'd carried since, years earlier, they had once had to jump off a dam. "This isn't going to be like Shasta," Chase said as they reached the exterior wall.

"No," Wen said. "Worse."

"I've worked on enough high-rises to know that there should be a maintenance . . . here." He reached into the water. "Yes! This ladder will take us all the way down."

"We are authorized to use lethal force if you do not surrender," the voice said.

"This is normally something that gets used when the waterfall is *off*, right?" Wen asked.

"Yeah, but it's enclosed with some steel caging."

"I still feel like we're going to plummet—"

Bullets shattered the glass not far from them.

"Come on, they still don't know where we are."

"You first," Wen said. "I don't want you slipping off and coming down on top of me. I'm lighter."

Chase dropped into the chute, gripping the rungs and finding a foot hold below. The force of the water cascading over him was making it difficult to not slip.

"Couldn't we find a shut-off valve before we go?" Wen called down.

"The water pump is at ground level," he shouted, water filling his mouth. "I'm sure it's down there."

Wen looked down more than a hundred feet. "Go!" she yelled, instantly following him.

Inside the water, they could no longer hear each other.

Climbing down through the waterfall with tens of thousands of gallons pouring down on top of them, they were momentarily invisible.

Knowing there would likely be FBI, Vintons, or shadow people waiting for them, Chase wanted to yell up to Wen about what to do at the bottom, but she couldn't hear him over the raging noise of the water. He couldn't even see her. It was impossible to look up without thousands of gallons raining down in his eyes.

Chase tried to go too fast. His hand missed. His body dropped almost five feet before his foot found purchase and jammed into a wet rung, his back wrenched into the frame. The pain bolted through him, and he used it to regain his focus.

Breathing was difficult in all the water. He had no idea how much farther they had to go, but it had to still be at least three stories—not the kind of drop he wanted to take.

Wen slammed into his shoulders. He somehow managed to hold on to prevent her falling further, or from taking them both down. It took a few seconds of struggling for her to right herself and take her weight off of him.

A few moments after that, they could see the far end of the pool reflecting distant lights of the strip. The area closest to the building was still shrouded in mist.

As they dipped below the mist line, they spotted four FBI coming at them. "If they're really FBI, we should try to avoid shooting them," Chase yelled, forgetting they still had tranquilizer bullets. "Killing federal agents is never a good idea."

Finally down into the pool, Wen had been counting agents, gauging their threat level. If her estimates were right, they were now well within range. Standing in the shallow pool, still hidden in the mist, she shouted directions into his ear. They both fired nonlethal rounds, getting at least fifteen shots off. When they emerged from the water, only two agents were left standing. Wen finished them.

"You never cease to amaze me," Chase said breathlessly as they ran, soaking wet, into the darkness, heading to where they'd left the Destino.

Chapter Fifty-Five

Wen checked the map on her wrist. They were four blocks from the Destino, and there was no sign of them being followed. They had ducked into a parking garage, where Chase had spent several valuable minutes scanning the pages while Wen began to upload the drive.

"I transmitted the last page," Chase said. "I'll do it again once we get on the road. The mobile scan app doesn't always get everything."

"Great. We've still got just over five minutes until the upload is done."

"Maybe this will finally give us the answer."

"We find these places where he operated from," Wen said as they continued walking briskly toward the truck, "but nothing we find leads us to anyone above Belfort."

"We've just been saved months of work, maybe *years*. We now have the names of hundreds of more shadow people."

"That's great, but they are all *below* Belfort."

"So you're guessing he doesn't know who he works for," Chase said.

"It sure looks that way. He's careful to clean up his trails, but this drive could be the key. He went to a lot of trouble to hide it."

"Maybe the FBI wanted it."

"These minor scraps left behind could be insurance for him, or could be disinformation to us. I don't know." She checked behind them again. "The Circuit is so powerful, would they really trust someone like Belfort, or anyone, to know anything that could hurt them?"

A crackle in her ear proceeded the Astronaut's voice. "Turn. Turn back," he said. "They are up ahead."

"Who?" she asked, freezing.

"Shadows."

"Did you get the scans?" Chase asked.

"Yes. Now get onto Ali Baba Lane. You can cut over and reach the Destino . . . uh-oh . . . "

"What?" Wen snapped, already backtracking.

"You need to forget the truck," the Astronaut said. "Too many. Get to Dean Martin Drive!"

"Dean Martin?" Wen said, checking her wrist. "We'll be running right back into the arms of the FBI."

"*Move!*" he snapped. "No choice!"

Chase and Wen jogged down the neon-lit streets. They couldn't help but think of the last time they were in Las Vegas, when they'd almost died in a manmade volcano. Each separately also recalled the miles of tunnels and storm drains mazed under the desert city, occupied by the "mole people."

Chase pointed. "I hope we don't wind up down there again."

"Only if we have to," Wen said, already using her wrist tablet to find the nearest entrance to the subterranean world.

"Think our Vegas luck has run out?" he asked, knowing it would bother her. "We got away with an awful lot the last time we were here."

"We make our own luck!"

"Even in Vegas?"

"Especially in Vegas."

"If you two are done," the Astronaut said into their in-ear transmitters, "I'd like to continue attempting to save at least one of you."

"How many FBI are we about to hit?" Wen asked.

"And why are the Feds coming after us?" Chase added.

"Working on it," the Astronaut responded.

"And how many shadow people are back there?" she asked, trying to develop an escape strategy for the noose closing in around them.

"Two groups after us," Chase said. "I'm never coming back to Vegas."

"I think there are three."

"Three what?"

"Take a look at your wrist."

He tapped the small screen and saw an image sent from the Astronaut. It showed three men in various spots around the city. To an untrained eye, they might have appeared to be casually dressed businesspeople, but even Chase could tell they were something more. "Who are *they*?"

Bullets hit all around them.

"Where are they coming from?" Chase yelled. "It's like we're in a damned shooting gallery!"

"What's happening?" the Astronaut asked.

"There are shooters everywhere!" Wen yelled, ducking into a grove of palm trees in front of a fast-food joint.

"We need a car!" Chase yelled to Wen as he sprinted through a gaggle of tourists.

"I've got seven parties," the Astronaut said. "Make that eight, nine, eleven . . . "

"Who *are* all these people?" Chase yelled as they ran between a fitness center and an adult entertainment place.

More shots. "We've got to get off the streets!" Wen yelled.

"Where?"

"There!" She slowed her breath and simultaneously hurled herself toward the entrance of the Smokewine Hotel and Casino.

The woman brought Vader a special herbal smoothie that he sipped like a fine wine. "Thank you," he said, as if she'd brought him oxygen.

"You need to keep your strength up."

"Why? So I can lure more people to the dark side?"

"You might be taking the Vader nickname too seriously."

"Really?" He pointed to four of the giant screens in the dimly lit circular room.

"Las Vegas?"

"Sin city," he said. "The dark side."

"I know. We're there."

"Of course," he said, knowing she wasn't talking about the corporate presence his organization had in the desert city. She meant the dark troopers, otherwise known as the Regulators.

Chapter Fifty-Six

Inside the low-end hotel and casino, Chase looked at his wrist again. More reports were relayed through the Astronaut. "Maybe a fourth group."

"Who?"

"Working on it."

Chase and Wen made their way to the back corner of a bowling alley off the lobby. Slot machines lined the walls. Old ladies and scraggly cowboy-wannabes worked the one-armed bandits, losing rent money, welfare checks, and yesterday's meager winnings. A cloud of smoke blanketed the room like a sadistic ghost ready to strike.

"The fighting continues," the Astronaut said.

"What's that mean?" Chase asked.

"The groups pursuing you are engaging each other."

"Wow, that adds to the fun."

"We seem to have stumbled into something a little bit different," Wen said. "There's an awful lot of guns in town, and they're not all shooting at us."

The Astronaut, trying to make sense of the scene, knew

things Chase and Wen did not. He'd heard rumors of rumors during his many years working in the most secret seams of the intelligence world, realms where the most dangerous and duplicate events occurred, places few alive even knew about. It had been in those gritty margins, the seedy underbelly of the calculated chess moves and shady side bargains, where he'd first seen glimpses of evil.

There had been traces of two opposing forces; both devoid of a loyalty, or even a connection, to any specific government, let alone any moral sense of right and wrong. The pair of indie-armies allegedly battled it out in the whispered preambles to events, invisible movements, absent oversight or repercussions. They were perhaps the most frightening groups on the planet—Skyggers and Regulators.

The Astronaut swallowed hard, daring not to believe his suspicion, lest it turn into a burning fear that the two dark forces were now locked in this shadow war with implied contracts against Wen and Chase.

The evidence of his theory was there, where only he could see in the patterns of what had happened, and the weighted trajectories of what was happening. Looking ahead with SEER and other AI programs, he saw more, worse, dramatic tectonic shifts, traumatic things he could hardly cope with, while trying to fight through the present. "The future will have to wait," he said, almost choking on the words.

The Astronaut touched the screens in front of him, issued voice commands, and relayed footage from traffic cams, images from casinos, and security feeds to their wrists, showing them shadow people getting shot.

"Looks like we're getting some help," Chase said.

"The campers are here?" Wen asked.

"Not yet, still approximately forty minutes out. Someone else is there."

"Grimes, Shelby?"

"No," he said. "Someone else."

"If it's not our friends, and not the guys we're paying, it can only be CISS agents. Why would Tess send IT-Squads?" Chase asked.

"Negative," the Astronaut said. "CISS has no one in the area."

"I really don't have time to worry about who it is right now. As long as they're shooting the guys shooting at us," Wen said. "That's all that matters for the moment."

The Astronaut disagreed, but kept his thoughts to himself. This was not the time to explain to Chase and Wen that the world as they knew it was ending with the almost biblical arrival of two dark forces in an epic contest for the fate of freedom.

His deeply analytical mind, crazy with ideas, was trying to figure out what was going on. *Why is someone helping them? Whose side are you on? How does this fit into the equation?*

And the Astronaut *knew* it fit into the equation. The equation was everything, and the only way to find his answers, to solve the equation, was to keep looking at the patterns, especially the ones newly forming in real time in Vegas, the ones that could end the life of his beautiful Wen.

"Don't die, Wen," he whispered to himself. "Don't let the shadows and dark forces kill you."

Chapter Fifty-Seven

Bursts of machine gun fire went over Chase's head. The Smokewine Hotel and Casino's neon sign, with its bright colored wine bottles and blinking cigarettes, exploded above him. Shards of glass, like fine needles, came down, along with a man, riddled with bullets, who'd fallen from the elevated parking garage, where the colorful sign had been. His machine gun and head slammed into the concrete sidewalk with a clanking *thud*, a bloody mess.

"Sorry I was a little late," Wen said. They'd been separated after a group of shadows had found them in the hotel's bowling alley. Belfort's men had all died, but in the confusion, Chase wound up on the street, while Wen had steered through a gift shop and cheap designer clothing store attached to the hotel.

"Let's go," Wen said while Chase brushed thin splinters of glass from his hair. She ran over the tops of a line of cars stuck at a red light as if she were running across stones in a stream.

Two black SUVs squealed around the corner, the

unyielding traffic blocking the big vehicles from going any further. Several agents leapt out, yellow FBI blazed across the backs of their jackets, and began pursuing on foot.

"I'm going to have to kill these guys," Wen said through Chase's ear.

Chase, still on the other side of the busy street, checked the images on his wrist. "Not a good idea . . . federal agents, we won't get another chance to undo that one," he said.

"Then tell them to stop following me."

"I'm trying to reach Tess," The Astronaut broke in. "It's 8:27 pm on the East Coast. She isn't answering her private cell."

"Try the office. She's always there."

"Not this time. I called twice. Talked to her deputy. Very cryptic, but truthful. I used the meter." The meter was an AI device he'd developed to detect when a person was lying just by analyzing their voice. "Tess has managed to keep her home address classified beyond even my reach since her boyfriend was killed at her prior residence."

People on the sidewalks scrambled as more shots were fired. Chase, too caught up in watching the images on his wrist, as if viewing an action movie, forgetting he was one of the stars, saw even more agents coming on the other block. "This way!" he yelled.

"I see them," she replied. "Split up."

He decided not to bring up the fact that splitting up was not a clever idea. "Remember, you can't kill them!"

"I won't," she replied, "as long as I don't have to."

Chase figured she'd slip into the nearby small stadium. *High Ground,* he thought, *she always goes for the high ground.*

The well-lit streets made the images on Chase's wrist almost perfect, but even the darker alleys and backlots were showing up clear. "How are we seeing all this?" he asked, dashing into a large paint store.

"I've developed a program to transform the video," the Astronaut explained. "It handles the light interface. With the extra dynamics, because it's all digital extract elites, it extrapolates the data contained in each pixel and enhances it."

"So you can turn nighttime into daylight?"

"At least through the cameras."

"I wish you could do it for real right now, so we could see all these people hiding without having to check our wrists."

"Chase, they saw you," the Astronaut said. "You're getting company. Four, no five . . . seven shadows, hitting now!"

Dozens of paint cans exploded all around him, a rainbow of spraying paint streaming out. Chase slid in the puddling paint as if he were going into home plate, but instead skidded behind a thick metal gondola holding assorted brushes, rollers, and other applicators.

The three employees and one customer fled into the back, and by now had probably escaped out a rear exit. Chase figured the police were busy enough with everything else going on, but wouldn't mind the distraction of their arrival. "Am I getting any help?" he whispered.

"Tied up," Wen said.

"Working on it," the Astronaut said.

No help, Chase thought. *I need another idea.*

That's when he smelled the fumes.

A conglomeration of solvents and other chemicals that had been punctured by bullets was cascading over the nearby shelves. Hundreds of gallons. Chase knew what Wen would do.

He crawled around the other side of the display and quickly picked off a couple of shadows with his Beretta. The other five had fanned out into the large store. Chase took out his Zippo lighter, checked that it worked, which took a few tries after the soaking in the waterfall. Next, he found a box of painter's rags sold by the pound and doused them in a gallon of paint thinner he'd pulled from the shelf.

He watched and waited. After his handy work with taking down two shadows, he knew the rest would come.

A few seconds later, four of them were there, in the middle of the pond of solvents. He lit the box and kicked it into the approaching men.

Flash point.

"When it all goes up in flames," Chase sang to himself. "The shadows become silhouettes and then they fade to black."

Chapter Fifty-Eight

Wen's years of training in hostile obstacle courses came back as she ran at full speed across a narrow wall separating a parking lot from the heavily trafficked street. Bullets blasted and chipped the painted concrete blocks at her feet. She scrambled and spun, crossing her arms in front of her, shooting in two directions at once. "I've got them on both sides," she said. "And I don't know who I'm shooting. Please tell me I'm not killing federal agents."

"Working on it," the Astronaut replied.

"If they *are* FBI, I'm beyond caring."

"Appear to be shadows."

Three men approached the wall. "Those looks like feds to me!"

"Yes," the Astronaut agreed. "Those are, but the others weren't."

"What a mess." Wen dropped to the other side, leaving the FBI agents trapped and lost.

Her landing led into a roll, and she came up ready to

fire. She missed shooting an old woman pushing a shopping cart. The lady screamed.

"That was close!"

She ran into the adjoining parking lot of a home improvement store, thinking that would be a great place to make a stand. However, she kept going, trying to get back to Chase.

"Wen, check your screen," the Astronaut said.

She looked down. The image showed four shadows. "Where are they?"

"Waiting for you, here." A map popped up. "Go this route and you can avoid them.

"Map me in behind them instead."

The Astronaut didn't need to ask why. In all his efforts to keep her safe, she always ran into the face of danger, looking to answer the fight rather than avoiding it. "Okay." He sighed. "Just don't die."

"Never."

"And please, never say never."

"I meant not today."

"Better."

Wen saw the route and veered off onto a side street. "Chase is right, we need a car."

"You have a truck."

"We keep getting farther away from it. We need a car to get us *back* to the Destino."

"Working on it."

Wen came up behind the four shadows, waiting in a cluster of palm trees around a tumbling fountain, its stone facade making an excellent ambush point if she'd come from the other direction. The budget hotel, wanting to look bigger and better than it was, trying to seem more Vegas, had commissioned the nice entrance.

"Looking for me?" Wen asked loudly.

She could have shot them in the back, but that seemed too much like cold blooded murder. Either way, they were all dead in seconds.

"Still alive," she said to the Astronaut.

"I see," he said. "Wave hello to the camera in the sign."

"Can you erase that little mishap those men just had?"

"Done."

"Where's Chase?"

"Picking up some groceries," Chase replied.

"Need some help?"

"Don't I always?"

"Can you map me?"

"Here you go," the Astronaut said, not knowing she would never make it.

Cranson landed at the Las Vegas airport, a car waiting. The driver opened the door, then handed him a phone. He knew who it was before he said, "Hello?"

"Why isn't your phone on?" Belfort blasted.

"I needed to sleep."

"Oh, poor baby. I'm so sorry I interrupted your night-night time. Are you all rested up now?"

"Good enough."

"How nice that you can sleep while our people are getting slaughtered."

"Slaughtered?" Cranson echoed.

"Yes, while you were napping in dreamy-land, Chase and Wen have raided my office and initiated a killing spree."

"I'm here now."

"Good. Why don't you go stand in front of Wen's machine gun."

Cranson said nothing while his over-sized laptop powered up. He clicked open an app. Live video feeds from shadow's chest cams began to fill his screen. He rotated through them, not knowing that his device had just been hacked by one of the Astronaut's AI programs. "It's not looking good."

"Oh, you think?" Belfort said, watching the same images. "Who's killing our people?"

"It's not Chase and Wen?"

"Watch some of the older footage, but I'll save you the trouble. Our operatives are dropping dead when they are nowhere near Chase and Wen."

"Dead from what?" Cranson asked, scanning rapidly through prior feeds.

"Gunshot wounds, what do you think!?"

"I assumed *that*, but what *kind*?"

"Snipers mostly."

"So Chase and Wen have support. They hired shooters to protect them."

"Good guess," Belfort said sarcastically. "However, if you'd been watching from the start, you'll see there is no coordination. Chase and Wen are definitely not communicating with them."

"Then who?"

"I don't know," Belfort said, sounding angry, but beneath that, almost scared.

"Have you alerted upper management?" Cranson asked.

"Why should I?" Belfort sneered. "I'm the final word."

"Oh-kay."
"Figure this out. Kill them."

Hundreds of miles away, Tane stood in the TV studio, watching local Vegas television stations collecting footage of the sudden guerrilla war taking place in their city. He let an experienced Circuit producer curtail the coverage, but it was not going to be contained for long—too much happening, too many reporters out there, but the big problem, as always, was the amateurs.

"All these idiots taking videos with their smart phones," Tane said. "Do you see the irony?"

Blanc, growing frustrated because shadow people kept getting in the way of Skyggers, ignored the comment. "Perhaps we should have coordinated with Belfort."

"Collateral damage," Tane said. "There are plenty of operatives there, the Skyggers can't kill them all . . . well, I guess they could, but they aren't there to do that."

"They *are* there to kill Chase and Wen, so why is it taking so long?"

"The wealthiest man in the universe . . . Darth Vader."

"You've seen Regulators?" Blanc asked.

"No, but they are there. More of Belfort's people are dying than can be accounted for with Skyggers or Malone and the Chinese woman."

"What about the army?"

"No sign of them either," Tane said. "If our intelligence is correct, and Malone really is raising an army to come against us, we've seen no trace of them."

"What about Los Angeles?"

"We have no film of how they escaped."
"Doesn't mean it didn't happen."
"It's the Regulators. Vader is here."
"How can you be sure?" Blanc asked.
"Because it's the End Game, and Vader is everywhere."

Chapter Fifty-Nine

The paint store in flames, Chase, trying to catch up to Wen, encountered a contingent of FBI agents, some of the same ones who had been at Belfort's. Although he believed killing them would not be as horrible an idea as he had thought earlier, instead he took refuge in a twenty-four-hour grocery store.

He tried to be incognito in the cereal aisle, reading the ingredients on a box of Cap'n Crunch. Corn Flour, Sugar, Oat Flour, Brown Sugar, Palm and/or Coconut Oil, Salt, Reduced Iron, Yellow 5, Niacinamide, Yellow 6—

He stopped reading and checked both ends of the shelves packed with boxes. Clear. *Why do you need food coloring in cereal, and two kinds of yellow?* he wondered. He looked up again as a lady pushed a cart past, but didn't head in his direction. Then he noticed a box of King Vitamin cereal, one of his favorites as a kid. "I didn't think they still made this," he muttered, checking the ingredients, which turned out to be very similar to the ones in Cap'n Crunch. *Two yellows in King Vitamin, too. Maybe that's why I turned out so strange.*

Suddenly, boxes of Trix, Fruit Loops, Frosted Flakes, Lucky Charms, Fruity Pebbles, Count Chocula, and dozens more ripped open in a storm of colorful sugar snow.

He dropped onto the crumb covered floor and got off a lucky shot. The man who'd somehow missed him turned out not to be an FBI agent, which was good now that Chase had killed him. Chase grabbed the dead man's machine gun, having learned enough about weapons from Wen to know it was an Uzi. Although Wen preferred Heckler & Koch MP7s, he thought Israel Military Industries Uzi's had the coolest name of any gun out there. He wasn't completely convinced the man he'd just killed was a shadow, but was sure he wasn't a Fed, as they didn't use Uzis.

Chase peered around the corner as the twenty or so shoppers and a dozen employees fled the store. Two men in the front corner of the store, near the milk and eggs, saw him and opened fire.

Those look like shadows... I need to get out of here before the feds do come.

"Twenty-one minutes," the Astronaut's voice said in his ear.

"Not soon enough," he whispered, wondering how many campers were coming. "Wen, where are you?" he asked, hoping she could help him find the express checkout.

"I haven't been able to get her to answer," the Astronaut replied instead.

Chase retreated back into the cereal aisle, knowing there would probably be a fourth shadow lurking somewhere. Machine gun fire erupted in the front of the store. Even without looking, he knew the Feds had just met the fourth shadow. He wasn't sure who to root for, but knew it was time to leave.

"FBI has entered your location," the Astronaut said.

"I know, I know!" he hissed. "What's it look like out back?"

Chase quickly climbed to the top shelf where the Cap'n Crunch and King Vitamin had been.

"Clear for the moment. However, Las Vegas Metropolitan Police Department has dispatched three patrol cars and a SWAT unit to your location."

"That's all I need." He slithered along the granular residue of sugar, flour, and food coloring, until the two shadows from the milk and eggs made their way to his end. *Shooting them from above is easy, too easy. But I have a feeling getting away from the feds without killing them is not going to be as simple.*

"Anything from Wen?" Chase asked while he climbed up into the rafters and began traversing the store on high.

"Nothing."

"I could use a hand here." From his vantage point, Chase counted nine FBI agents.

"Prepare to get soaked and to run to the back door."

"Soaked?" Chase asked.

Two different alarms sounded, one a deep wail, the other high-pitched whines. At the same moment, the sprinklers system started spraying what, to Chase, felt like ice cold water. *I've had enough water for one day,* he thought, having still not dried out from the waterfall. The paint covering his clothes, face, and hair began running, dripping into his eyes and mouth.

"Back door is accessed through the employees only receiving room near the end of aisle twelve," the Astronaut's voice informed him.

Chase wiped the colored paint water from his eyes and

dropped to the top of aisle nine, detergents and cleaning supplies, knowing he could move faster on the ground.

Two agents spotted him. Chase opened up with the Uzi, hoping not to hit them, or at least not to kill them. One went down, but even in the soggy blur, Chase was fairly sure the injury was to the man's leg.

The deafening whir of alarm sounds seemed to grow louder. Emergency lighting and the continuing indoor rainstorm gave the store's back room a horror movie vibe. Chase, at first, couldn't make sense of the place, but then he found the emergency exit that promised to sound an alarm as soon as he opened it. "What's one more?" he said, pushing the bar. No new alarm came.

The cool night air greeted his wet body like an arctic shock.

"Wen?" he tried the comms.

"Nothing," the Astronaut said. "But I have an idea where she is."

"Where?"

"FBI custody."

Real Truth - Internet Fact Based News

Posted by JI Right

We are still trying to get to the truth of what happened in Taos. And now we have Las Vegas, Nevada. FBI agents injured, many bystanders killed. We have word from hospital workers—unofficial, since they will not confirm this count—that they've seen more than two hundred casualties. Yet no official reports have been made. Is it related to the events in Taos? We don't know.
But there's more: we've uncovered events in Los Angeles. Seventeen dead. No reports there either. No explanation.

Kentucky—up to sixty dead. Thirty more in Houston. What happened there? We've got reports of unexplained deaths of former military members all across the country. Who is doing this? Why?

It seems to me the country is in the middle of some sort of silent Civil War. Who are the two sides? Are there more than two sides? These events are not conspiracy theories or speculation, these are facts. The list below shows the dates and times, the number of dead.

These controversial events have not had one bit of coverage in the mainstream media. Why?

Chapter Sixty

Wen scanned in every direction, searching for what she knew was not there—a way out. It had been a vicious fight, with too many against them. The seemingly endless supply of shadow people coming meant they were out-gunned, out-ammunitioned, out-everything. She continued searching, but knew it was lost.

The restaurant had been full of people enjoying dinner before the shooting began. They were gone now, the ones that hadn't been hit in the crossfire.

Chase. She wondered where he was. Her communications weren't working for some reason. Surely the Astronaut could track her. *Chase will come.*

There were twelve guns pointed at her, fourteen if she counted the two on the balcony. Wen knew the makes of each weapon, could wager a fairly accurate guess as to how many rounds remained in each magazine, but the biggest number that mattered was there were only two bullets left in her gun. *I can kill two, maybe even three or four, if I get the angles right, but not twelve or fourteen.*

She dropped the gun at her feet. Surrender was never an option, until it was the only option remaining.

Rough hands quickly found her, shoving and pulling at her, patting her down, searching for the weapons that she undoubtedly carried. These professionals knew what they were looking for, and in less than forty seconds, had stripped her of everything, even her throwing stars.

The police will be here soon. She began calculating how she could use that commotion. *Will we already be gone by then?*

"I'd like nothing more than to execute you right here, right now, you dragon witch," a man said.

Wen recognized him as a long-time shadow. She'd escaped his murderous attempts in the past, and no doubt killed some of his buddies. "Do it!" she said, knowing he could not, or she'd already be dead

"They want to talk." He suspected his bosses would also be using her as bait against Chase. Yet everyone knew that Wen was the truly lethal one. Chase would be much easier to capture or kill without her.

The restaurant was now completely cleared out. Most of the employees had escaped, but she'd seen a chef take a bullet and at least two servers and a busser were dead—not by her hand, but she felt responsible. Tables had been knocked over during the gunfight, remnants of the meals they'd held all over the ugly carpeted floor.

One of the men put his hands where they didn't belong. He might have been looking for something, but it wasn't weapons. Instantly, she sent him down into the floor, face first, and with broken fingers. The other men backed off a little, but didn't shoot her.

"Kill her!" the man with the mangled hand screamed as he rolled in agony.

Someone shot him instead.

"Get her tied!" the one in charge barked.

Knowing in a few seconds her arms and legs would be bound, and she'd be carried hogtied out to the trunk of a car and driven off, she maintained all calm and logic, calculating every possible way to resist, to attack. A man came marching toward her with zip ties in his hands.

Now or never. With no gun close enough, Wen reached to the nearest table and, in one swift motion, snatched a butter knife and sent it straight toward the man in charge. It soared ten feet, as if on a line, and landed in the middle of his neck, piercing the external jugular vein and sending him backwards.

From her standing position, Wen flew into a backflip, landing on a group of three startled men. They crashed to the ground, tangled and easy targets. She came up with one of their machine guns, quickly ending their lives, along with four more standing nearby.

She whispered a quick thank you to Four Arrows, an old Native American man she'd encountered in Mexico who'd taught her the knife throw. Wen often said that one never knows where wisdom comes from, that people should always think of learning as borrowing the knowledge of others.

The shadows quickly recovered their shock and returned fire. Using the cadavers as cover, and two fresh machine guns, she fought with the fury of someone who'd lived to die another day. Clearing a path through the room, she made her way to the kitchen. After another skirmish that left two more shadows dead, Wen staggered out the back door, unaware that she was bleeding heavily.

Chapter Sixty-One

Vader sat in the dark room, almost none of his features distinguishable in the glow from the monitors, just a mere silhouette. There was no one else physically there with him. Times had grown far too dangerous for that. He'd sent the woman away to attend to other affairs.

His keen eyes moved from one screen to the other. Occasionally he gave voice commands to switch the images. This was how he kept track of operations, how he attempted to control the world.

Skyggers involvement in the Vegas affair told him the severity at which his rivals deemed the situation. His Regulators were no match for the Skyggers one-on-one, but he knew he could provide the edge through monitoring and insurance. And he had other forces to draw upon, but that would reveal his identity to those he sought to destroy, and then he would lose his final edge; an edge he was counting on, the only real chance he had to succeed.

And he *had* to succeed. There was so much at stake.

Still, in the end he knew it was likely the Skyggers would

do more damage than he could repair. It seemed increasingly likely that soon Chase and Wen would be dead. But until then, there was always hope. He had the advantage in Las Vegas because Tane and Blanc still hadn't figured out what was happening, but they would, and by then, it would be too late. Too late for who, he did not know.

Chase, still wet and covered in paint, arrived at the front of the restaurant and found the bodies of more than a dozen FBI agents. He knew Wen hadn't done it, because they'd mostly been shot in the back.

Inside the dining room, he found her victims and quickly replayed the horrific scene in his head, guessing how it might have gone down. Then he hurried to the rear exit.

Noxious scents of fried grease and rotting garbage filled the cool air. "Wen, where are you?"

No response.

He wandered the well-lit area for several minutes. *Careful*, he told himself, *shadows lurk in the darkness*. There was blood and bodies, but no sign of life, and no sign of Wen.

"Wen . . . *Wen*?"

Nothing.

"Nash! Are you there?"

Nothing.

"Can anyone hear me?" he asked, his voice a hoarse whisper. He jogged cautiously around the parking lots connecting a motel, a carpet store, and a boarded-up gas station. A helicopter in the distance seemed to be heading in his general direction, concerning him. Otherwise, there appeared to be no visible threats.

The Astronaut finally came through. "I've just picked up

Wen's locator. She's not far from you. Fifty-seven feet north."

"Are you sure?" Chase said, looking to the north, seeing nothing but a short service road leading to an overflow lot for a nearby used car dealer.

"She's not moving," the Astronaut said. "I retraced the beacon . . . she hasn't moved for eleven minutes, sixteen seconds."

"Maybe she lost her transponder," Chase said, running now. They both knew that would nearly be impossible unless her arm had been ripped off. The transponder was a band worn just under her shoulder.

"Wen would not remove it."

"Yeah," Chase said. "I know. But she's not there." Less than fifteen feet from her supposed location and he could see nothing. "She's not here."

"She is there."

Chase, now two feet from where the Astronaut said, shined his light across the ground. A concrete base to an old burned-out sign was the only thing there. Chase walked around it. "Wait." He knelt down. Two curbs joined, forming a drain. *There isn't enough space . . . Wen!* He reached into the void and felt her back, sticky and wet with blood. Chase pulled her out as carefully as he could. *Check her breathing.* "I have her."

"Is Wen okay?"

"She's unconscious, but breathing."

"Closest hospital is Spring Valley Medical Center."

Chase looked up. That helicopter was closer now. "How far?"

"Eleven minutes if you have a car."

"I don't."

"Get one."

"I don't know if we have eleven minutes," Chase said, cradling Wen's limp body in his arms as he jogged to the closest vehicles, a row of low-end cars parked at the motel.

"You don't," the Astronaut said. "They know where you are."

"Who?"

"Shadows, FBI, the others . . . they all know your location, and they'll be there in less than two minutes."

Chapter Sixty-Two

Chase ordered the driver of the Destino to meet him at the hospital and then broke a window of a 2008 Toyota Camry. After gently strapping Wen into the front passenger seat, he hot-wired the vehicle and pulled into light traffic.

"Police are all over the area," the Astronaut said, "responding to your many messes."

"They're mostly Wen's messes."

"How is she?"

"Same."

The helicopter hovered at an intersection. Men with machine guns hung out of each side. Chase swerved into the oncoming lane just as they began firing. Now in a residential neighborhood, traffic was almost non-existent.

"Road divides, and you're crossing the Bruce Woodbury Beltway. After that, you can return to your proper lane. It's a good idea."

"You think?" Chase steered the Camry into the concrete walls of the overpass to avoid a semi heading straight toward him.

Bullets from the helicopter tore into the trailer being pulled by the semi, which turned out to be a tanker filled with thousands of gallons of gasoline.

The explosion physically moved the Camry. Chase fought to regain control before swerving back into the correct lane. "That ought to slow down our friends," he said, checking the rearview.

"Not the chopper," the Astronaut said.

The helicopter appeared above the flames, and one of the shadows onboard shot out the Camry's back window.

At the same moment, Luke and Leia fired simultaneously from the ground and killed both shooters in the chopper.

A few seconds later, the pilot's head exploded. "Bird coming down," Luke said. "Our work here is done."

"Not necessarily," Leia said, pointing to the two black Suburbans that passed them.

"Who took out that chopper?" Chase asked.

"Not us," the Astronaut said. "Maybe someone helping us . . . but who?"

"They *definitely* helped us."

"Perhaps they meant to, perhaps it was a side effect of a very different intention."

"Either way."

Chase looked over at Wen, still unresponsive. He slammed the accelerator, and passed a limousine on Decatur Boulevard. Before he could get back on the right side, a dump truck pulled out of Patrick Lane, completely blocking the road. Chase slammed on the brakes to avoid the collision, then saw the guns come out of the truck's covered bed."

"Trouble!" Chase yelled, cranking the wheel to the right, plowing into a VW Bus, before bouncing up the curb.

"You're at the Tropicana Detention Basin."

"What is that, a prison?"

"No, water management—wash, dam, floods. The desert is—"

A silver SUV slammed into the side of the Camry. Chase pulled the Uzi off his lap and fired through the window. The SUV veered away. Chase, trying to figure out if he'd hit the driver, missed seeing the earth berm. The airbags deployed as the Camry plowed into the mound.

Chase used the blade from his multi tool to puncture the bags, unbuckled Wen, then ran around to open her door.

"Why are you covered in paint?" she asked woozily.

"You're back!"

"Where was I?"

"Long story." He scooped her up, along with the three machine guns she'd had with her, and ran for cover.

There was a break in the berm, with a tall, heavy wall. Luckily, there was a door. Unluckily, it was locked with a keypad.

"Nash, I need a key code."

"Working on it."

"What's with the paint?" Wen asked again, still only half there.

"Picked the wrong place to hide," he said.

A sudden explosion sent gravel and sand spraying into his head and back, but he was able to shield Wen. Chase turned to see the obliterated frame of the Camry on fire. *The next RPG is coming in here.* "I need that damned code!"

"One-seven-two-seven-three-seven."

Chase hit the digits and the door opened. He pushed through and closed it behind them. The small space served as a makeshift storage area, but was really just a way through the long berm. *This place won't withstand an explosive attack.* "How's it look on the other side?"

"Clear."

"Paint?" Wen said.

Chase opened the door. The Astronaut had been right. He carried Wen across the dusty field and then saw something that both annoyed and delighted him. The Las Vegas Metropolitan Police Department had a station right next to the Tropicana Detention Basin.

"Put me down," Wen said, sounding like a little girl who'd fallen asleep on the couch watching TV.

"We need to get you to the hospital."

"No we don't," she said. "I'm fi—"

Chase eyed the squad cars in the nearly empty station lot. *A siren and flashing lights would sure help me get to the hospital faster . . .*

He hit the ground, rougher than he would have liked with Wen in his arms. "Do you have visuals?" he asked the Astronaut.

"Working on it."

"Well, work a little faster. I just spotted at least twenty shadows." He peered up. "Make that forty." He looked back at the berm, planning a retreat, and saw two dozen more. "Oh man, we're surrounded." He glanced down at Wen, unconscious again. "Sorry to say this," Chase whispered to her, "but I think we're going to die here."

Chapter Sixty-Three

Chase slowed his breathing, as Wen would have done. He pictured in his mind the entire area he had seen, where the lights were, the roads, the police station, the number of shadows. He looked at the four machine guns, counting his Uzi, and there were two pistols between them, but she was out, and he could only fire two at once, so it was like having just two and a bunch of extra ammo. He tried to find the escape—the '*seam*', as Wen often called it. It would be even harder to get out because he'd have to carry her, *and* shoot, *and* not get killed . . .

He took one last look, deciding which way to shoot to at least kill as many of the shadow bastards as he could on his way to the grave.

That's when he saw the robots.

Ten black and white advanced humanoid robots and three agile robotic *dogs*.

For a moment, Chase felt like he was in a science fiction movie, and that he was going to die even faster than he'd originally thought.

An instant later, he realized they were *his* robots, part of his army. Somehow, he'd forgotten the campers existed.

I have an army, and my army is here!

"Enemy analyzed," a robotic voice said. "Seventy-eight armed human personnel. Engaging in three, two, one."

"How did that get in my ear?" Chase asked the Astronaut.

"Patched in," Blitz said. "Hope you don't mind."

Chase hardly heard him. Gunfire was tearing up the basin. Chase's wrist screen lit up with a green-tinted view of the action coming from one of the bot's chest cams. He marveled at the precision of their shooting. While the desperate shadows were firing at anything and everything, the bots were hardly missing a shot.

"Where did they come from?" Chase asked.

"Dark skies hide all kinds of things," Blitz said.

"I need to get to the hospital," Chase said.

"You're injured?"

"Wen."

"Damn."

"Closest vehicle at Las Vegas Metropolitan Police Department, 5880 Cameron Street," an AI voice said.

"I've already figured that out," Chase said. "It's getting there that's my problem."

"We'll open a lane for you," Blitz said.

The battle was raging all around them, and Chase had no doubt police would be responding soon, but they had been kept quite busy that evening. He'd find out later that most of the department's resources had been purposely diverted to two Casino mass shooting and hostage situations on the strip, events created by the Skyggers.

Following behind two of the multimillion-dollar bots his money had paid for, Chase felt almost invincible. Their armor, an advanced composite ceramic and titanium alloy, had been developed by DARPA. The AI-target acquisition system was nearly ninety-eight percent accurate in close nighttime combat conditions such as these. By the time Chase and the pair of dynamic fighters reached the police station, two thirds of the shadows were dead.

Chase took the first patrol car he reached and left the bots to return to the battle, having no doubt the shadows would be history before he made it to the hospital. Sirens blazing, Chase broke every traffic law during the short trip.

Inside Spring Valley Medical Center, Chase found a doctor exiting the ER. "I need your help," Chase said. "I have a gun, but don't want to hurt you."

"Not a good way to begin," the doctor, a youngish looking man with an Indian accent, said.

"I'm a deep undercover agent with the government. No time to explain, and no time to be polite."

"What do you want?" the doctor said, studying Chase, his paint-covered clothes, the scrapes on his face, some obvious blood on his hands, but it didn't seem like his. "You look a mess, but not enough to pull a gun on a doctor."

"My partner, she's hurt. Gunshots and knife wounds."

The doctor stared at Chase, stunned.

"Rough night," Chase moaned.

"Are you part of all this trauma we've been seeing? We've been getting gunshot victims for hours."

"People have been trying to kill us for hours," Chase said. "I need you to help her, *now*."

"Okay," the doctor said. "Where is she?"

Chase led the man out to the parking lot.

"Your car?" the doctor asked sarcastically when he saw the LVMPD cruiser.

Chase didn't reply, instead opening the passenger's door.

After only a few seconds of examination, the doctor told him Wen needed to be inside immediately.

"I can't admit her. They'll find her, they'll kill her."

"I don't know what will happen if we take her in, but I do know that if you leave her out here, she will die."

Chapter Sixty-Four

Chase gave false names for both he and Wen, prepared aliases from the multiple identities they always carried.

Two bullets had entered her body, both had exited, and a couple of knife wounds furthered her trauma and loss of blood. An hour and forty minutes later, and only thirty minutes post-surgery, and *definitely* against the doctor's firm advice, Chase and Wen left the hospital.

In the back of the Destino, laying in a comfortable hospital bed Chase had procured from Spring Valley, while a well-rested driver navigated them out of the city, Wen recounted the events that led to her hospitalization.

"I left the restaurant, already injured, I must have caught a bullet . . . and right outside five or six people jumped me . . . "

"I saw the bodies," Chase interrupted. "It was seven."

"Right, and they didn't make it easy. I handled them, but . . . they got some hits in. I staggered around, indecisive, cloudy . . . then walked a little way before realizing I was in real trouble. Tried to reach you . . . no response. I went to hide behind a big . . . and saw the drain . . . then I went blank."

"Good thing I happened along when I did."

"Yeah," she said weakly. "I knew you'd be looking for me."

"Always."

She squeezed his hand. "Where are we going?"

"Santa Barbara," Chase said. "A new lead on Belfort."

"Can I sleep until we get there?"

"That's all you're allowed to do," Chase said. "I think I'll do the same."

Before he could close his eyes, the Astronaut called to check on Wen again. Chase repeated his earlier assurance that she would be fine. Next it was Blitz checking in. Chase went to the other end of the trailer so he wouldn't disturb Wen.

"Amazing, huh?" Blitz said of the footage he'd just sent Chase of a group of bots loading into a rental truck.

Chase glanced at the images, still partially creeped out by the bots. "It's crazy. They're a cross between the dancing robots from Boston Dynamics, and something out of the Terminator movies."

"More like Star Wars. These babies are precision-driven AI autonomous advanced weaponized soldiers," Blitz said. "Plus, they don't really look anything like a cyborg from Terminator."

"No, not really," Chase agreed, still uncomfortable with the idea of armed autonomous robots on the loose. It was exactly that kind of abuse of technology that he had spent the past few years fighting.

"The Terminators has a nice ring to it, like killer

machine bounty hunters going after shadow people and their Circuit overlords."

"Bounty hunting is a complicated profession," Chase said. "Don't you agree?"

"We're going to *terminate* the Circuit . . . get it? *Terminate* the *Circuit*. You know, like the electrical term?"

Chase, being an engineer, certainly understood. "Yeah, I get it, but if you have to explain a joke, it's not really funny."

"But it sort of is."

"Killing is serious business," Chase said, exhausted and trying not to sound as impatient as he felt.

"Yeah, sure, but it can also be a lot of fun, too. Especially if you're one of the good guys."

"As long as we're sure we're the good guys in this movie."

"Hell yeah, of course we're the good guys."

"Everyone always thinks they're the good guys," Chase said.

"Really?" Blitz asked. "You're telling me that those evil sadistic Nazi bastards thought *they* were the good guys?"

"Nazis don't count," Chase said.

"I'm sorry I wasn't alive back then," Blitz said. "Love to kill me some Nazis."

"Goodbye, I need to sleep."

"I hear you. But before I let you go, let's agree to drop the name '*campers*'. That makes them sound like a bunch of Boy Scouts. *Terminators*, that's the name of a terrifying army coming to drag their enemies into hell."

"Are we that close?" Chase asked. "Because from everything we've learned, the Circuit is huge, their reach has no limits, and they've got influence over the president."

"You're forgetting one thing."

"What's that?" Chase said, tired of the conversation.

"The Circuit has never faced any real opposition. The Terminators aren't just thirty-six of the most advance AI fighters in existence, they are more than a thousand of the most highly trained covert special ops soldiers in the world. We're coming."

Chapter Sixty-Five

Chase got a little sleep before they arrived in Santa Barbara at dawn. He took two more calls prior to Wen waking.

PeacePipe phoned from Taos.

"It's not safe for you there," Chase said, glad he was recovering.

"Not safe anywhere these days, and if I have to be in danger somewhere, I'd rather be in Taos."

"I understand," Chase said, recalling that Tess often quoted the line from Michael Hearne's song *New Mexico Rain*, "If I ain't happy here, I ain't happy nowhere."

"A lot of talk about the virus' origin, and the real threat coming from Remedy, on the alternative internet sites," PeacePipe said.

"Hardly anyone believes it."

"That's because it's easier to fool people than to convince them that they have been fooled, a quote that is ironically falsely attributed to Mark Twain."

"The propaganda is so good, so polished, and the population is so conditioned, that even skeptics believe it in some form."

"Everyone believes their news source," PeacePipe said. "That they have found the one source that gets it right, the one that's telling the truth. The idea is easy to sell because they like to believe that *they* were clever and lucky enough, or smart enough, to identify the one or two remaining accurate media sources with journalistic integrity."

"Right."

"And the media that they watch constantly reenforces that idea by regularly pointing out all the mistakes and biases of the other side, the other channel."

Chase sighed. "It's always an us-against-them mentality. Keeps us looking at something other than what we should be looking at."

"If the population ever figures that out, it'll be too late."

"Why?"

"Because it's already too late."

Chase's next call was from the Astronaut. After asking about Wen, he launched into an update. "The twenty terabyte drive you found in Vegas is still eluding us, but we are close to finding the key."

"How close?"

"Maybe in a few hours. The eleven photos and the twenty pages are more promising. When we cracked the pages, we have what appears to be a complete list of shadow people. I've sent it to you, and to Blitz."

"Great, thanks. And the photos?"

"Turns out they aren't below Belfort, they are above him."

"Circuit?"

"We think so. Should be able to confirm it soon."

"Very promising."

"Yes, but at the same time we are getting close, so are they," the Astronaut warned. "Someone is bombarding us with millions of cyber-attacks a minute. Bull and Dez are handling it so far, but we may run out of time before we discover the answers."

"Why?"

"I'm afraid to say that in the technology field, as in all other areas, our enemies are stronger than us."

The two wealthy Circuit leaders were awash in covered-up footage of the events in Vegas.

"This is not how we use Skyggers!" Blanc said. "This is too much, it will leak. The people—"

"I decide what the people think!" Tane interrupted. "Traditionally, yes, Skyggers are used to create events, to manipulate them, and to make the people react in certain ways; divide them into factions, move the needle of public opinion, distract the masses with the boogie man de jour." He stopped and stared at the monitors. "That's all changed!"

"But why?"

"Perhaps we flush out Darth Vader."

"Really? This is about Vader? About who has the most power?"

"It's always about power," Tane said, as if appalled he had to explain.

Blanc sighed. "Ultimately, of course, and yet we find

ourselves in this mess. How can these amateurs be allowed to inflict this much damage? And what do we gain by going all in?" Blanc asked, horrified by everything that had happened in sin city without it even yielding a positive result. "I mean, with what's at stake, why take the risk?"

"Risk?" Tane responded as if the word was foreign to him. "There is no risk. We control everything!"

Real Truth - Internet Fact Based News

Posted by JI Right

We need new conspiracy theories; the old ones have all come true.

The authorities are trying to shut us down. We have once again had to find new servers. They raid the offices and homes of our anonymous reporters. They identify us and find our hiding places. They have technology and power you would not believe. It may be too late to win, but it is never too late to fight, to resist.

Today, more questions than answers. Ask yourself...

Why don't they want us having open discussions? Why do they need to censor?
Sure there will be liars and crazies who make up stories, but the important thing about the truth is it will always find a way.
Smart people will know the crazies are lying. But if you censor them, when does it stop? Who gets to decide?

Who benefits from us fighting amongst ourselves?
What do they want us talking about?
Instead of what? What are they distracting us from?

Look back at the controversies and stories, how easily our attention ping pongs from one thing to the other while the erosion of freedoms and theft of the treasury continues.

Focus on weapon manufacturers, pharmaceutical giants, banks.

Chapter Sixty-Six

Chase checked all the exterior monitors of the Destino while the Astronaut took another call.

"I'm back," the Astronaut announced. "That was Tu. His end of Flash-burn is set. He says the fuse is ready to light."

"Good. Coordinate with Mars, do it whether you hear from me or not."

"I don't like that talk."

"I just mean we might be in custody," Chase said, and then asked the same question he'd been asking since they made it out of Vegas. "Why is the FBI after us?"

"The charges are classified," the Astronaut said. "So far I haven't been able to get in deep enough to discover any more than that."

"I know someone who can," Chase said. "Someone who owes us a big favor."

"Whatever it is," the Astronaut said, "just remember Tess could be part of it."

"Yeah." In spite of everything they'd been through

together, including the recent events in Taos, they'd always had difficulty trusting Tess.

"The woman whose life you saved may be involved in a plot to end yours," the Astronaut cautioned. "Knowing where loyalties lie can be more difficult than dodging bullets."

Tess grimaced as she reached to push the speaker icon on her private cell phone. She had set up voice command, but kept forgetting to use it.

"We were just pursued by the FBI," Chase told her, trying not to sound angry, trying not to believe the Astronaut's warning.

"The FBI?" Tess echoed, sounding genuinely surprised. "What have you two done now?"

"We haven't done anything—at least nothing *they* should be bothering us about," Chase said.

Tess paused, realizing it was part of the same operation that was trying to kill her. Not many stood in the way of the End Game, but she did, and so did Chase and Wen.

"Tess, they were shooting at us," Chase said. "We're lucky we didn't kill any of them."

"You didn't though, did you?"

"No, but it was close. And it wasn't just a couple of agents."

"How many?"

"It's hard to know, but more than twenty."

Tess leaned forward and stifled a cry. The pain came from so many places, she couldn't pinpoint its source. She typed into the computer. "I see they have warrants out for you."

"We knew that much," Chase said. "Why?"

"We'll find out in just a second," Tess said, continuing to open windows. "This is really strange. It's saying I don't have the clearance. There must be some kind of mistake . . ."

"You don't believe that, do you?" Chase asked.

"I would have if it wasn't something to do with the two of you. That just seems a little too coincidental, and I can't see what charges they have against you. I'll call the director and get right back to you."

After the call, Chase tried to decide if he believed Tess.

We've known her a long time, he thought. *We saved her life… she sounds legitimately surprised.*

He glanced at Wen, still asleep, wondering what she would think. Then a disturbing thought hit him. *What if the shadow people that tried to kill Tess, also found a way to block her? That would mean the Circuit's power truly has no limits.*

It took longer than usual for the FBI Director to come onto the line. He was the last person she wanted to speak with, knowing he would likely be hunting for her soon.

"Tess, what can I do for you?"

"Chase Malone, Wen Sung."

"What about them?"

"Don't give me that. Why are there warrants on them?"

"Sorry Tess, that's above your clearance."

"What are you talking about? There is *nothing* above my clearance levels. They certainly exceed yours."

"Apparently not."

"We'll see about that," she said, ending the call.

Tess called her assistant and told her to get the president on the phone.

Ten minutes later, the assistant informed Tess that the president was unavailable.

"Call back. Tell them this is a Red-99 Situation."

Another fifteen minutes. "The president remains unavailable," the assistant said.

Tess nodded, no longer surprised as she called her deputy, Linda.

"The president always talks to me," Tess said. "But he doesn't want to tell me something."

"About Chase and Wen, or you?" Linda asked.

"I don't know, but clearly Chase and Wen are in real trouble. They have to know Chase and Wen will not allow themselves to be arrested."

"They know they'll fight back," Linda agreed.

"Then this isn't an arrest warrant, it's a kill order."

Chapter Sixty-Seven

Belfort glared at the images as if the dead operatives were personally killed by those seeking to destroy him—because they were. His hands clenched, hiding a slight tremble. "This threat," he muttered. "It's real. They're coming for me." However, it scared him less than it offended him. Belfort had long considered himself one of the Masters of the universe, but now he had to admit that his sense of invincibility had really only come from working for the Circuit.

Chase Malone and Wen Sung have been trying to stop me, trying to destroy me, and yet, I'm still here.

"See-saw forty-four," he said, giving the order to implement an operation that had been in the planning stages for months. There were always "events" ready, sitting, waiting, at various stages; things like refinery explosions, airplane crashes, pandemics, mass shootings at schools, at shopping centers, at workplaces, major forest fires, residential gas explosions, political scandals, Hollywood scandals, shocking news of all kinds. Each were packaged to be addicting to watch.

"Certain?" the man on the other end asked.

"Confirmed."

It's not that stories like these weren't real, it's just that they would normally occur far less frequently. Belfort knew the Circuit orchestrated many of these events as needed to distract the public, sway their opinions, keep them entertained. The final result was usually to camouflage other moves.

That's what I need, Belfort thought. *A little camouflage.*

Even when events occurred organically, the Circuit moved in to enhance them, or simply to utilize the occurrence for their own objectives.

"Never let a good crisis go to waste," he muttered after his underling was off the line. Belfort knew that often repeated quote was first attributed to Winston Churchill, but it had since become the mantra of the Circuit.

A school shooting would have been a good idea right about now, he thought, enjoying the memories of the last one. *The shock, the tears, such dramatic images. Riveting. But these are more delicate times. The tragedy I've arranged will still keep the news cycle clogged while we go to war with Chase and Wen.*

A school would still be involved. Belfort had ordered an "accidental" natural gas explosion. When it was all over and the toll was tallied, the initial blast and subsequent fire would result in the deaths of more than four hundred elementary students at P.S. 361 in New York City. Nearly a thousand more would be injured, some critically.

Even without controlling media outlets, there would be instant round-the-clock coverage, many investigations and reactive school closings all over the country.

As a result, and as usual, the Circuit's bought-and-paid-for politicians would immediately enact more restrictive measures that ultimately did little for public safety, but did fit the organization's objectives.

Less than an hour after Belfort's order, the incident occurred, and right on cue, the massive outrage began. The media companies knew how to do this; the grieving parents, the theories, the blame game, the heroes and villains.

As the news of the school explosion broke, like everyone else, Tane and Blanc watched the coverage unfold, although they also saw extra footage, unvarnished, uncensored, raw.

"Almost looks like one of ours," Blanc said, knowing they had not initiated the incident.

"It *is* one of ours," Tane said, staring at the screens, but not watching, his thoughts a thousand miles away.

"But . . . " Blanc began, confused for a moment, until it registered. "Belfort pulled this trigger?"

"Uh-huh."

"Because he still has the authority to be our middleman, but . . . why?"

"It appears our man is desperate."

"Not good." Blanc stopped short of saying, '*I told you so.*' "He should've been handled before this."

"Perhaps, but he's given us an opportunity."

"Never let a good crisis go to waste," Blanc said, "as Obama's chief of staff once said."

"It was Churchill."

"No, it was Rahm Emmanuel. I was in the Oval Office when he said it."

"I know, but he stole the line from Churchill."

Blanc didn't care if it was Charlemagne who said it. "Either way, the point is, we should send in the Skyggers."

"We'd be fools not to."

"Explode another school?" Blanc made a face, as if the idea of killing innocent children bothered him. It didn't. He considered them a commodity, like any other raw material.

"We need to amplify the situation."

"Not a real one this time."

"Oh, no, no. What a distasteful mess that would be." Tane laughed as if he cared. "We've got plenty of footage and outtakes from this one. We'll produce it, all the interviews with the grieving parents and whatnot. We'll have Bruce short the stock, might as well make some money, pay for the whole thing. He can get in a big order just prior to the second explosion in the morning. Investigators will quickly find that there is a damaged valve found to be installed at the same time as the one in that school." Tane pointed to the screen.

Blanc knew the drill. They'd done it so many times. Underlings would quickly find the site for the alleged explosion, the location of a warehouse fire six months earlier, where no school had ever been. It wouldn't matter, no authentic reporters would be allowed anywhere near the scene, so few real journalists existed anymore anyway. There would be little chance of discovery, and even if someone tried to find the actual truth instead of the Circuit's lies, they would be discredited, de-platformed, and labeled conspiracy theorists before their stories caught any traction.

"Always nice to make a profit on these things," Tane added.

"I'll find a company to blame that belongs to one of our rivals."

"A neat package. Make sure there were bribes paid to get the valves installed."

"Evan knows the way we like it to go down," Blanc said. "He's been doing these for us for more than twenty years. He did Building Seven."

"I know. Let's pin the valves originating with the Chinese."

"You always like them for a scapegoat."

"It's a necessity. We have to keep them in check. They don't play by our rules. They cheat, steal, and lie." Tane laughed again. "You can never trust a liar."

Blanc laughed, too. "Evan will see to it. Paid-off inspectors let it happen, that's our little swipe at the city government. A neat and tidy package. The media will keep the public outraged and distracted. They'll call for full safety audits of every school building at every educational level, K-12, colleges, and universities. So many opportunities for profit and drama."

"Not necessarily in that order."

Tane picked up his phone and explained everything to a voice on the other end.

"A full secondary blast, produced and ready in the morning?" the man asked, sounding a little overwhelmed, but knowing it could be pulled off.

"Do it," Tane said.

"And Belfort?" the man asked.

"Yes."

"Understood," the man said before Tane ended the call.

Tane looked at the flames on the screen and nodded slowly.

Blanc smiled.

Chapter Sixty-Eight

A fortified guard station greeted Chase and Wen at a twenty-two-acre coastal estate outside of Santa Barbara.

"You sure you're up to this?" Chase asked.

"Yes," Wen lied.

The incredible home sat on five parcels and clung to the unspoiled bluffs with unmatched views of the Pacific.

"Trouble," Wen whispered as they approached a partially open security gate.

"What?" Chase asked, scanning quickly for threats.

"It shouldn't be open . . . where are the guards?" But as she peeked inside, she realized it was worse than she thought. Wen motioned him forward with her head.

Chase looked in the direction and saw the body.

"Someone got here first," Wen whispered while stepping over the dead man.

"Who?" Chase asked as they encountered two more bloody victims.

"My guess is shadow people." She took a machine gun off one of the bodies. "Still bleeding. Fresh kill."

"If it's shadow people, why would they be killing Belfort's security?" Chase asked. "Because we're getting too close?"

"Probably," Wen said as they made their way cautiously to the mansion. "Someone in the higher echelon of the Circuit is afraid our friend Belfort is going to talk."

"Well that's good news. They know him better than we do, and if they think he'll talk, maybe he'll tell us—"

"Only if he's still alive. Dead men can't talk."

They moved along the hedges. Wen remembered the ambushes of the past, how many times she and Chase had been up against surprise attacks of a dozen or more shadow people. *They always send more than they need. How many are inside?* she wondered.

"We have to get to Belfort in time," Chase said as they found three more dead men near the front door.

Wen looked at their injuries. "It hasn't been long," she whispered. In that instant, she realized she and Chase would've had to kill these men if someone else hadn't done it first. The deaths always weighed on her. She felt no less responsible for these than if she had pulled the trigger herself.

The sound of gunshots brought her back. She and Chase bolted inside the open front door. A full-scale gun battle raged inside. More bodies were scattered about. They joined the fighting.

"How do we know who's who?" Chase said through gritted teeth.

"Doesn't matter. In order for us to get to Belfort, they are all going to have to die."

The foyer of the opulent beach home was not nearly as elaborately decked-out as some of Belfort's previous dwellings, but its main feature still provided a strategic advantage for the shooters already in the house. Sweeping staircases went up to another floor, linked by a bridge that appeared carved from a tree-sized chunk of driftwood. Up there was the million-dollar view of the Pacific. Both grand staircases also descended into a lower level that opened to lavish gardens.

Chase and Wen donned gas masks as she tossed in tear gas and colored smoke to "soften" their opponents. Minutes later, the carnage ended. Chase found himself on the lower level facing a locked door.

"I think I found our target," he said into his comms. "He's probably hiding under the bed."

"Be right down," Wen responded after finding no one left alive on the upper floor."

Chase kicked in the door and discovered a man pointing a pistol at him from behind a sofa.

"It's Belfort!" Chase yelled after checking the photo on his wrist tablet.

Belfort fired five rounds before disappearing. Chase was well into the large room by the time Wen arrived.

"There!" Wen pointed to a hall opening off the far side of the room.

"Damn!" Chase snapped, spotting the French doors in the hallway that Belfort had escaped through.

"He's running into the trees!"

From her brief time upstairs, Wen knew there was nothing between them and the ocean except trees, rocks, and cliffs.

"What kind of gun did he have?" she asked Chase as they pursued him.

"How should I know?"

"He shot at you with it, didn't he?"

"Yeah, that's why I didn't stop and study it."

Wen fired several shots. Belfort dove to the ground. By the time he recovered, they were there. He unloaded the rest of his gun.

"It's a Ruger LCP, standard seven plus one. Poor choice, and now you're out of bullets, Belfort."

"You've got the wrong guy."

"Shut up," Wen barked, pointing her MP7 at his head.

Chase checked again. "It's him."

"What a coward," Wen said. "For more than two years, you've sent countless people to assassinate us, and I've had to kill them all. So. Many. Deaths."

He shook his head. "Listen, that wasn't me. I didn't order anything."

"That's not true. Now I'm going to kill you unless you tell us who you work for. Who is your contact at the Circuit? Where do we find them?"

"I can't tell you."

With Chase covering, Wen, slung her gun across her back and grabbed Belfort by his collar. "You tell us, *now!*" She slammed him back onto the ground.

"You won't kill me," he said. "You need my information too badly."

"What are we going to do?" Chase asked. "I mean, we don't have a jail we could stick him in."

"Oh, we'll build a jail," Wen said. "A crummy little concrete cell on a cold little island far from anything, and we'll keep him there, starving, suffering, freezing, until he talks. I don't care if it takes years."

Chase couldn't tell if Wen was being serious, but Belfort was right. They needed to do deep interrogation on him, and this wasn't the place. Chase pulled out zip ties, ready to cuff him.

Belfort looked at Wen. "As soon as you take me out of here, I'm as good as dead. I have some information you need, but I need something, too."

"What?" Wen asked, disgusted, wanting so badly to kill him, even knowing it wouldn't end her nightmares.

"Money. Ten million in Bitcoin. Another ten million in a numbered account."

"Give us something now. We need proof that you have information worth twenty million."

He got half a syllable out before his head blew apart.

"Sniper!" Wen screamed.

They both hit the ground. The bullets kept coming.

Real Truth - Internet Fact Based News

Posted by JI Right

We have several sources confirming that the NoLiv virus originated in Israel. It was not accidentally created, but intentionally fused with AI to create the international crisis.
Astaria, a former Mossad agent, claims she has been inside secret computer labs in remote areas of Israel and others in Morocco where the origins of NoLiv can be found.
She, and others, have traced REMEDY to those same labs. Virus and cure developed together.
"Remedy was not made to counter the virus. Remedy is the virus," Astaria stated. "The whole crisis was fabricated so that Remedy could be forced upon everyone."
To be clear, she is not saying that the virus didn't do great damage. She is saying that it did what it was intended to do—damage, instill fear, and foster obedience.

"We are told Remedy must be installed," Astaria went on to say. "And the public doesn't realize that once installed, Remedy gives the government access to all their files: photos, mail, phone calls, browsing history, even what is deleted, even if your device is not connected to the cloud."
We have documents showing Remedy gives full and easy access to every computer, tablet, smart watch, and smart phone in the world. They have set up giant facilities to monitor and record all of this information in real time.
"The most dangerous aspect of this," Astaria warned, "is that they can also create, insert, and change the data on your device."
We have also begun to identify those who are responsible.
Bill Doorset, Haris Tane (aka the Maestro), Timothy Blanc, Maxim Miner (aka the Judge), and there are many others.
A full list of what we've been able to compile will be posted to this site later today, including the identity of a man so dangerous he is known as Darth Vader.

We will also have an exposé detailing the exploits of two ultra-secret groups known as the Regulators and the Skyggers.

Chapter Sixty-Nine

Three thousand miles away, in another mansion, Whitley and Belfort watched the man Chase had thought was Belfort die.

"I took a page from their playbook," Belfort said, still watching the footage, proud his body-double had fooled them and not caring in the least that the man was dead. "Chase and Wen think they killed me!"

"The sniper was a nice addition," Whitley said, touching his leg.

"Not part of my plan."

"Yeah, well."

He was confused for a moment, but let it go. "Anyway, I survived, and they think I'm dead. Problem solved."

She kissed him, more passionately than before. It was the most incredible kiss he'd ever imagined. He had to have her.

"How about some drinks to celebrate?" she said.

He nodded. "Yes, please!"

"I'll be right back."

He was still nodding while she headed to a bathroom. As soon as she was out of sight, he barked for the butler.

"Yes, sir?"

"We need drinks. I'll have a gin and tonic, and get Whitley whatever it is that she normally drinks."

"Which is what, sir?"

"I don't know, you idiot, that's *your* job."

"Well that's an amusing turn of words," the butler replied. "Ms. Whitley doesn't drink, and with all my time waiting on you, Belfort, today is the first day I actually *like* my job."

"Why's that?" he asked impatiently. "Wait, if she doesn't drink, then why—"

The first bullet hit his thigh. The second hit his other thigh. His screams, high pitched whines, were like an animal being tortured in the wild. "My god, you shot me! You piece of—"

The next bullet hit him in the abdomen. He clutched his stomach as blood spilled through his fingers.

"The Circuit is finished with you, you rude, *racist* little man," the butler said. "Thank you for your service."

Belfort went white. He shook his head and stared bitterly at his killer. "The damned butler . . . I should have known . . . It's always the butler who does it."

"True, that is often the case," the butler said, firing again. This time the bullet hit Belfort's mouth. "Enjoy your lemonade in hell."

Once inside the Destino, Wen collapsed back into bed, exhausted. She didn't tell Chase one of her wounds had started bleeding again. She quickly fell asleep.

While the driver headed to a secluded piece of coastline, Chase called Mars.

The images of burning children and the tortured faces of parents filled the screens. Contrary to what the media was reporting, SEER analysis had suggested the school explosion was an intentional act.

"Flash-Burn is ready," Mars said. "One final chance to say goodbye, or change your mind."

"Go with full initiation," Chase said bitterly. "All flags flying, all guns blazing. End these bastards."

It started small at first, what a falling domino of global catastrophe would look like. Half a dozen blue-chip stocks simultaneously fell five percent from their daily highs. Within minutes it was twelve percent off, then the momentum kicked in. Top tier companies plunged between six and eight percent more. At that point, some shoppers appeared, bargain-hunting and buying the dip. But it wasn't enough. Those unfortunate amateurs had no idea of the storm that had been programmed against them.

Soon leading equities crashed nearly twenty-five percent. The thundering stampede of funds exiting those stocks turned into an avalanche and took the rest of the market with them.

Chase accepted a non-video call from the Astronaut as the Destino pulled into a parking area near where Chase had instructed the driver to take them.

"I sure hope you cracked the codes," Chase said while

checking the exterior monitors, something Wen would be doing if she were awake.

"It's not computer code," the Astronaut said. "How is Wen?"

"Asleep. What is it, then?"

"Tu figured it out. It's a roll of sequential numbers that change when they are plugged into certain instruments. Is she going to make it? I want to know the truth."

"She's just sleeping. So it *is* a code."

"A code, yes, but not computer code. This is the most sophisticated manipulative working cypher I've ever encountered. Why are you avoiding my question? Your evasiveness regarding Wen indicates that you are concealing the truth about her condition."

"What is a sophisticated manipulative whatever you said?"

"I'm surprised with all your programming experience you are not familiar," he replied. "The program was built to adapt. That would have been pre-AI, but now with AI, its capabilities are nearly infinite. Are you taking her back to the hospital?"

"No. That's her decision. What does the program do?"

"It does the whole game," he said.

"Game?"

"The program does the entire financial system. This is how the Circuit does it."

"What?" Chase asked.

"Robs us."

"You know how it's rigged?"

"Yes. There is no way for the average person to ever win. They're running a feudal system."

"Where are they?"

"That we don't know yet, but with the crash, they should be showing themselves any minute."

"The code thing—"

"It's called a siphon."

"Yeah, the siphon," Chase amended. "Can you use it to crumble their companies faster than what Mars is doing?"

"I believe that is the case, but there are risks."

"Such as?" He wandered back to check on Wen.

"The siphon is the system. If we destroy it, there will be nothing left. I mean *nothing*. It will be like living in caveman times."

"Survival of the fittest."

"Yes. Wen better be okay."

Chase looked at her battered body and hoped the same thing.

Chapter Seventy

Chase waited while Tess wheeled her way toward him from the helicopter. She had requested the meeting at the last minute. Wen couldn't be there; she needed to sleep. If she woke up before he returned, she'd be busy coordinating with Blitz and Mars as they readied phase two, a full deployment of the Terminators and the criminals.

Four armed women stood guard around the area.

"You've gotten good at the chair," Chase said, pointing to her high-tech ride.

"It's not permanent," she said, as if offended. "It's mostly automatic, quite sophisticated . . . but only for four of five more weeks."

"Good."

Tess looked out at the ocean, the sun reflecting off thousands of points in the water, gulls in a frenzy, their cries blending with the pounding waves. "It's like a lullaby," she said.

"It's not Taos," Chase said, standing next to her.

"No . . . Taos is in my heart, but I wish I could stay at

this beach. It would be a good place to heal, to devise a way to survive the world that's coming."

"We need to change that," Chase said, touching her shoulder.

"I wonder if that's really even possible anymore."

"I need the truth about Turkey."

She inhaled deeply, taking in the salt air and its calming properties. "Turkey never said they were keeping the nukes," Tess said. "It was all done with deep fake videos."

"They've advanced too far with that technology," Chase said. "Can't believe anything you see anymore."

"Especially when they control the media. Six companies control more than ninety percent of everything the public watches, listens to, and reads. Who controls those six companies?"

"The Circuit?"

She nodded. "That's another conversation. The nukes were meant for Iran."

"I don't understand… why didn't the US give the nukes to Iran in the first place if that's what they wanted?"

"The nukes are all accounted for and kept track of—people tend to do that with things that can destroy the world. They needed a smokescreen, and like with everything the Circuit does, it all gets down to money and power."

"Still, it doesn't make sense."

"The complexities of the moves are difficult to break down. It's one of the reasons they are so successful and never get caught. They make these interweaving decisions and movements that play out with ramifications all calculated to the last move."

"So you're saying I can't understand?"

"I don't even understand, and I get the briefings." She

laughed, but it quickly changed to a different sound, something like choking, before it passed. "People wonder why it's gotten so much worse in the last ten years, and even before that . . . "

"It's technology," Chase said.

"Exactly. Computers ushered in far more abilities for them to control and manipulate. Then the Internet gave them immense power to track, control, and manipulate. Finally, artificial intelligence . . . " She looked accusingly at Chase. "Now with advanced AI, they can see far more. Every chess move is played out into infinity, so they know what the results will be, and they take the actions leading to the most reward for the Circuit."

"So they decide to transfer a series of nukes, and they can see what will happen."

"Yes. And when you think about it, what is *really* fascinating, they probably didn't *start* with the idea of moving nukes. Maybe they simply wanted to take over another company or sell a few billion dollar's worth of weapons, but to achieve those objectives, the AI tells them to do this or that. One thing leads to another, and ultimately their programs tell them if Iran would acquire nuclear weapons, then Israel would do this, and the United States would do that, troops would be sent in here, sanctions would be implemented there, governments would fall over there, and on and on . . . each step leading to another until the action is taken. Turkey leaves NATO even though they never wanted to. It's frightening in its efficiency, and how it can never be undone."

"And now with deep fakes, it's like a giant video game that they play," Chase added. "One where they create the events, then just broadcast them over the Internet or across the media they control. They show the public both sides, sway them into what to think with slogans and fake stories."

"And it all looks so real, but none of it ever happened."

"That's why it feels like we've been chasing lies."

"Because you have," Tess said. "And not just you. Everyone in the world is chasing lies. The only ones not chasing lies are the ones at the top, the very few who pull the levers and push the buttons to make it all happen. That may be the scariest part of all. Only the Circuit knows what the real reality is anymore."

"And even some of them may be duped by their own creations," Chase said. "Frankenstein's monster."

"Exactly," Tess said. "It may already be out of their control."

Chapter Seventy-One

Tess gave the pilot the signal by making a twirling sign with her finger. The helicopter started up again.

"So what about you?" Chase asked. "What now?"

"I'm going to disappear for a while," Tess said. "They'll kill me otherwise."

"I've never known you to run from a fight."

"It's not a fight when your enemy is the Circuit, it's a burial."

"I've got an army. I can keep you safe."

"Thanks, but that army is for a different purpose than keeping me safe. You're going to need everything you've got."

"Money? Are you all right with money?"

"I've got resources. I've known this was coming for a long time, did everything I could to avoid it, but knew those odds against us were big. I'll be okay."

He looked at her, the woman he'd shared so much with —life and death and back again. She looked somehow less invincible than before. Maybe it was just the casts, cuts, and bruises, but there was something in her eyes, something bordering on fear, yet laced with sadness.

"You *sure* you're okay?"

"I wanted to see you in person to say goodbye," she said, ignoring his question. "But it was also the safest way to give you this." She handed him a small, business card size envelope.

"What's this?" he asked, flipping it over, noticing it was sealed.

"Instructions." She paused, gave him a hard look, one he'd seen from her before. It expressed danger, uncertainty, like a parent giving a teenager car keys for their first solo drive on a Friday night. "If you really want to continue this, to go down the rabbit hole, I mean take it *all* the way . . . "

"I have to."

She nodded, not surprised. "Then this is where you need to go."

"Do I open it now?"

"It's self-explanatory." Clearly she preferred he *didn't*. He opened it anyway.

"These are directions to a cabin in the woods?"

"Yes."

"Seems ironic, doesn't it? That after all these years, the answer to all of this high-tech war, killings, conspiracies, and everything else, would all end in a cabin in the woods."

"It never ends," she said.

"Yeah."

She studied him. "Wen is going to think it's a trap."

"Is it?"

"You should be beyond asking that, Chase. But I'll allow it this last time." She glared at him, as if she might suddenly burst into tears. Of course, she did not. "But never again!"

They were silent for a few long minutes.

"I know how they find people," she finally said, "and they are never going to find me."

"Wen and I tried to disappear."

"I told you the secret, years ago. If you don't move, they can't see you. If you don't go out to play, they can't see you. Stay out of the system, out of anything digital, and you're free."

"Not free while all this is going on, none of us are."

She looked at him and smiled. "I learned that before you were born." Tess motioned for him to lean down, then hugged him. "Stay alive," she whispered in his ear. "Make sure you don't screw that up."

Chase watched as her helicopter flew away, expecting it to explode into a fireball at any moment, but it didn't. It just faded into a small black speck in the distance over the ocean until he could see it no more.

His phone vibrated. A text from PeacePipe: **In trouble. Two names. The Maestro. Darth Vader. Two groups. Skyggers. Regulators. Unveil them and you will have your answers.**

Where are you? Chase texted back while returning to the Destino.

No response.

Do you know the identities?

No response.

Are you okay?

Chase forwarded the texts to the Astronaut, and asked him to look into the four names and to track the location of PeacePipe's phone. "If you find him, have Blitz send a team."

Inside the truck, Wen was still asleep. He checked the news. The major networks and cable outlets were playing down the turmoil and financial calamities occurring across the globe.

The alternative sites, however, were warning of a complete collapse of the system, food shortages, and potential anarchy.

Maybe I should have listened to Mars and the Astronaut.
Maybe we pushed too hard.

Chapter Seventy-Two

Wen had slept for sixteen hours. Unbeknownst to Chase, beforehand, she'd restitched the worst of her wounds.

"You look good," he lied. He wasn't sure they should continue, but they were so close.

"Thanks," she said, even though she knew he was lying. "You still have some blue and white paint on your neck."

He self-consciously rubbed his neck, having no doubt he'd missed a lot of the paint. "Are you ready for this meeting?"

"Yes." Her voice was firm. Wen was always ready, so he didn't know she was also lying.

Just prior to her waking up, he'd received word that PeacePipe was dead. Shadows, or someone else, had gotten to him. His phone, laptop, and whatever other electronics he'd had on him were gone. Chase hadn't told Wen yet. There would be time after the meeting.

The two biggest alternative news sites were down. Their founders had disappeared, likely not by choice. Militarized police departments were combatting rioters and looters in more than two hundred cities and towns across the US. The same was happening worldwide. Chase glossed over these details. They hardly mattered, at least for the moment.

A cool breeze blew. Leaves, still clinging to their branches, fluttered like prayer flags. Others, already brown and lost, swirled across the forest floor. Wen surveyed the area, holding her MP7 as if it were a shield, a Glock 19 ready at her side. "I don't like it," she said again. "It's too quiet."

Chase stared into the distance, searching for the trouble that she sensed. His intuition, not as finely tuned as hers, was certainly on alert. He'd learned to rely on Wen's feelings more than his own during situations like this. "What do you want to do?"

"Leave."

"We can't leave," he said. They both knew the stakes were too high. This might be their only chance to discover who was behind the Circuit.

"But we should."

Chase nodded, trying to recall any other details that Tess had provided.

"There," Wen whispered loudly. "Ten o'clock."

He looked up ahead to his left and saw a small cabin, a stone chimney adding to its picturesque setting.

"There should be a fire burning," she said.

"Yeah," he agreed, noticing there was no smoke coming from the chimney. "It's certainly cold enough for a fire."

"I don't see any other heat sources." As they got closer, Wen motioned toward a small, open-sided woodshed, filled with split firewood neatly stacked to the ceiling. She studied it carefully. It was a place she might hide for an ambush. Satisfied it was empty, they continued to the cabin.

"Strange place for a meeting," Chase repeated Wen's earlier concerns.

"Heavy wooden door," Wen said, deciding if she would shoot it apart. "Appears well-milled."

Walking slowly in a wide circle around the cabin, they noted every potential weakness. "The windows are covered with some kind of opaque sheeting... I can't see inside."

They found the back door equally sturdy. It was time to enter. She scanned the trees one last time and saw nothing unusual.

"The canopy is so thick," she said. "It bothers me."

Back at the front door, Wen raised her gun. Even the heaviest of wood would splinter and fall apart against the MP7.

"Shouldn't we just knock?" Chase asked. "Or maybe . . . " He tried the knob. It turned.

Wen moved in front of him and pushed the door open with her foot. She grimaced in pain from one of her many injuries. Chase missed it.

The well-lit interior smelled of cinnamon and apples. Wen's finger held steady, resting on the trigger, awaiting the nerve impulse from her brain; an instant beat, the nano transmission and micro flick of her finger would send forty rounds into the small space in less than three seconds, destroying any living thing unlucky enough to be caught in the line of fire.

Her finger, expecting the pulse, twitched, ready to exercise the muscle memory of thousands of situations like this one. Wen knew a firefight was waiting as she stepped inside. Her eyes darted a hundred miles per hour, seeing in every direction, looking for every hiding spot, calculating every angle. It all occurred in an instant, her expert gaze taking it all in.

And yet, she found nothing.

Wen swallowed her apprehension and fear. "Empty," she said, keeping the submachine gun ready.

Chase lowered his Beretta. "It could still be a trap."

"Of course it could still be a trap," she said, now studying the furnishings more closely—a leather sofa, a couple of oversized leather chairs. They looked comfortable. Behind that, a large, handmade stone fireplace, logs cross-stacked inside, waiting for a match. In one corner, a small kitchen, separated by heavy slabs of polished wood serving as a counter. On the other end, near the back door, was a bed covered with a blue and white quilt. Wen thought it seemed like an afterthought, and may have never been used.

Chase shivered. "It's freezing in here."

"That's out of place," Wen said, pointing to a small table in the center of the room. A computer and large monitor sat on the glass top. "What is it?"

Chase, being the computer tech, walked to it. "My department."

"Careful," she hissed.

"It's modern," he said, examining it. "Too modern." Before his fingers could touch the keyboard, the screen lit up.

"Hello Chase," a male voice said. "Hello Wen. Thank you for coming."

Real Truth - Internet Fact Based News

Error 404. Site could not be found.

Chapter Seventy-Three

Wen whirled around looking for cameras, aiming her MP7 at every corner. "They see us!"

"Yes, I do," the voice replied.

"That's an excellent AI generated voice," Chase said.

"Chase, Wen. I'm, of course, not surprised you brought weapons, but you won't be needing them here."

Wen continued checking the room.

"No need to worry," the voice said, "we are alone."

"Who is we?" Wen snapped. "I don't see anyone else here."

"My friends, you must agree, these are dangerous times. We need to be extra careful. I'm sure you understand."

"We are not your friends. We don't understand," Wen said, still searching for cameras. "Who are you?"

Chase, checking the computer more closely, decided it was an extremely sophisticated machine. He noted custom power cables leading into it. "How is it getting power?" he asked. "I saw no solar panels, heard no generator. This far out in the middle of nowhere, there are no electric utility lines."

"Things are never quite as they appear. You should know this by now, with all you have been through."

Suddenly, videos seemingly came from everywhere, the room filling with projections of news stories. They were barraged with images of assassinations, wars, student demonstrations, mass shootings, killings, and more disturbing events.

"Do you know what all these had in common?" the voice asked.

"They are all biased stories," Chase said.

The voice laughed.

The response surprised them. "Computers don't laugh," Chase said.

"Don't they?" the voice asked. "But that's a topic for another time. Right now you need to answer my question about the news stories. Your first guess was incorrect."

"We're not here for games." Wen said.

"Ah, Wen, your answer is much, much closer, but still not enough for the $64,000."

Wen, annoyed, crouched next to the computer and examined it as if it were her enemy. Using the position as cover, she took another visual sweep around the room.

"Allow me to tell you the reason you are nearer to the truth," the voice began again, seemingly unaware of Wen's maneuverings, or not caring. "In some ways, it is a game. An insidious and calculated game that they are playing."

"Who?" Chase asked.

"The correct answer," the voice said, ignoring Chase. "All of those news stories are false. Instead, they are fabricated to create a narrative that will result in a specific outcome."

"Wait a minute," Chase said, "I remember almost all of those stories. I don't believe you."

"And that proves the depth to which even you, a skeptical, intelligent, cynical person, has been compromised, propagandized, corrupted."

"It is possible I am many things," Chase argued. "But I am not corrupt."

"Are you that naïve to believe what you just said?" the voice asked. "You have very much been corrupted. You are simply unaware it has happened."

"How are you so sure?"

Wen paced in front of the windows, then slowly raised one of the shades and peered out.

"It is what they do. They broaden their conspiracy by unwittingly involving you."

"How?"

"By getting you to perpetuate the lie."

Chase, beginning to feel as if he were in some mad man's version of the Wizard of Oz, was growing impatient. "I don't lie."

"But you do, every day, when you *interpret* the news and debate current events with colleagues, friends, family. You are repeating and authenticating the fabrications. You legitimize the lies."

Chase shook his head.

"The people you are looking for know your every move. They know everything. They know what positions you will take on any given subject and they know equally how your friends and colleagues will respond. By controlling events in the news, they control you."

"Get to the point."

"Was the virus real? The events in Turkey? The school explosions?"

"No," Chase said, partially based on what he knew, a little of what he'd learned in the cabin, and the rest realizing that maybe most of what he thought he knew was a lie.

"You're learning," the voice said. "There is always a little truth in the best lies. The politicians and bankers know this well, but it is the experts in the media that make everyone believe."

"Why do they do this? What do they want?"

"As is often the case, the answers are contained in the question."

The voice paused. Chase wondered if the program was rebooting. Had they suddenly stumped the AI? Wen pointed to Chase, and then at the front door, then aimed her MP7 at the back door. As instructed, Chase covered the front.

However, no attack materialized. Instead the voice continued. "They control the events, they control what you see, and they control your responses to it, because . . . It. Is. All. About. Control. That's what they want, to control everything. And that's what they do."

Chapter Seventy-Four

Wen sneered at the computer, as if it were a real person. "Why should we trust you?"

"You should *not* trust me," the voice responded. "You should not even trust yourself. Because you have been propagandized so long and so efficiently that you can no longer trust your own mind and its responses."

"This is ridiculous," Wen said. "He just told us that we shouldn't believe him." She looked over and gave Chase a *'let's get out of here'* look.

"I did not say you should not *believe* me, I simply advised you not to *trust* me," the voice said.

"What's the difference?"

"The difference is you should believe the information, since you know it is true."

"How do we know that?"

"You know because trusting your instincts is all you have left. Your intuition tells you that I am telling the truth."

She frowned. "These people you're talking about . . .

what you're telling us about their abilities, their motives, their intentions . . . how do we know *any* of that is real?"

A man stepped out into the open, seemingly from thin air. "Because I am one of them," the man said in a real-life version of the computer's voice.

Wen spun and pointed her gun at the man.

"Your guns don't work here, Wen. Put it down."

She stepped closer, keeping the gun aimed at his head.

"Well then, if you insist on keeping it pointed at me… go ahead and pull the trigger."

"Chase, anyone else?" Wen asked, never taking her eyes off the man.

"All clear," Chase said, waving his gun toward the doors and windows.

"If you are afraid to pull the trigger, then put it down," the man said firmly, still smiling.

"Not going to happen," Wen said.

Chase studied the African American man, sensing something familiar about him, but before he could ask, the man suddenly produced a pistol and aimed it at Wen. Without hesitation, she pulled the trigger. Eight rounds exited in a rapid burst, but the bullets arced wide, missing their target.

Stunned she had missed, Wen's mind told her finger to fire again, but in the same instant, the MP7 flew out of her hands.

The man smiled and tossed his gun into the air; it also went zinging toward a corner. "I told you, guns are no good here."

Wen looked at him incredulously and pulled her Glock. Instantly, it was wrenched from her grip by a seemingly magical force and followed the other weapons through the air, disappearing in another corner.

"It's all done with magnets," he said. "You can't trust anything." He stepped back from the spot from where he'd first appeared and vanished again, then waved his hand while the rest of his body remained invisible. "I was here the whole time. You just couldn't see me, because you didn't believe anyone was in the cabin."

Wen shook her head, still uncertain.

"I say cabin, but in fact, we're not really in a cabin at all. We're not even in the woods. Nothing about this scene is real." He snapped his fingers. Suddenly, the entire cabin disappeared, and they were standing in the open woods. "We can create reality, decide what is real, and you . . . believe what you see." He snapped his fingers again. All the trees disappeared, and they found themselves in the middle of a vast field.

"What's going on?" Chase asked, totally disorientated.

"We're on a soundstage, and all of this has been created—"

"By magnets," Wen said. "Magnets, smoke, and mirrors."

"Now, you're catching on," he said.

Suddenly, hundreds of soldiers charged at them. Helicopter gunships surfaced on the horizon. Wen searched frantically for where her guns had gone.

"Relax," the man said in a soothing voice. "Although it appears we are under attack, and our deaths are imminent, you should know by now, it's all make believe. If I snap my fingers, it will all vanish."

The soldiers stormed closer.

"Snap your damned fingers, then!" Wen yelled, but the loud engines and whopping rotors from the helicopters drowned out her voice. Now positive they'd fallen into a trap, that the man was lying, and they were about to perish, Wen lunged toward Chase. "We have to get out of here!"

Chapter Seventy-Five

The invasion closed in so fast they could not move. The shouts, the hum and buzz of the machines coming at them. The smell of sulfur, diesel, and sweat. *It's over!* Wen thought, suddenly feeling weaker than she could recall feeling before.

"See!" the man shouted. "And believe!"

It all vanished. Once again, they found themselves in the empty field.

"Wen, do you now understand that you cannot even trust yourself?" the man asked. "Not what you see, not what you hear?"

He snapped his fingers again, instantly returning them to the cabin, but now there was a fire in the fireplace. It felt warm, even cozy.

Wen, furious at being played, but grateful to still be alive, turned to the man. "These people that you are a part of, how many are there?"

"Presently, there are forty-eight of us, but the number is constantly changing."

"Changing how?" Wen asked. "As more get invited to

join your little club? Or is it an inheritance thing? Rich families? What?"

The man smiled. "They die. Some by natural causes, others by more sinister means, and new ones rise through the billionaire ranks, accumulate the requisite wealth, power, connections, then develop insatiable lust for more of those things. They are human, so . . . well, allegedly human. Power corrupts, and most humans already possess a burning desire for control."

"This group, does it have a name?" she asked.

"Oddly enough, no. As I said, it's not really an organized club. The participants aren't always friendly with each other. In fact, quite the opposite. Most of the time they are ruthlessly competing with one another."

"Sounds like a sweet bunch of guys," Chase said.

"No," the man said gravely. "They are not. And you two have stumbled into the middle of a war. It's long been anticipated, but many wanted to avoid it—kind of how the world's nuclear powers abstain from war with each other because of that mutually assured destruction thing."

"But now they don't care about destroying each other?" Wen asked.

He shook his head. "We're in the End Game now. A few of them are making a run at the top spot."

"And that's new?"

"There's never been one person in total control before."

"But you're one of them," Wen said.

He nodded.

"That means you are our enemy."

"It's complicated, but Tess sent you here because I am actually your only hope."

Wen studied him. She had never had more difficulty

reading a person. Her training told her not to trust him, but her gut said otherwise.

"I told you we don't have a name," the man continued. "However, conspiracy theorists and writers have, over the years, coined a few terms for us: the Illuminati, the Aylantik Foundation, Omnia, and there are others . . . 'Remies' is the one I use."

"Remies?"

"They are not one cohesive organization working as one. Although Remies share a common goal to control everything."

"Rule the world?"

He smiled. "Yes, an ambition as old as humanity."

"But is it really possible?" Chase asked.

"Remies use what we refer to as MADE events. The acronym stands for *Manipulate and Distract Everyone*."

"It's all lies and propaganda?"

"Most of it. Wars, riots, scandals, natural disasters, financial meltdowns, pandemics, mass shootings, terror attacks, anything. It doesn't matter if the things occur naturally, or are completely contrived. Remies will use them to consolidate wealth and power."

"The virus is just the latest example," Wen said.

"Yes, but the most important thing they do is a trick used every day by the media called SAD: *Scare, Agitate, Divide*. Everything is a battle. Every crisis is politicized. Fifty years ago, we all got along. Now it's all tribalized. Us versus them."

"The Remies are winning," Chase said.

"Constantly," the man agreed. "Overwhelmingly."

"Then the Circuit, the group who sent the shadow people, are the Remies?" Wen asked.

"Yes, the Circuit is the most powerful block of Remies,

and they are extremely dangerous—but you already knew that part."

Chase suddenly clapped his hands. "I've finally figured out how I know you," Chase said. "You're Booker Lipton."

The man, perhaps the wealthiest human alive, smiled. "Guilty as charged. Although, many of my enemies call me Darth Vader."

Chapter Seventy-Six

Booker, Chase, and Wen met at a more traditional location several days later. The three of them were aware they needed to form an alliance. Although Chase and Wen entered the discussions reluctantly, they saw great advantage in working with someone from the inside, and tapping his enormous wealth and resources.

"This war between the Remies," Booker began as they strolled in a forest of Redwoods on the Northern California coast. "It has been anticipated for decades. You have to understand that these men are seriously conspiring to control the world."

"They seem to be running things already," Chase had said, in awe of the magnificent trees. Booker had told them he occasionally held important meetings among the giants, noting how they offered a type of spiritual safety and also granted a special kind of perspective.

"The Remies may seem in charge, yet they are not really there yet. The world is big and complex, difficult to hold," Booker said. "Some Remies have considerable power, but they are also competing with each other. Think of it as how some countries are more powerful than others. Some, like the US, have immense influence, but there is also China, Russia, other competitors. Now think of one world government. That's what the Remies are after—one king, behind the scenes, running the show."

"So it's a bigger deal than just some rich guys fighting over a larger slice of the pie."

"A lot bigger," Booker said. "These people look at everyone else as pawns, as disposable sheep. Haris Tane views the earth as a farm. He once told me, 'The masses are no different than any other animal. They are here for us to use.' He went on to say, 'Half of them are below average intelligence, a considerable number are barely above average —they are a herd. The ones possessing a little more intelligence are better consumers, a bit more useful as generators of wealth, which is simply another resource for us to mine.'"

"Nice," Wen said sarcastically.

"The goal of most Remies is to transfer any private wealth generated into their hands. They do this through the public filter; mainly taxation, income, sales, and other taxes. For decades, they've also used the invisible tax called inflation."

"You can judge a man by the company he keeps," Wen said. "Your fellow Remies are evil."

"Like you, I am fighting them, only my methods are different."

"So it's a who-can-take-it-all competition between the Remies?" Chase asked.

"First and foremost, it is them, the Remies, above all others, enriching themselves as a group. But now, the evolution of their policies and manipulations, SAD and MADE events, have taken the world to the brink, to a point where they each see the possibility of total control. So they are at war with each other. They are called the CapWars. Many thought that would be years from now, but it is happening now."

"And who will win?" Chase asked.

"There are a group of serious contenders: Titus Coyne, Haris Tane, others."

"You?"

"Yes," Booker said. "But I aim to win. Not for my own enrichment, but to prevent society from slipping into a dystopian world."

"Really?" Wen said. "And what will you do instead if you win?"

"Change everything. End the pursuits of greed, teach people to let go of fear, to unlock the great untapped human potential. Find our place in the stars, seek enlightenment, see how far our minds can take us, return to the authentic place of our souls."

"And why should we trust you?"

He looked over at her benevolently. "I thought we already established that you should not."

"Then?" she pressed.

"I will show you," he said, sounding as if he were about to unveil something magical. "The keys to the kingdom, an item so extraordinary you will forever know."

"What is it?" Wen asked, skeptically.

"A piece of truly remarkable technology unlike anything you have ever seen before."

"That's unlikely," Chase said. "But even if you have something fantastic, how will it convince us?"

"Because it will allow you a glimpse into the future."

Chase thought of his secret AI program, SEER, and assumed it was something similar.

Booker summoned a man they had not noticed before. He approached and withdrew a basketball-sized sphere from a black case. "It is called an Eysen."

Chase and Wen spoke about it later. The Eysen, a kind of crystal ball, had projected incredible images, shown them several possible futures. The technology seemed many decades, even centuries, ahead of anything Chase had ever imagined, but they remained unsure.

"Booker, by his own admission, is a Remie," Wen reminded Chase often. "He is probably just using us to win the war with the other Remies."

"Can there be such a thing as a good Remie?" Chase asked.

"I don't know… seems unlikely. Power corrupts."

"What about the space guy, who makes electric cars?"

"Is he a Remie?" she asked.

"He was on the list."

"If there *is* a good one, he's probably it."

"What about the founder of AweSum?"

"He's on the list. Could be good, pretending to be bad."

"Like Booker?" Chase asked.

"Maybe. We'll just have to tread lightly, see where the road takes us."

"One day we might have to kill Booker Lipton."

Wen sighed. "On any given day, we might have to kill anyone."

Epilogue

For more than a week, the economy spun out of control from operation Flash-burn, until the government-imposed Martial law and was able to rein in the crisis through stimulus, money printing, regulations, and temporarily taking ownership of more than eighty too-big-to-fail corporations.

The economic catastrophe was blamed on the NoLiv virus, which officials declared had originated in Russia. Sanctions were being imposed.

JI Right, or whoever was behind RealTruth, disappeared. All records and past posts from the site also vanished. Dozens of other alternative news websites were taken down, their staffs prosecuted under newly enacted disinformation statutes enforced by the Department of Homeland Security.

A special fact-checking commission was established to determine what was true and what was not. Through this "truth initiative" the government assumed full control of communications—television, cable, radio, satellite, and internet. This was done in the interest of creating a more peaceful and harmonious society.

"Never let a good crisis go to waste."

More than a third of the Remies were destroyed. However, Tane, Blanc, and many others were too resourceful and powerful to fall easily. Although they suffered huge financial losses, these ruthless men had contingencies in place. Their control of politicians and bankers shielded them and allowed them to put some things back together. Although these new empires were smaller and more fragile, it seemed certain they would be back.

Tane and Blanc, like most of the surviving Remies, saw the opportunity to advance and consolidate their power. The flash-burn attacks and ensuing global economic meltdown were viewed as an opportunity. The End Game wasn't over, it was just beginning. The Remies' CapWar among themselves would continue until one of them sat atop the pyramid.

Wen's physical injuries healed. The psychological toll of continuously killing and being nearly killed was a different kind of pain that would take much longer to recover from, if that was actually possible.

Still, Chase and Wen were not done with the Circuit, or the larger organization of Remies. They continued developing the army necessary to defeat them. Utilizing their growing roster of special ops mercenaries, AI-Terminators, and the rogues recruited by Mars, they planned to join the CapWar.

Tess Federgreen kept her promise and slipped into the night, lost to the whispers and dark realms where secrets and lies remain still in a heavy fog. Numerous teams were sent to find her, to kill her. They were unsuccessful.

However, Tess wasn't just hiding, she covertly maintained control over several IT-Squads. She'd been preparing for years, knowing the End Game was coming. Tess had large quantities of sophisticated weapons and technology hidden away. She'd traded favors and built loyalties over her lengthy career, leaving her with a black book of trustworthy contacts in most parts of the government.

She'd carefully chosen a series of safe houses in Mexico and Central America in order to remain close to the United States, "Because that's where the fight is."

Booker Lipton, the reclusive billionaire who had provided so much information to Chase and Wen, had proven to be something of an enigma to them. They needed him, but worried their alliance was like getting an arsonist to help extinguish the fire.

"Time will tell," Wen said.

"Yes," Chase agreed, "but Time is a funny thing."

Blanc and Tane sat on one of Tane's private jets, reviewing the state of the world. "What a mess they made," Tane said, as if discussing red wine spilled on a white carpet during a cocktail party.

"Obviously Chase and Wen are not afraid of us," Blanc said. "In fact, Wen seems to have no fear at all."

"Really?" Tane said. "Well, they are about to find out the true meaning of the word 'fear.'"

"What are we going to do?" Blanc asked. "Have you invented a new way for them to die?"

"No, we aren't going to kill them. But very, very soon, they will wish we had. They'll be choking on so much fear, Chase and Wen will be begging for death."

Next in the Chase Malone Thriller series

vinci-books.com/chasing-fear

Escaping was the easy part. Surviving is the real nightmare.

After a daring escape marked by explosions, chaos, and a staggering loss, Chase Malone and Wen Zhou are thrust into their most perilous ordeal yet.

Turn the page for a free preview…

Chasing Fear: Chapter One

NEW YORK CITY

Sunday - 5:57 am - Eastern time

Chase and Wen stood on the abandoned antique concrete platform of New York City's first subway station. The wide, arched opening above them read CITY HALL, just as it had on its opening day in October of 1904.

"This is such a bad idea," Wen said, adjusting the straps of her backpack.

The ghostly, yet elegant space they found themselves in had sat unused since it had closed just after the end of World War II.

"Should have brought Terminators," she added. The private army they'd formed to fight in the shadow wars had recently taken on the AI-inspired name.

"We need this guy, and he wouldn't come unless we were alone," Chase said, not happy to be rehashing this debate minutes before their contact was expected to show up. He thought it was a moot point anyway. They both knew half a dozen Terminators were just above them in City Hall Park.

For two years, since the *End Game* had begun, Chase had been trying to get someone on the inside to talk. Finally, someone had agreed, someone high up in the corruption tree: the Deputy Chief of Staff to the Mayor of New York. However, the mayor was more than a city official, he was one of two candidates running for president of the United States with the general election less than ninety days away.

"Back when I was on the wire," Wen said, referring to her time with the MSS, China's equivalent to the CIA, "we called this type of situation *dinner at a slaughterhouse*. The meat might be fresh, but it's going to be your last meal."

Chase laughed. "It must make sense in Mandarin, but I think something got lost in translation."

She glared at him. "Point being, this is a deathtrap."

"No." He pointed up at the vaulted Guastavino tiled ceilings, natural light filtering in through vintage, leaded-glass skylights. "Don't you feel like we've traveled back in time? Imagine the history that came through here."

"I *know* the history!" Wen always researched everything. "The City Hall Station originally served as the southern terminus of the Manhattan Main Line, designed by Heins & LaFarge and built by Interborough Rapid Transit Company. It's been closed since 1945, and thus earned its nickname as 'the ghost station' or 'the lost stop'. Because of the chandeliers, curves, and arches, in its day it was likened to a miniature Grand Central Station." She pointed to the features to which she referred. "Though, after the final Brooklyn Bridge stop, the tracks are still used as a turn-around for the 6 train, but the station itself remains closed, and given its proximity to City Hall, is considered a high-security location. No one gets in without clearance."

"Except us."

"Us and the Deputy Chief of Staff." She checked the tunnels again, then eyed the staircase. The once magnificent setting, decorated with glittering chandeliers and other accruements, was now muted by a thick layer of dust, rust, and water damage. "Why here?"

"Just what you said. No one gets in here. No cameras, no way he gets seen talking to us."

"He's late."

Chase checked his phone. "Three minutes is hardly late." But he knew it was to Wen, who valued precision and professionalism. Many times he had seen her calculating and achieving incredible feats only because she understood how much could be accomplished in each of the sixty-seconds contained in a final minute.

"Here he comes," Wen said. "Or it better be him." She listened to the footsteps and immediately deduced it was only one person, male, between one-hundred eighty and two hundred pounds, tall, probably six-two. Unfortunately she couldn't tell if he was armed, but experience told her he was not. The stride was quick, tense, and civilian.

"Chase?" the man called as he emerged from the arch.

"Yes, and this is Wen."

He nodded to her, but did not make eye contact. She summed him up quickly. She already knew from his profile on the NYC government website that he was fifty-four years old, and a graduate of Columbia Law School. Other online sources revealed the man to be married with three kids.

"I'm not sure I should have agreed to this," he said. "It's just that we're out of time to stop it."

Chase wasn't surprised. The Deputy Chief of Staff had been waffling for months. But he was here, so although nervous, he was still going through with it, in spite of his protests.

"We're fine," Chase said.

The deputy gave him a look that suggested he might be insulted that mere words from Chase could assuage his fears, but the Deputy had also done his research and knew Chase was a brilliant engineer who had become a billionaire from his breakthrough in AI before he'd turned thirty. The man respected both big brains and big money. He nodded. "Did you bring the cash?"

Chase handed him a briefcase.

The Deputy opened it, looked at the stacks of banded hundred-dollar bills, considered counting it, but changed his mind. "You know I'm not doing this for the money."

"I know," Chase said.

"Why are you doing it?" Wen asked, to the chagrin of Chase.

"They're taking over the world. It may already be too late, but at least now we can still pretend it's like it was before. The money is so I can disappear before they realize it was me."

"Thank you," Chase said.

"Everything you need is on this flash drive," he said, holding it up. "What's not on it can be acc—"

A bullet penetrated his head. The flash drive flew from the Deputy's hand as he fell forward.

Chase dropped to the platform. In his peripheral vision, he saw the drive slide over the edge onto the tracks. Bullets struck all around them, ricocheting off the many hard surfaces. Wen, already returning fire, yelled, "Call in the Terminators!"

Chasing Fear: Chapter Two

Chase jumped down to the tracks, desperate to find the precious flash drive. Wen, firing a Glock 19 pistol, followed, looking for something else—the only decent cover in the station.

Dropping the pack off her back, she quickly unzipped the black, military-grade bag. Among the throwing stars, knives, and other small weapons were a couple of H&K MP7 submachine guns, extra magazines, and another Glock. She whipped out the MP7 as if it was an extension of her own arm—which, after the thousands of times she'd used one in training and real-world gunfights, it practically was. Her first four bullets killed three black-clad fighters.

"I need more light!" Chase shouted, still scavenging for the drive.

"I need more guns!" Wen yelled back. "There are at least fifteen hostiles. Forget the drive."

Just as Chase was about to do just that, the light from his phone passed over a silver glint. He snatched the precious drive and slipped it in his pocket, then grabbed the other machine gun.

"That looks like more than fifteen to me," Chase yelled as he started firing. Scores of rounds came in every second as the death-squad of now nearly twenty men barraged them with machine-gun fire.

"That's because they keep coming!"

The green and gold tiles shattered and chipped in the hail, adding to the clouds of dust and debris already forming from the shot-up ancient concrete.

Chase took three men down, but six more appeared from the stairs. "Where are they all coming from?"

Wen replaced the exhausted magazine in her MP7. "Your Deputy led them to us."

"Not knowingly," Chase yelled. "He was the first to die."

"You know how the Remies work. No witnesses, no exceptions, ever!"

"Let's shoot now and talk later."

"Now you're talking my language." She looked over her shoulder, concerned additional hostiles would funnel in from the subway tunnels. "Keep an eye on that opening. I'll watch this one."

"I'm more focused on the guys in front of us right now," Chase barked, shooting the legs out from under two more advancing men.

With the advantage of their cover, it didn't take long for Chase and Wen to pick off more of the attackers, soon reducing their numbers to six, and, at least for the moment, no more seemed to be coming.

"It's been kind of like a shooting gallery," Chase said. Though the easy targets were gone now, the survivors were sandbagged behind the bodies of their comrades.

"Apparently they expected to kill us on the platform," Wen said, still trying to figure out the play. The standoff grew more dangerous each second they didn't finish it.

"Just got a text," Chase said. "The Terminators are having a hard time reaching us in the tunnels."

"Are they encountering hostiles?" she asked between taking single shots at the men on the platform, hoping to prevent them from charging.

"Not yet."

"Have them blow the skylights."

Chase looked up at the rows of leaded crystal panels and relayed the message. Minutes later, Terminators above in City Hall Park began blasting the skylights, quickly killing several of the now exposed men below. Chunks of glass and debris rained in on the opulent station, but the operatives outnumbered the Terminators and soon began picking them off.

"I'm out of ammo," Chase announced, rummaging through the duffle.

"Glock or the HK?"

"HK," he said.

"Then it's a good time to run," Wen said, knowing their attackers would be distracted with the Terminators above for at least a few more minutes. "On three."

"Okay, but where does this tunnel lead?"

"Two, three!"

Chase took off with the Glock held high while Wen fired a cover burst with the MP7, then followed.

Chase stumbled, the soles of his shoes slipping on the slick tracks. "What about the third rail?" he panted, eyes darting towards the lethal electrical conduit running alongside the tracks as they sprinted down the dark, dank tunnel, their footsteps echoing off the concrete walls.

"Just stay away from that side," she said. "It should be covered."

"Oh, great, then we're relying on the efficiency of city government workers, because the third rail carries a constant electrical current of at least six-hundred volts—*more* than enough to kill a human."

"Don't touch it then!"

"Good advice."

Chase and Wen continued running. The smell of damp concrete, the flickering of the lights in the tunnel, and the sound of the men now coming up fast behind them confused their senses.

"They're gaining on us," Chase said. "Let's find a place to fight."

"We need to outrun them to daylight."

Chase thought his lungs might explode and doubted he'd last that long. There was no light at the end of the tunnel even visible yet, and the men were closing in fast.

The air was thick with the metallic tang of electricity, and the sound of an approaching train filled the tunnels. A red and black hazard sign warned of the exposed third rail ahead. Wen grabbed it, yanking it from its rusted bracket. "Ancient Chinese proverb says it's difficult to catch a black cat in a dark room, especially when it's not there."

"What the hell does that mean?"

"We do not need to help our enemies survive so they can make sure we do not survive."

Chase and Wen rounded a bend in the tunnel and were faced with a section where there was no platform, or "shoe", covering the third rail as it crossed into the open.

"That's going to either kill us, or save us," Chase said, pointing to the rail as the vibrating clatter in the tunnels was suddenly interrupted by the sounds of gunfire and ricocheting bullets.

Grab your copy…
vinci-books.com/chasing-fear

About the Author

USA TODAY Bestselling Author Brandt Legg uses his unusual real life experiences to create page-turning novels. He's traveled with CIA agents, dined with senators and congressmen, mingled with astronauts, chatted with governors and presidential candidates, had a private conversation with a Secretary of Defense he still doesn't like to talk about, hung out with Oscar and Grammy winners, had drinks at the State Department, been pursued by tabloid reporters, and spent a birthday at the White House by invitation from the President of the United States.

At age eight, Legg's father died suddenly, plunging his family into poverty. Two years later, while suffering from crippling migraines, he started in business, and turned a hobby into a multi-million-dollar empire. National media dubbed him the "Teen Tycoon," and by the mid-eighties, Legg was one of the top young entrepreneurs in America, appearing as high as number twenty-four on the list (when Steve Jobs was #1, Bill Gates #4, and Michael Dell #6). Legg still jokes that he should have gone into computers.

By his twenties, after years of buying and selling businesses, leveraging, and risk-taking, the high-flying Legg became ensnarled in the financial whirlwind of the junk bond eighties. The stock market crashed and a firestorm of trouble came down. The Teen Tycoon racked up more than a million dollars in legal fees, was betrayed by those closest to him, lost his entire fortune, and ended up serving time for financial improprieties.

After a year, Legg emerged from federal prison, chastened and wiser, and began anew. More than twenty-five years later, he's now using all that hard-earned firsthand knowledge of conspiracies, corruption and high finance to weave his tales. Legg's books pulse with authenticity.

His series have excited nearly a million readers around the world. Although he refused an offer to make a television movie about his life as a teenage millionaire, his autobiography is in the works. There has also been interest from Hollywood to turn his thrillers into films. With any luck, one day you'll see your favorite characters on screen.

He lives in the Pacific Northwest, with his wife and son, writing full time, in several genres, containing the common themes of adventure, conspiracy, and thrillers. Of all his pursuits, being an author and crafting plots for novels is his favorite.

Acknowledgments

In recent months, during the writing of this book, my family has lost two loved ones - Marty and Mollie.

Saul Martin "Marty" Goldman has left behind a legacy of creative work, laughter, and a fascinating life well lived. He will be greatly missed. I'll always be grateful for his input and generous "director's eye," to my first novel. I enjoyed our many lively debates and discussions on so many issues. And, I will always see the artistic influence he had on my son. Read the incredible story of his rise from an award-winning illustrator to Hollywood motion picture director in his memoir, *From Mad Ave to Hollywood*

We also lost another dear member of our family. I've known Mollie Gregory since my early childhood. Along the way she transitioned from friend to family, as those remarkable people who find their way into our lives often do. Mollie was a New York Times bestselling author, and wrote across several genres in both fiction and non-fiction. She critiqued and coached some of my first attempts at writing a book, then continued to encourage and support my work all her life. She never shied from telling anyone the unvarnished truth. I loved that about her. One of the great compliments I think can be said of someone is that their loyalty never wavered. Mollie's never did. She was a remarkable woman. Mollie's most recent book, *Stuntwomen: The Untold Hollywood Story*.

Another important person is honored in this story. My

late father's oldest friend, Edward Holmes Underhill Jr., was the inspiration for the character of Ed Underhill. They have a lot in common, both were amazing wood carvers, both worked in intelligence, both had a quick sense of humor. However, the real Ed Underhill was funnier and kinder than the one in *Chasing Lies*. After the untimely death of my father, Ed was someone I always knew could be counted on. He had a way of making people feel safe and special. I've always considered his daughters, Susan and Anne, to be the sisters I never had. Ed lived a good life, 1932 - 2020. Rest In Peace.

Below, I've included the collected wisdom of Glenn Legge, who, if we traced it back three or four centuries, might be a relative. In this lifetime, we crossed paths through my books. He became one of my trusted beta readers. Recently, doctors told Glenn he might be running out of runway. We all know doctors can make mistakes, but I hope in this case they are wrong, and that Glenn will be reading my books (and lots of other ones) for years to come. When he sent me this list, I thought it would be of value to my readers, so I included it here. I've always found lists like this to be good reminders, especially when accumulated over nearly eight decades of living.

<u>Glenn Legge's collected wisdom</u>
Build memories.
Tell the truth.
Give to charity.
Take responsibility for your actions.
Contribute your non-monetary resources freely.
Never stop learning.

Many people won't think doing your best is adequate.
Confront people when something is wrong,
and hold them accountable.
Always practice "Lagniappe"
Have fun and share it.
Always seek input from thoughtful people,
but make your own decisions.
Learn who George Carlin was,
and sometimes look at life the way he did.
Integrity must not be compromised.
Value true friendship. It is rare.
Seek interesting people, and ask interesting questions.
Every morning, decide to have a good day.
If you do good and you feel you need credit, you may take it.
If you do bad, you must take the blame.
Marry carefully, and for keeps.
Believe in something greater than yourself.

In communicating with Glenn, I also gleaned some other useful lines from his emails:

The surprises of childhood are waaay more fun than those of old age.
Contact those people who mattered in life,
and reinforce your gratitude.
Enjoy yourself while you can, and document the good times, the ancestors you remember and why, and your basic beliefs for your descendants. It will all die with you if you don't.
I am willing to bet that whatever is next is even better.

Glenn also wrote his own epitaph(s):
"He was fun while he lasted."

"If you enjoyed this service, copies are for sale in the gift shop on your way out. Drive carefully."

Chasing Lies was a lot of fun to write, partially because I got to finally reveal the identities of those behind the shadow people. It also allowed me to revisit (in my mind, at least) one of my favorite places in the world, Taos. That high desert town is so important to me, it often seems to find its way into my stories.

This book would not be out in the world if not for the many people who help me do this work (what, to me, is the best job I've ever had). That I am sitting in front of the Pacific Ocean, feeling a warm tropical breeze as I write these acknowledgements, is a whole other dream come true.

To the wonders of my world, Ro and Teakki, who make the adventure so amazing. Teakki has become quite a technical advisor, and will talk for hours about plots, gadgets, and tactics. And Ro, who inspires me a thousand ways every single day.

My mom, Barbara Blair, who seems to really believe I am a great writer. I hope to prove her right someday. I am fortunate to have known her so long.

Joan Osborne, for her gifts of words and ability to craft an understanding from an unintended confusion. Gil Forbes, for his unique insights and clever mind. Jack Llartin, a patient copy editor, who fills the gaps of my education and gets it the way I wanted all along.

And, finally, to Teakki, who patiently waited to show me a newly created comic, or latest video creation, until I finished writing each day.

Most of all, to all of my readers, the ones that have read

everything I've published, and the ones who have just finished their first Booker thriller or Chasing adventure. You make it possible for me to live this dream, to create these worlds, to live with these characters and tell these stories. Thank you for the time you've shared with me via my books. Please drop me an email anytime. Responding to reader emails is one of my favorite parts of the day!

I'd like to give extra thanks to some special readers and/or members of my street team for their support, kindness, reviews (I love reviews), suggestions, and encouragement.

(If I left anyone out, I apologize. Please forgive me, and let me know. I can fix it!)

Please don't let the fact that there are so many of you do anything to diminish your importance to me. This ever-expanding group is the fuel to my creative fire.

In alphabetical order (by first name):

Adam Tanner, Alec Redwine, Amber Hunt, Anne Kaplan, Bill Borchert, Billie Harkey, Blake Dowling, Bob Browder, Bob Dumas, Brian C. Coffey, Brian Schnizlein, Cara Johnson, Carl Howard, Carol M, Cathie Harrison, Cheryl Olson, Chet Keough, Chis Bond, Chris Tomlinson, Christine Moritz, Christopher Bowling, Chuck Gonzalez, Cid Chase, Claudia Wells, Consuelo Ashworth, Debra Harper, Dennis Lowe, Derek Redmond, Diane Smith, Diane Whitehead, Doug Wise, Douglas Dersch, Douglas Meek, Elaine Dill, Ernest Manpino, Ernest Pino, Frank Fusco, Frank Murphy, Gary Human, Gene Leach, Gene Legg, Gil Forbes, Gillian Charlton, Glenda Dykstra, Glenn Legge, Ingo Michehl, Irene Witoski, Jacky Dallaire, Jan Dallas, Janice Gildea, Jean Sink, Joan Osborne, John McDonald, John Nicholson, John Nunley, John Oliver, John Wood, Judith Anderson, Judy Hammer, Julie Price, Justin

Lear, Karen Mack, Karen Markovitz, Kat Heyer, Katherine Atwood, Kathleen Robbins, Kathy Creecy, Kathy Troc, Ken Clute, Ken Friedman, Kevin Burton, Kyle Dahlem, LA Dumas, Leslie Royce, Linda Loparco, Linda Petty, Liz Miller, Marcel Roy. Gerry Adler, Mark Perlmutter, Martha Heckel, Martin Gunnell, Melanie C. Hansen, Michael Ferrel, Michael Picco, Mick Flanigan, Mike Brannick, Mike Lauland, Nancy Lamanna, Nigel Revill, Normand Girard, Pam Gilbert, Patricia Ruby, Paul Gyorke, Peggy Gulli, Randy Howerter, Rick Ferris, Rick Woodring, Rob Weaver, Rob Zorger, Robert Smith, Robyn Shanti, Ron Babcock, S. Michael Smith, S.W. Kelly Myers, Sam Rhoades, Samantha Jackson, Sandie Parrish, Sandra Zuiderhoek, Satish Bhatti, Sharon Moffatt, Stephane Peltier, Sue Steel, Susan McGuyer, Susan Moore, Susan Norlund, Susan Powell, Terry Myers, Tom Strauss, Tony Sommer, Tricia Turner, Vicki Gordon, Vivienne Du Bourdieu.

Many authors I've met along the way have impacted my craft and career as well. This is far from a complete list, but each one included has made a difference to me: Robert Gatewood, Mike Sager, Craig Martelle, Michael Anderle, Mark Dawson, Nick Thacker, Ernest Dempsey, John Grisham, A. Kelly Pruitt, Eric J. Gates, Dale DeVino, Phil M. Williams, Jennifer Theriot, Haris Orkin, Brian Meeks, Jennifer Theriot, Michelle McCarty, Mollie Gregory, Judith Lucci, and Zoe Saadia.

There are so many friends of mine who are creatives as well, many from Taos, where parts of this story are set. Their work inspires my work (and my life): Tony Schueller, David Manzanares, Geraint Smith, Michael Hearne, Don Richmond, Lenny Foster, Jared Rowe, Jimmy Stadler, Scott Thomas, Carol Morgan-Eagle, Deonne Kahler, Bart Anderson, Ernest James, Jenny Bird, Angelika Maria Koch,

Brad Hockmeyer, Verne Verona, Brooke Tatum, Markus Kolber, Terrie Bennett, and many others!

Speaking of reviewers, the prolific readers and top Amazon reviewers who have been a great support of my work, deserve extra recognition. Thank you so much, and special gratitude to the remarkable Grady Harp, and to whoever the reviewer "Serenity" is!

There is a goal among some authors to turn readers into fans, fans into super fans, and super fans into friends. I am fortunate to have been able to achieve that goal on numerous occasions.

Thank you.

www.ingramcontent.com/pod-product-compliance
Ingram Content Group UK Ltd.
Pitfield, Milton Keynes, MK11 3LW, UK
UKHW041854120925
462873UK00003B/71